The Twelve Dares of Christmas

Lisa Maloney

ISBN 979-8-9889205-0-2 (paperback)

ISBN 979-8-9889205-1-9 (ebook)

First edition

Cover design by Erin DeMoss Creative, LLC

Copy and line editing by Charlie Knight (cknightwrites.com)

To my childhood self: you'll get here.

And to everyone who feels like they're bursting at the seams, filled to the
brim with stories and magic:
I see you.

Contents

DAY 0: CATALYST

"Is it wrong to hope your parents get eaten by a shark?"

"You're being a little dramatic, Haley," Anna yelled back to me from the kitchen. She wasn't wrong. Even I could admit that I was leaning into it a little too much, but I didn't know how to fix my attitude.

I was sprawled across the couch feeling sorry for myself, covered in Cheeto dust and seriously reconsidering my recent choice to be the type of woman that doesn't immediately take her bra off when she gets home.

In my defense, Cheeto dust was a force of nature, the wire from my bra was stabbing me in the boob, and my parents had just broken the news to me that they'd decided to take a trip to Jamaica over Christmas instead of hosting me and my brother for a week of Christmas cookies and pretending Santa was real.

I'd offered to switch up cookies for chocolate bark and to stop acting like a tubby old dude was going to break into the house (in a nice way!), but no. Apparently, the tickets were already booked and nonrefundable, and my feelings didn't matter. Rude.

I stared aimlessly around the apartment Anna and I shared, grumbling at the decorations we put up earlier in the week when I was still filled with the holiday spirit. Not twelve hours ago, I was plotting an additional wave to add more tinsel, more snowmen, more everything festive. Now

I couldn't help but scowl at the reindeer lining our mantel and the lights sparkling under fake snow lining the TV stand. Christmastime, especially the part I got to spend with my family, was the thing that kept me going all year through my nice, but ultimately boring and predictable day-to-day life.

"What did Jake say when they told you both?" Anna's question brought me back to reality. "Are you two going to do something without your parents while they're away?"

"Ugh, no." My brother barely chimed in during the video chat earlier that evening. You'd think that, as an attorney, he'd be more impressed with my determination to believe everything is negotiable, but instead, he just kept telling me to stop arguing. "He was actually happy about it! Relieved that he didn't have to deal with trying to figure out schedules and how to see our parents as well as his new girlfriend's family over the holidays. Little brat didn't even consider me other than suggesting we have brunch sometime to exchange presents."

He'd be lucky if I even brought him coal now. The drone that he wanted to get himself but was reluctant to buy considering his girlfriend's dislike of them was already wrapped in snowflake paper, sitting in my closet. I knew I wouldn't be returning it, but I could lie to myself for a bit. Maybe, once I'd accepted the change in our plans, I'd get a kick out of giving him some coal first for not backing me up with our parents. He could have the drone after we had a good laugh.

"In fairness, navigating the holiday how-to-split-family-time landmine is pretty stressful." She smirked at me. "And you are a lot to deal with for longer than a few hours."

Grumpy enough to keep pouting, I tossed a pillow at Anna who dodged it before she sat down on the couch and handed me a mug of cocoa.

"You know you're more than welcome to come to my mom's house for Christmas." Anna offered. "She and my grandpa adore you." Anna and I met early on in college, and after our first visit back to her parents' house over a long weekend, they'd always sent two care packages to the dorms, one for each of us.

I'd spent increasing amounts of time there each year, celebrating birthdays and joining family dinners. I had helped Anna plan a fortieth wedding anniversary party for her parents, was part of the welcome crew when Anna's grandpa immigrated from Japan after his wife passed away, and I grieved with them and supported them however I could after Anna's dad was involved in a fatal car accident two years ago.

Even now, when we lived barely forty minutes from their house and visited regularly, Anna's mom and grandpa sent Anna care packages just for the fun of it. Every time, there were snacks and things that Anna didn't care for but that I loved. They felt like a second family, and I knew I was always welcome.

"I know, and I'm grateful for the offer, but it's not the same. Maybe I'll just stay here, watching movies and stuffing my face full of candy." Sometimes a girl just wanted to feel sorry for herself and pout. Not exactly a healthy coping skill for disappointment, but I just couldn't get excited about not being with my family for the first time ever on Christmas. It wasn't something I was going to voice, but I felt betrayed. It felt like my parents leaving meant they valued me less than a vacation they could take any other week.

"No." Anna's decisive tone left no room for argument.

"No?"

"Nope. If you stay here, you're just going to mope, and then when I get back after having a lovely time, you'll still be here moping. You'll come with me, and you can watch all the movies and eat all the candy you want, but there will be no moping." Anna grabbed the remote and started scrolling through channels until she found a cheesy holiday romance. "Now," she said, handing me a notepad and a pen, "make a list of made-for-TV holiday movie stereotypes, and let's turn this watch party into a drinking game. I'll grab the wine."

Anna wasn't known for budging once she'd made her mind up, so I'd have to find an excuse to stay home and wallow later. For now, a list needed to be made.

Anna had already written out a few items. There were a few frequent but not guaranteed items, like a reveal that one of the characters was the *real* Santa Claus, as well as things that were almost certain to pop up in every movie, like the characters walking through a Christmas market.

I almost suggested that we go out for the night instead just to avoid getting as drunk as we were bound to get, but one look outside, where it was snowing and already dark, changed my mind. Besides, I loved a cheesy holiday movie, and you had to hand it to the writers who kept coming up with slightly different spins on the same plot lines and raking in viewers despite the predictability of it all.

Anna came back into the room with comically overfilled glasses of wine, and we settled into blanket nests on the couch, snacks on a platter between us. Friday night movie marathons really could not be beat.

0.2

"You know the worst part?" I sighed, Anna glancing over at me with glassy eyes as the couple on screen kissed in the falling snow, basking in their assuredness after the woman decided she didn't want to go back to her job in the big city but would instead stay and help her new partner run a toy store. "The worst part isn't even spending Christmas alone; it's the next two weeks. We should have been decorating gingerbread houses, planning a menu for our Christmas brunch, and wearing silly sweaters." I released another exaggerated sigh.

The last several hours of movies were supposed to make me feel better, but I hadn't been able to shake the disappointment about my parents abandoning me for Christmas and ruining my favorite season. Anna stayed quiet, and I didn't continue, the buzz of the two bottles of wine we'd gone through not exactly helping but not hurting either. Maybe I should have just gone to bed early after getting the news from my parents, but Friday night movie marathons were our time to unwind and catch up after long weeks.

Anna stared at the now-muted television before her hand snapped out and started tapping on my arm like she always did when she had an idea she was trying to piece together. She looked at me with excitement in her eyes. "Why don't we turn the tables then?"

"You want to go to Jamaica?"

"No, no, that's not what I mean. But let's do something different than normal. See those people?" She gestured at the TV where a new movie had begun, one we both recognized. "That woman is about to get stuck in a time loop and go on dates with someone new each time Christmas Eve repeats itself. She's about to have twelve dates before she can get to Christmas!"

"So, you want us to go find twelve people to date? Or a handful of men to date twelve times? I'm unlikely to pull that off, but it's more likely than a time loop."

"Oh, hell no. Something more fun than that. Let's do twelve days of festive games! Or challenges or something. We're two weeks out from Christmas, so we can start tomorrow, and then we'll be done in time to be lazy on Christmas Eve and celebrate Christmas morning at my mom's house."

I could feel myself grimace, even though I loved games and Anna's suggestion definitely had the potential to distract me. I tried to force a smile onto my face, knowing Anna shouldn't have to deal with me being in a bad mood for two weeks. I could at least make an effort when my best friend was trying to help me. "Okay, but are we just doing these for fun, or what's the deal?"

"How about our usual bet: loser has to read a book of the winner's choice, no matter how bonkers. To make things interesting, we could throw in the loser having to be stuck with bathroom deep cleaning duty for all of January."

My grimace was back. Deep cleaning the bathroom, a weekly task we usually alternated, was by far my most hated chore. Anna knew that if I agreed, I'd have to actually try, which was probably her plan all along.

I sighed again. Even I was getting sick of hearing myself sigh. "Okay. I'm in. Let's figure out the challenges."

"Yes!" Anna shouted before frowning. "Challenges? We need a cool name for our list. The twelve bets of Christmas? The twelve games of Christmas?"

"What about the twelve dares of Christmas?" I could see Anna thinking it over, but she didn't say anything. Finally, she nodded and leaned back into her corner of the couch, unmuting the television. We each settled in to watch, tossing out silly dare ideas as they popped up throughout the movie.

0.3

"Hales? Hales, come on," I heard Anna say from somewhere above me. I'd fallen asleep on the couch at some point during the third movie of the night, but I hadn't slept well, and I really had no interest in actually opening my eyes. "Haley!"

"Why are you yelling at me? Just let me become one with the couch."

"It's already 10:00 a.m. Do you really want to risk only being stuck with crummy, end-of-the-afternoon Christmas tree options?"

It took a minute for my brain to catch up before I remembered that we had plans to get up early and drive out to a tree farm to pick out a Christmas tree for the apartment. I grew up in a fake-tree home, and Anna was more than happy to agree to get a real tree when I brought it up. I'd ended up with wonky, patchy trees over the last few years because I had waited too long to get one, but not this year. The streak would be broken.

Even so, it was with more than a little grumbling that I got myself upright. Anna, a hangover angel, handed me a plate with a breakfast sandwich and hash browns. A few bites in, I was already feeling signs of life again.

"So," Anna started, drawing out the first word, "the dares start today."

Thirty seconds was all it took for my mind to clear the fog of sleep and remember the wine-fueled decision-making that resulted in a list of twelve so-called dares meant to prevent the next twelve days from becoming a daily invitation to a pity party. Anna handed me a piece of paper that neatly outlined a list of twelve challenges—excuse me, dares—that I vaguely remembered deciding on last night.

Scanning through each dare, I had to admit that I was a little excited, even if the part of me that wasn't used to having constant plans or things to do wanted me to rebel against the whole plan. Anna had pointed out last night that I'd been complaining a lot lately about being bored, and I realized she was right. I was just letting life go by with minimal effort, more often restless than energized. I was going to do these dares even if I had to give myself daily pep talks. Resolved to dive in, I took a photo of the list and set it as my lock screen.

<u>The Twelve Dares of Christmas</u>

1. Pick the best tree (have a stranger judge).

2. Win an ugly Christmas sweater contest.

3. Three kisses under the mistletoe.

4. Sneak the names of popular holiday songs into every conversation.

5. Five acts of kindness.

6. Eat only Christmas cookies and drink only hot cocoa and eggnog all day.

7. Get your picture taken with a live reindeer.

8. Work for a day as Santa or an elf.

9. Win a gingerbread house contest.

10. Win a snowball fight.

11. Get kicked out of a group of carolers.

12. Twelve Days of Christmas scavenger hunt.

"So," I said, looking up from my phone to where Anna was washing dishes in the kitchen, "your real motivation for getting to the tree farm early was so that *you* would have the best tree options to pick from."

"When I win dare one, I don't want to spend the rest of the day listening to you whine and try to make excuses about how you would have won if the good trees hadn't already been taken."

I had to admit that I probably would do that.

"You're pretty confident about winning this one, and obviously one of us will, but what about the rest of these days? Like tomorrow, for instance. Where are we going to find and get invited to participate in an ugly Christmas sweater contest on such short notice?"

"Already handled. Check your texts."

Opening up my messages, I noticed a text that had been sent to the group chat by our friend, Maddie that I somehow missed earlier. Last week, Maddie, the planner of our friend group, had organized brunch for tomorrow. Her latest texts to the group suggested that we turn brunch into an excuse to wear our silliest holiday apparel by having an ugly sweater contest. "That was lucky."

"Not really." Anna shrugged. "I texted Maddie this morning suggesting it. You know she loves a themed event."

"Okay, but are we going to make everyone vote? What if everyone votes for themselves or if the votes are even, or if neither of us wins?"

Anna's head snapped up at that. It was clear that neither option had occurred as a possibility. I doubted she even considered that she wouldn't win. The woman did have one heck of an ugly sweater collection, and it wouldn't be the first contest she'd won with ease. There wasn't much point in me even trying to win that dare, but I was confident about my superior tree-choosing abilities, so it would even out.

"I guess we just ask the waiter to pick their favorite, and if it's neither of us, it'll just be a wash? There are things on the list that both of us could achieve and win in the same day, so maybe rather than making it a race to who does it first we just do an accumulation of points? Dares like today's can have a winner who gets a point and the other person gets none, but other days, we can both get the points or neither of us could get points. Maybe on the last day, we should get a point for each of the twelve days of Christmas items that we manage to get. That'll give you a chance to catch up after I shut out the first eleven dares." She flashed me a grin to make sure I knew she meant it in jest. Neither of us was obnoxiously competitive, but I'd need to come up with some good smack talk nonetheless.

"Okay," I said, clapping my hands together as I got up to get ready for the day. "Game on."

DAY 1: PICK OUT THE BEST CHRISTMAS TREE

After a thirty-minute drive, Anna and I pulled into a parking lot packed with other cars. Booths selling hot cocoa, cider, and spiced nuts sat between rows of checkout lines and merchant booths, beyond which rows of trees filled the open space. A line of excited kids led the way to where Santa was waiting to hear about what each child was hoping to find under their tree—once it was purchased from the tree farm, of course.

Stopping first for cocoa topped with whipped cream, sprinkles, and candy cane pieces, Anna and I browsed collections of hats, ornaments, and nutcrackers. A woman was adorning wreaths to replenish her dwindling supply next to a booth displaying a rack of holiday sweaters.

I people-watched as Anna looked through the rack but walked away without one, so I had to assume that whatever she was planning to wear tomorrow put everything at the booth to shame, which was saying something considering I spotted a sweater with a reindeer face that had antlers sticking up from the shoulders. Sometimes, I wondered if people actually intended to make charming apparel, but there was a very thin line between tasteful and horrendous when it came to holiday sweaters.

We kept wandering around, and I eventually had to try to talk myself out of buying mittens made of alpaca wool so soft that I might never take them off. I felt my resolve crumbling.

"Should we head to the trees," I asked, turning to Anna.

"You make it sound like we're going on a quest."

"We are, m'lady!" I exclaimed, my expression serious as I gestured to the lines of trees. "Out there, our treasure awaits."

Anna looped her arm through mine, and we headed back to the trees. There was a section of pre-cut trees as well as access to rows of trees still planted and dusted with snow. We headed straight to the back, where the two sections met before continuing into the lines of planted trees. It felt a bit like we were in a corn maze made of pine trees, albeit the easiest one possible since it was just straight lines of trees with intersecting pathways to let people move between the rows.

The woodsy smell of pine was inescapable, and the air somehow seemed fresher than it was just a few hundred feet away at the booths. I took my (sadly not alpaca wool) mittens off to run my hands against the prickly branches, feeling more grounded than I typically did in the city, and the further we walked from the noise of the crowds, the calmer I felt.

Admittedly, as much as I always liked the holiday season, the chaos of it all sometimes overwhelmed me. Being out among the trees, listening to the branches move in the wind and birds sing from somewhere beyond the wandering patrons, let me release tension that I didn't know I was carrying.

"I don't suppose you have a chainsaw in your purse?" And just like that, I was back in my body, realizing how cold my toes were becoming, and thoroughly confused until I looked around and realized that Anna had a point. How were we supposed to cut down a tree?

"Do you think they have them up front where we check out, or were we supposed to bring one?" I was betting on us being responsible for our own supplies, but a girl could hope.

"No clue, but either way, we're going to need to head back to find out."

"I don't suppose anyone is going to put up with being dragged to multiple different trees to judge which is the best, even if they would come out with a saw for us, though."

"Probably not. We might be stuck with the pre-cut trees. Let's search through those, pick our contender, and then we can have them both side-by-side for whomever we get to be the judge." Picking out a tree from the woods seemed great in theory but not worth the extra work, and we weren't going to cut down multiple trees and then only buy one. We split up, each starting our search.

People were very particular about Christmas trees, and I realized that if I was going to win this dare, I'd need to find something outstanding, something so perfect it couldn't be refused. Still, what if I brought a pine to the judge, and they preferred a fir variety? What if they were the type to be sympathetic to a tree that needed more love and attention over fuller, more symmetrical options? I couldn't choose based on the whims of an unknown judge, though, so I had to find my ideal tree. After all, it would be in my apartment for the next few weeks once I won.

In minutes, I went from looking at and judging each tree I passed to letting my mind wander as I roamed through the aisles, barely scanning the options. The scent, not nearly as good as it was out in the organized forest of uncut trees, still settled something inside me, and the added bonus of people-watching provided me with endless entertainment.

A little girl was telling her mom fun facts about why people started decorating trees in the first place. As a connoisseur of fun facts, the only option was to pretend to inspect a few nearby trees while I listened in as she chattered away. A laugh burst loudly out of me when the feisty little girl flatly refused her mom's instance that Christmas trees were intended to let Santa know where to put presents. A scowl from the mother had me moving on, but I threw a quick thumbs up to the little girl as I went.

Turning a corner, a puppy was getting scolded by its owner, and I started walking up to ask if I could pet their dog when my phone vibrated with an incoming text message.

Anna: I found the perfect tree and am ready to win this dare

Laughing at Anna's text, I reluctantly turned away from the puppy that was now chewing on low tree branches. I must have zoned out because a quick glance at the time confirmed that I had been wandering around longer than I expected to and without anything to show for it. Honestly, I was surprised Anna had taken this long to pick a tree; I definitely should have already found one. "Focus, Haley."

Haley: Let's meet by the entrance to this section of trees in 15 minutes

Having bought myself a little time, I needed to pick my champion. Most people probably picked a tree before getting to the end of the aisles, so I moved quickly through the rows, not stopping for anything that looked patchy or dried out. I wanted something lush that ornaments could be hung from and settle on, but also something a bit squat. The trees that looked like someone closed an umbrella and just put it on a stand? Not for me.

Realistically, narrower would be better for our apartment, but the idea of our living room being twenty-five percent Christmas tree was appealing. After all of the holiday romance movies Anna and I had watched over the years, I probably should have had a list of ways to test out whether a tree is *the* tree, but I didn't. I just wanted something that made me happy. I wanted something fluffy, if a tree could be such a thing. I want something that—

I wanted that one.

Someone was holding my perfect tree, looking between it and another, skinnier option. Making an attempt at casually walking over, I threw out a comment about how nicely the branches of the tree I didn't want were laying as I forced myself to inspect other nearby options. The misguided fools left with the tree I hadn't set my sights on.

I scooped up my prize before they could change their minds and made my way back to the front to find Anna. My mittens went into my pocket so that they wouldn't get dirty from the tree as I used both hands to reach between the branches and grip the trunk. Ten seconds later, this proved foolish when my hands were sticky with sap.

"There you are," Anna said as I turned a corner near the front section of trees, "I was wondering if you'd admitted defeat and were trying to make a break for it instead." She was leaning against the back of a booth, a tree beside her. Grudgingly, I could admit that it looked good.

"Not a chance. I was just giving you time to come to terms with having to put your tree back before I brought up mine."

"Is this your friend?" A man in his early thirties walked up and stopped beside Anna. He had dark curls poking out of the sides of his beanie and an easy smile that he flashed to Anna before he looked back over at me. "I hear I'm going to get to pick out a winning tree for you two."

"This is Jason," Anna said, pointing her thumb in his direction. "He helped bring my tree up here, and I filled him in on the dare. He volunteered to be our judge."

"Oh, no. Nope, nada, nuh-uh. I know two people in cahoots when I see them!" Who knew what Anna actually told Jason, but I wasn't giving her the upper hand of having buddied up to him in advance.

He gave a good-natured chuckle, shrugging and holding his palms up in defeat. "Fair enough, though I never promised to pick Anna's tree, stunning as it is." Anna's self-satisfied grin shifted to surprise before a blush formed on her cheeks. Jason was looking down at Anna, completely ignoring the tree beside her.

"That solves that," I declared, "Jason, you've been a fabulous sport, but I insist upon an impartial judge."

"A judge for what," a newcomer asked from behind me, making me jump. Turning to respond, I ended up looking up into the eyes of a man about six inches taller than my five-foot-five height. There was a slight resemblance to Anna's new friend, though this guy seemed a bit younger.

He looked curiously between each of us, so I turned to the side to form a small circle between the four of us. I'd like to believe that I wasn't staring at him awkwardly for more than a few seconds, but by the time I snapped out of it, his expression had started to change from curiosity to concern. Oh, right, I hadn't responded, and Jason was whispering something to Anna.

"We're, umm, trying to pick a tree," I stammered.

"Hmmm," he said, looking around at all of the trees behind us and the one I was holding. "If you're going to make up a story, at least make it believable. You don't need to tell me about whatever secret mission you're undercover on."

After a few seconds of confusion, I realized he was joking, and the ridiculousness of it managed to erase the weird tension hanging in the air from my ogling. It was a little unfair that someone could be both funny and so good-looking. The man's chocolate-brown eyes crinkled at the sides as he smiled, and I realized I'd started ogling him again.

"Looks like you caught us. I'd ask you to judge who found the better tree, but I can't trust that you just happened to show up ready to judge."

Jason's laugh surprised me. I hadn't thought he was paying attention. "This is my brother, Adam. Anna and I were chatting while I was waiting for him to show up, so he really doesn't know what's going on." Anna nodded her confirmation before turning to Adam.

"We need someone to choose which tree we should get for our apartment," she explained.

"Isn't that something you should pick together? What type of trees do you both like and want?"

"Usually, sure," I supplied, "but we decided to make a game out of it and see who could find the best tree here. Your brother is biased, so it's up to you."

"Okay, let me see the contenders," he said, rubbing his hands together. Years of dating apps had really lowered the bar for my expectations of men, and it was refreshing to have a conversation with someone clearly willing to have fun with whatever he unwittingly ended up involved in.

I subtly checked him out as he looked back and forth between the trees Anna and I were each holding. After a minute, he reached out to touch a few branches of each tree before stepping back and requesting that we turn them slowly so that he could get a 360-degree view. All four of us did our best to try to remain stone-faced and serious, but no one could keep it up when Adam shoved his face into the branches of first one and then the other tree, taking a deep sniff of each. That could not have felt good on his face.

Stepping back and rising to his full height, Adam brushed off his face and gave a slight nod. "I have come to a conclusion."

"And?" Anna pushed after he didn't immediately continue.

"I'm trying to decide if we should get a wreath or something to crown the winner." He looked around before snatching a pinecone from the ground and turning back to us. "The winning tree belongs to," he took a deep breath, clearly enjoying himself, "Anna."

"Yes," Anna shouted at the same time I exclaimed, "What?"

Anna stepped forward, accepting the pinecone, before doing a little dance that had Jason smiling. I, on the other hand, was standing with my mouth hanging open.

"I don't understand. Did you see how lush my tree is? Look at how round it is!" I brushed the bottom of my tree with my hands, not sure if I was trying to console myself or the tree for losing a competition it didn't even know it was in.

"It's a good tree," he began, correcting himself after I shot him a look. "Umm, it's a great tree? But I like a tree that's a bit more uniform. This one looks like someone forgot that they were supposed to trim its branches before bringing it here." I spent a few moments mourning the loss of this, the perfect tree, before finally considering the one Anna brought up. It was pretty similar to the one I brought up, though it was standing a little straighter.

"Fair enough," I conceded. I was feeling weirdly insecure about hanging around after my defeat, especially with Adam watching me quietly, clearly unsure whether I needed to be consoled like a child. In his defense, I might have been pouting. "Anna, let's bring your prize home."

"Here," Jason said, plucking the tree out of Anna's grip, "I'll help you get this wrapped up and on top of your car."

"That would be great." She smiled at Jason before turning to me. "Hales, will you grab the car and meet us up front?" She was already walking away as I agreed, so I started heading to the parking lot, Adam beside me. I didn't need help driving the car up to the front, but I assumed he didn't want to just stand alone waiting for Jason, and I wasn't going to turn away handsome company.

"So," he said after a few feet, "Hales?"

"Haley. Hales is just a nickname."

"I like it. If you ever wanted to be a meteorologist, you'll already have a topical name."

"I'll keep that in mind in case I ever want to pivot, but for now, I'll stick to what I know."

"Which is?"

"Project management. Though maybe I need to start teaching classes on how to judge competitions. I hereby offer you a free introductory course on Christmas trees." I was trying to be funny, but I may have still been a little salty. Normally, Anna would have just gone with whatever tree I wanted because she didn't really care much so long as it fit in the apartment and smelled good.

"I take it I won't be in the running to judge any future competitions?"

"No, sir, you will not."

"Wait, are there actually any future competitions?" He got a rundown of the twelve dares list that Anna and I had come up with, glossing over the original reason, in part so as to not ruin the light mood and in part because I was embarrassed. I was constantly trying to tell myself that there was nothing to be ashamed of, but it felt uncomfortable telling a near-stranger that your parents would rather go on vacation than spend the holidays with their daughter.

"What's taking you both so long," Anna yelled out behind us. She and Jason were walking up, Jason with both arms full of our mesh-wrapped tree. Adam and I slowed to a stop, though we were already walking about as slowly as possible. We were only a few feet from Anna's car at this point and waited until they reached us. Jason lifted the tree onto the car's roof, wrapping it with rope we brought for this purpose. Anna and I shot glances at each other and then at the guys while they secured the tree. The sharp honk of a nearby car's horn interrupted the awkward silence that formed once the tree was secured, and we all awkwardly shuffled our feet and rubbed our hands to stay warm instead of splitting up.

"Thanks for your help," I said to the guys. Anna opened her door, and I moved to the passenger side, hiding a smile as I caught the wink Jason shot Anna before waving to us both.

"No problem," Jason acknowledged my thanks before shifting his attention back to Anna, "make sure you text me a picture of that award-winning tree all decorated." The car we were blocking honked again after that, so Jason and Alex were forced to move across the lane to get out of the way. Reluctantly, Anna and I plopped down into our seats and shut the doors.

"So," I said, turning to her as I clicked my seatbelt into place, "you got his phone number, right?"

1.2

"How have you managed to store this many decorations in our apartment without me knowing about it," Anna looked at me as I brought out yet another tub, this one filled with various tinsel and lights.

I'd never understood how some people only had one set of holiday decorations. I mean, sure, everyone should probably have a base set – enough lights in either white or multicolor for your tree (plus an extra strand for when you inevitably realize some are burnt out), enough ornaments to provide some interest on the tree, something to top it with, a tree skirt, and then at least one or two free-standing items to pull the room together – but is that really enough? How do you handle the years when you decide to change up your base lights? And who doesn't end up buying at least one or two cute ornaments each year? Not to mention, who wants just one room of the house decorated? If you don't celebrate Christmas, fair, but if you do? Well, okay, my standards were probably a bit inflated.

I had always been a multicolored lights devotee for the tree. Do what you want around the rest of your home, but the harsher, brighter light given off by strands of white lights just never appealed to me. I wanted a cozy glow, something that you wanted to settle in by with cocoa, a blanket, and a book to read for hours on cold winter nights. I really tried one year to like white lights on the tree, thus the several untouched strands of them in the tub I began unloading, but when it came down to it, I always went back to multicolored lights.

With N*SYNC's first holiday CD playing (a classic), Anna fluffed branches and rifled through tubs until she found a tree skirt covered in tiny Christmas trees decorated with matching tree skirts that she started wrapping around the six-foot pine sitting in the corner of our living room. If you looked really closely, there was a pattern on the tree skirts of the trees on the tree skirt, and I liked to believe that the pattern repeated itself indefinitely.

Eventually, we reached my favorite tubs. The ones that, at first glance, appeared to be filled only with bubble wrap and tissue paper. The ones that really weren't holding much physically, but they were filled with a lifetime's worth of memories recorded in the form of ornaments. I had a tub filled with various matching baubles somewhere, but those rarely got used.

Growing up, I woke up each year on Christmas morning to a stocking hung on the wall next to our tree, above a construction paper fireplace. The stocking, filled with candy and small gifts, was handed out as soon as I woke up to placate me until my brother woke up an hour or two later (it'd be four if he was allowed, but I always managed to find a way to wake him, accidentally of course). Next to each stocking hung an ornament, personalized to each of us and commemorating something special that had occurred that year in our lives: a tiny dog bowl the year I begged my parents to let us get a dog, a guitar for Jake the year he started learning to play.

"Tell me about this one," Anna pulled me out of my internal reminiscing to bring her along with me down memory lane. It was my favorite part, she knew, unwrapping each ornament and retelling the story behind it. She'd heard them all before, but she indulged me.

"The jellyfish," I laughed at the little glass sea creature with fluttering ribbon for tentacles, "as you already know, is because my family will never let me live down the year we took a trip to Florida, and I got stung by a jellyfish."

"Are you sure it was getting stung that they won't let you live down," she questioned, "or the fact that you came out of the water insisting, loudly, that someone pee on you?"

"I was seven!"

Anna smirked at me before unwrapping the next ornament. Most of the ornaments were more benign, like the Italian flag from the first year I went on an international trip, but they were my history. My parents boxed up each of the ornaments when I first moved out. I was going to have a Christmas tree in my own home, and they'd ensured that I still felt a connection to my family in a new place. It worked, but each year, I got closer to needing to put up a second tree due to my penchant for buying myself a new ornament or two (or three) in addition to the yearly ornament they still gave me. I wondered sadly about what would happen this year, whether an ornament was waiting at my parents' house for me that they'd give me when they returned or if this was the year that more than one tradition ended.

A few hours later, Anna and I lounged on the couch, admiring our ability to fill the tree we had brought home earlier with a truly absurd amount of decorations. Mine were enough to already push the tree to over-decorated, but we filled the tree with Anna's small collection of ornaments as well. Her love of haphazardly flung tinsel knew no bounds, and between that and our combined collection of ornaments, very little of the tree could actually be seen. The lights were sparkling through, though, and the smell of pine was starting to fill the apartment. We sat quietly for a long time, appreciating the ambiance we'd created.

Later that night, I was back in the same spot, reading and drinking cocoa while I tried to decompress. Anna had gone out with some friends, and I appreciated having the apartment to myself. A few hours passed before I put my book aside and plopped myself down on the floor. Thankfully, someone at the tree lot earlier had cut off the bottom few rows of branches because I had always loved to lay underneath Christmas trees.

I wiggled my way below, taking a deep breath in and gazing up at the lights from a different vantage point. I wasn't one for wishing upon shooting stars in the sky, too unpredictable and wild, but every year, I did make one wish. I peered up and found the star topping our tree, its glittery coating glinting through the branches thanks to the lights surrounding it, and I made my yearly wish, a Christmas worth remembering. The tree star hadn't let me down yet, so if my luck held, this year would be no different.

DAY 2: WIN AN UGLY CHRISTMAS SWEATER CONTEST

What was it about Saturday mornings? They always came too early. Even when I slept in later than normal, Saturday mornings still showed up much too soon after laying down to sleep the night before.

There was no question why I was currently awake, though. Anna's quiet knocking at my bedroom door sounded like a gavel slamming down on a desk. "Hales? You awake yet?" I could only groan in response to her question from the other side of the door, but that seemed to be enough for her, given that the door swung open and a roommate-sized weight bounced on the foot of my bed. "Oh, good, you're up!" I groaned again, making a decent attempt at opening my eyes, but speech was still too much to ask of me. "I was going through my collection of holiday sweaters, and nothing is really speaking to me. I need a second win under my belt," another groan, "so I can't leave today up to the chance that one of the other ladies has a secret weapon sweater stashed away for just such an occasion as today's brunch."

"What about me? I could have a secret sweater collection."

Anna shot me a look, managing exasperation and resignation simultaneously. "We both know you're not a contender. For all your holiday spirit, you've never gotten on board with the ugly sweater trend. Your holiday sweaters are actually cute. I was genuinely surprised that you agreed to this being one of the dares."

She had a point. I liked seeing other people in silly holiday sweaters, but they were always so itchy or lumpy or both. Plus, ugly sweaters were...ugly, and I didn't like being laughed at, even if people thought they were laughing with me. "I was just trying to give you one easy win so that you don't fall too far behind."

"I'm undefeated!" I resisted pointing out that we were only one challenge in. "But, more importantly, I've decided that you have to actually throw your hat in the ring today. No cute red and green stripes, no tasteful threads of tinsel-like sparkle. I told my mom we'd send her photos of us when I convinced you."

I couldn't disappoint Mrs. Koyama. Not only would Anna never let me forget it, I knew her mom loved having silly pictures of us. I grumbled my assent as I forced myself to finally sit up.

"Good," Anna nodded happily, "be ready in fifteen minutes, and we'll head to the thrift store."

"What? Why can't I just use one of your four-million sweaters that you won't be wearing?"

"Because you need your own, even if you just tuck it in one of your Christmas tubs for next year. Think of it this way: once you have one, you'll always be prepared when there is, inevitably, an ugly sweater party each year." She had a fair point. Normally, I just showed up to those parties wearing my normal clothes and feigned either ignorance or an inability to find where my sweaters were tucked away. People always seemed annoyed, like I'd ruined their good time, so maybe having a sweater that I could deal with would get people off my back about it.

"Plus, I need to find something fresh. Hop to it!" With that, Anna bounced out of my room.

Thirty minutes later, we were sitting in the car waiting for the thrift store to open. We were only a few minutes early, and thankfully I had the forethought to grab a thermos of cocoa before I was enthusiastically shepherded out of the apartment. Anna was looking at this as a serendipitous mistake because it would mean that we got the benefit of looking through all of the sweaters before things got picked over later this morning.

I sipped my cocoa while half-listening to Anna list the attributes of her ideal sweater. She wanted something silly but not childish, something that was impossible to see without making the viewer laugh. I planned to just look around and pick something palatable. If I was going to be keeping this around for a few years' worth of ugly sweater events, it needed to be just weird enough that I could reasonably argue that it was an ugly sweater, but not stand out enough that I'd be uncomfortable every year.

We spotted an employee at the doors, presumably unlocking them. Time to head in. Apparently, the store had an inventory of holiday sweaters that they dug out this time each year because the only other explanation for the number of racks of them up front was that everyone decided to donate their ugly sweaters before the season ended. We split up but were still close enough that the next thirty minutes were filled with one of us laughing, holding up a sweater, and then both of us cracking up.

I got distracted and ended up going through other sections, looking around for anything that would make a good gift. Most of my gifts were already purchased, but I liked being able to add extra goodies.

Anna eventually found me in the book section, flipping through the pages of a Jamaican chef's cookbook. The recipes sounded and looked delicious, and I figured my parents would enjoy having them when they got back. A miraculously-unopened build-a-robot kit was tucked under my arm that my brother's girlfriend, a mechanical engineer, would love.

"Those don't look like sweaters," Anna's flat tone jerked me out of making a mental grocery list to try out a few of the cookbook's recipes before wrapping it up for my parents.

"I was just letting you have first pick," I joked as I started heading back over to the racks of sweaters. "Give me ten minutes or so, and then I'll come find you."

I scanned each option quickly before moving onto the next, but nothing called to me. I decided on a red sweater with a giant Christmas tree on it. Other than the torso-sized tree emblazoned on the front, it wasn't too outlandish, but it would do for brunch. Anna was always going to win this dare, so I considered it a known loss.

Obviously, I'd need to up my game after this to catch up, but that was a problem for tomorrow me. The wrinkle I didn't expect was the look of disappointment on Anna's face when I got to the register. She had already checked out, her purchase tucked away in a bag, but her smile crumbled when she saw the relatively plain and definitely tame sweater that I handed to the teenager ringing up my items.

"That's what you picked out? I saw the other options, and there were tons that were goofier than that."

"Goofy wasn't exactly what I was going for," I shrugged as I tapped my card to pay. We walked back to the car in silence.

"I was really excited about you getting into the spirit of an ugly sweater party for once." Anna's quiet confession broke the silence a few minutes later. I looked over and was surprised to see that her disappointment seemed to actually be bordering on hurt. I had assumed that she'd roll her eyes at me and that would be it, but the feeling of shame running through me was enough to realize that I'd messed up. I needed to fix it.

We were getting pretty close to our apartment, just about to turn down a nearby street filled with little shops that I knew included a small yarn and crafts store. Without any real plan besides hoping I could somehow make my new sweater something ridiculous, I had Anna pull over. I shot her a grin in response to her confused look as I unbuckled my seatbelt.

"I have one more stop, but I can walk home from here. I don't want to ruin the surprise." Anna looked ready to push for more information, but a car honking behind us jolted her focus away from me. "You didn't really think that I was going to wear this sweater as-is, did you? This is just the canvas on which I will create my masterpiece!"

I gave her a wave as I shut the door, watching as a flicker of hope lit up face. I hadn't meant to do anything more than add some kind of star to the top of the sweater's tree, but obviously I had to put in more effort. It was the smallest possible concession to make my best friend happy, so I walked back a few shops to the yarn store, hoping that they sold things other than just yarn since I needed beginner level adornments.

The tinkling of dozens of bells attached to the lacy curtain hung on the door greeted me. Sounds of chatter from a corner filled with a group of women all sitting together and working on various projects momentarily stopped and looked over. Still holding the door handle, I was trying to decide if I should just slowly back away and deal with disappointing my friend.

The silence lasted barely long enough for it to register before everyone started saying hello and waving me inside. I explained my predicament, and the excited chatter that followed eased my discomfort. I skirted around ever calling what I needed an "ugly" sweater, just in case, and the ladies all seemed on board to make my sweater so silly that it would be the talk of the town.

One of the women, about my age, put aside what looked to be a baby blanket and pulled a contraption out of her bag. "I can show you how to make a quick puff-ball out of yarn to top the tree with," she offers.

"A puff-ball?" One of the older women rolled her eyes. "A tree needs a star!"

"Why not a star with puff-balls," a third woman suggested.

"A star made of puff-balls!"

"A puff-ball made of stars!"

"Why not an angel?"

"How are we supposed to make an angel out of puff balls?"

"Obviously, we'll also need decorations for the tree."

"What about presents for under it?"

"And snowflakes above!"

"It doesn't snow inside."

"You don't know where the tree is."

My neck swiveled between the ladies as they volleyed ideas between them. I seemed to be in good hands, even if I had no idea what half of the ideas and techniques they were discussing meant.

"I see you've met the Knittie Bitties," someone said from behind me. I turned to face a middle-aged woman in a knit cardigan. The confusion must have been clear on my face because she clarified, nodding her head toward the still-arguing ladies, "those are the Knittie Bitties. When I opened this store, I considered hosting classes or social hours to try and bring in new customers, but they arrived the second week the store was open, started their own group, and they've claimed my shop sitting space as their own. If they're already rallying to help, you must have won them over."

"I'm not sure how," I admitted, "I just stood in the doorway and then got pulled inside. I'm completely hopeless with anything crafty."

"We do love a project!" The eldest of the group, a woman with a distinctly mischievous glint in her eye, laughed as she yelled over to us as she set her yarn down. "The chaps can wait. I'll get a star going for you."

"Did you just...are you making..." I looked at what she set aside, what I first assumed to be extremely long arms for a sweater, that did now look suspiciously like pants, or, at least, most of a pair of pants.

"You see," she said in a conspiratorial whisper that wasn't any quieter than when she yelled over before, "Irma, from my bunko group, well, her grandson was visiting last week, and the three of us had lunch together. I mentioned wanting someone to model the hats and mittens and sweaters and such that I've been making since my grand-niece got me set up with a website to sell them. He's a nice young man, and he offered to be my model! I may as well see just how nice he and his behind are and put him in some drafty chaps. I'll tell him they're part of my cowboy collection!"

While I was stunned into silence, the other ladies seemed to be used to this woman's antics because they all gave her a smile and then continued discussing my sweater. The cowboy collection knitter waved to the aisles of yarn as she pulled a yellow-gold ball out of an enormous bag. "Go on and find supplies for your sweater. We'll start working on your star."

2.2

An hour later, I walked back into the apartment and jumped in surprise when Anna popped up from lying on the couch, peering at my bag. Before leaving the shop, I had asked the shop owner, whose name I later learned was Jean, if she had any bags that didn't have the store's logo on them. She didn't, but for some reason Bernie, the grandma with plans of objectifying her friend's grandson, had a paper bag from a recent grocery store run in her yarn bag.

Jean took me around the store to look through yarns and the variety of other craft supplies. Raquel, the Knittie Bittie that first offered to help, joined us long enough to point out the puff-ball device she took out earlier sitting on a shelf and to suggest a few different types of yarn to create different textures in puff-balls. Maudette, another of the Knittie Bitties, appeared out of thin air to plop a glitter-threaded chunky yarn into my basket. Tinsel for the tree, she said, before peering at a wall of gadgets and adding what looked like a velcro ring with a hook on top into the basket. Nodding, she headed back to her seat.

I took it upon myself to add a bag of jingle bells and a few other things that seemed similarly familiar and simple to use to my basket. A few of the other Knittie Bitties popped over to add various things as Jean and I made our way around the store.

When we made the rounds and returned to the group of ladies, I stared at a bright yellow star sitting on the little table next to Bernie, another attached to what looked like a metal chopstick with a hook in progress. Without looking up from her work, Bernie tilted her head to the completed star on the table. "You'll need to get some stuffing, dear. We'll attach these two stars together so it's 3D."

"No need," a forty-something man that must have arrived as I was wandering the aisles added while giving me a friendly wave. "The ladies got me up to speed. I've got tons of tails that I've saved for this type of thing that you can use instead of buying a full bag of stuffing."

"Come on now, Dale, the rest of the group was doing so well at upselling," Jean joked. I had my suspicions that my nearly-full basket was ninety percent items that I didn't need to jazz up my sweater, but every time someone added something, usually without even explaining why, it felt like I was being taken care of by each of them.

"And look," Raquel said, proudly holding up five completed mini puff-balls in the same bright yellow, "these can go on each of the points!"

"Do you know what yarn they're using," I quietly asked Jean, "I'd like to get some to replace it and thank them."

"I do. I'll grab some and bring your basket to the register." I stayed put, watching everyone work on various things, still stunned that a few of their projects were meant for me. Jean waved me over to the register with everything already scanned. I guess I wouldn't be sneaking anything back onto the shelves. For now I was just grateful for the help.

After paying, I returned to the Knittie Bitties and Bernie passed over a completed three-dimensional star made from the two flat star pieces she'd been making, filled with the yarn tail scraps Dale offered up earlier, and mini puff-balls attached to each point of the star. "This is incredible. How did you make this so quickly?"

"It was a group effort, dear," Bernie said, smiling at Raquel who beamed with pride at the acknowledgement.

"Everyone here helps each other," Dale stated fondly. "They took me under their wing when I needed something to keep my hands and mind busy after a knee injury that kept me mostly sedentary during recovery. My wife suggested knitting and had seen this group here when she'd come in to get a book for beginners and asked if she and I could join them for an afternoon."

I looked around the group subtly, trying to guess who Dale's wife was. There were a few younger women, the closest in age to Dale was probably Raquel, but they hadn't been interacting as anything other than new friends. I clearly wasn't being as subtle as I was attempting, though, as Dale chuckled and clarified. "My wife isn't here. Although she is cautious to leave me here with Bernie, the scoundrel."

"Is she coming by later?" I asked Dale, curious if I'd get to meet his wife before I had to get going. Dale was instantly likeable, and I had a feeling his wife would be too.

"Nah. She came with me the first two or three times I showed up here after she asked if we could join, but she didn't have the patience for knitting or crocheting. I'm not that skilled yet, but I really enjoy it. She's been on the hunt for a new hobby now, and we've both been embracing the time we spend apart, me here and her trying out new things, as a fulfilling aspect of our mental and social lives where we're not tied to each other at all times."

"That's..." I stalled as I tried to think of the right word. I was impressed, but that didn't seem quite right.

"Healthy?" Dale offered. "It's important to us both that we're not solely wrapped up in each other. That we have a support system outside of our relationship, and learning a new craft has been wonderful for not feeling stagnant. We moved here a few years ago when Lily, my wife, got a new job, and we realized we didn't have a ton of true friends here yet when I didn't have many people nearby to call or have visit when I got hurt."

"That's tough, but understandable. Making new friends as an adult is a nightmare." I didn't want to wallow in it, but I'd been thinking lately about how I needed to branch out. Anna was always meeting new people and having fun, but I felt like I just stayed stagnant, relying on Anna and other long-term friends when I wanted company. More often lately I'd been noticing that I'd been just spending time alone instead of making an effort, and I didn't love that realization. "What types of new hobbies has she tried so far?"

"She tried crochet and embroidery when we came here together, stained glass and candle making at workshops she found at various studios around the city, and she recently took a one-night pottery workshop. She has since signed up for a four-week class. She's been watching videos on her phone and computer every day on different tips and tricks or projects to try to make ever since, and I have a gut feeling that she's going to be sticking with it for a long time. Maybe one day we'll end up with a whole set of beautiful dishes that she made!" Dale beamed, clearly happy for and proud of his wife.

We sat in comfortable silence for a few minutes, content to watch the rest of the group. I started looking through the things in my bag, trying to make a plan when Bernie interrupted. "Don't just sit there, girly, get out that sweater." Suddenly everyone was looking at me expectantly, so

I pulled the sweater out of my bag and held it up, showing it around to the group.

"Wow," Raquel said before letting out a low whistle, "you really did find the most boring holiday sweater possible."

"I was trying to find something I could use year after year, not a statement piece."

"Whether you want it to or not, it's making a statement."

"That you're boring, dear," Bernie chimed in when I didn't reply, smacking her hands on her knees, "we've got a lot of work to do. Empty out that bag of goodies and let's get to it."

I did as I was told, noticing as I did that a few extra items had made it into my bag. I checked my receipt when I got it and didn't notice anything extra, so Jean must have added these herself. Dale was right, the people here really did take care of each other, and they seemed to have taken me under their wing, although I was struggling to figure out why.

Raquel motioned me over to the now-open seat beside her, where she started explaining and demonstrating the best way to attach the star to the sweater before handing over a needle and more of the yellow-gold yarn to me to finish. Patiently, she watched as I fumbled my way through, lightly teasing me when I was doing well and gently guiding me on how to recover when I accidentally tried to stitch too far apart or where the attaching yarn would show instead of being tucked behind the star. When I finally tied everything off, the sweater was passed around until everyone had added their own touches of flair.

"Now that," Bernie declared as we all admired the now ridiculous, but still cute, sweater, "is a statement piece worthy of the statement it's making."

2.3

"Hales?" Anna's voice snapped me out of memories of this morning and back to our apartment. "Were you at the grocery store this whole time?"

"Oh," I said, patting the paper bag my sweater and various other craft and yarn leftovers and tools were hiding in, "I was just getting things for my sweater so that I can win today's dare." I left Anna to try to wrap her mind around what I might need at the grocery store for my sweater and headed into my room.

We only had about twenty minutes before we needed to leave, so my hair went up into a bun for a quick body shower before washing my face, moisturizing, and putting on mascara. Years of teenage and early-twenties acne led the skincare gods to finally cut me some slack, so I left the makeup at that and moved over to my closet. I toyed with the idea of putting on the black leather skirt that some version of me in the past purchased with grand intentions, thinking the dichotomy of the skirt and sweater would be fun, before grabbing my favorite pair of jeans. This was going to be uncomfortable enough, no need to pretend to be a whole new person.

"Anna, are you almost ready?" I shouted, cracking my bedroom door enough to peek out.

"Ready when you are. Ari already texted that she's running a little late."

"No surprise there, but I am surprised that she's texting in advance of already being late," I said, chuckling.

Ari was always late. Years ago, we met her when she was working as a waitress at a restaurant that Anna and I frequented. She'd said hello, but then hadn't been back to the table for so long that we thought the restaurant had forgotten that we'd been seated. She came over just as we were about to leave and go somewhere else, telling us about back-of-house drama that she had been unwilling to skip out on witnessing before ordering us a pitcher sangria, telling us that it would be better than whatever we were going to order for drinks. She was right.

At the end of our meal, Ari told us that she decided we were all going to be good friends and gave us each a slip of paper with her cell phone number. She had us set up a group text thread before she left the table, and that was that.

She was constantly running a few minutes late, though, and it had become a running joke, especially since she always came with an absurd tale about what caused her tardiness. Lion tamers had been searching for a lost lion that she found and befriended, she had eaten all but one flavor of donut and needed to wait until the store made more of the missing flavor, and let's not forget about the time she decided to follow a duck that she was certain was saying things other than "quack."

Once, I walked up to a museum we and a few others were meeting at and saw her leaning against the wall outside. After we said hi, she told me that she'd be inside in a minute or two but that she couldn't risk her reputation by being on time. She "arrived" a few minutes later, with a wink for me and a fanciful tale about getting a lead for tracking down a piece of sunken treasure supposedly hidden in the city.

I hated when most people were constantly late, but since that day I had the sneaking suspicion that she'd being doing it purposely, knowing that trying to guess about what had stalled her had become a fun game for the rest of us. Plus, she was typically less than five minutes late, and never when it would truly inconvenience us.

As I stepped into the hall, Anna turned and proudly held out the bottom corners of her sweater so that I could see it in its full glory. At first glance, it was just rows and rows of reindeer in all different stances, but there was no way Anna would be satisfied with that alone. It took a few seconds, but I finally realized that each of the rows of reindeer were doing a different dance. One row was doing the Y-M-C-A, one the macarena, the next what I think might have been the electric slide. "I love it, but what's the last row's dance?"

"Ah, I think that might just be individual, notable dance moves. See," she said, pointing out different reindeer, "Those two are doing the Charleston; that one's dabbing; that one is—"

"Twerking! Incredible. Truly a top tier thrifting find."

"Thank you, thank you," Anna said while taking a bow. She stood back up, finally looking me over, before making a noise somewhere between a laugh and a screech. "Look at yours! There's no way that's the same sweater you had when we left the store! Is this what you were doing after I dropped you off? Why did you have a grocery bag? Look at that star! Where did you even find that? Are those jingle bells? Jingle, woman, what are you waiting for?"

I was laughing so hard that I was shaking, unintentionally jingling the bells that lined the collar and bottom hem of the sweater. Anna plucked at the tinsel that someone twisted up each when she finally stopped to take a breath. I still had no idea where that came from since the yarn store didn't sell any that I'd seen. "I'll tell you the story on the way." We had planned to walk to the restaurant, and thankfully it was sunny enough to combat the chill. I filled Anna in on my morning adventures, telling her about the Knittie Bitties and how they sneakily set me up with a starter kit of materials and tools. Anna was, as anyone would be, especially interested in feisty, wonderful Bernadette.

"I want to be her when I grow up," Anna said as we walked through the front door of the restaurant.

"Who's Bernadette," a familiar voice asked from behind us. We turned to one of our friends, Sita, before we all exchanged hugs and hellos. "Maddie just texted me. She's got a table for us already."

As a budding content creator, Maddie's habit of finding places to try that had both great lighting and excellent food was unparalleled. She avoided places that had already gotten a lot of online attention to avoid the crowds and places relying on their popularity but where service or quality declined, so we all trusted her restaurant recommendations implicitly. She wasn't rigid or pretentious about her online aesthetic, though, so it was no surprise when she was all over Anna's suggestion to make brunch an ugly sweater contest.

Maddie stood up to greet us, giving us all a view of the short-sleeved shirt she was wearing under an open cardigan. A picture of Santa and Mrs. Claus kissing took up the whole front, with Mrs. Claus's hands on Santa's butt.

"You go girl!" Sita laughed, pointing at Mrs. Claus. "Where on Earth did you find that shirt?"

"Remember last month when I had that art center partnership and took their screen-printing workshop? I stayed in touch with the artist who taught the class, mostly exchanging graphic novel recommendations when we heard of something worth picking up. I asked if she'd be willing to make a shirt last-minute at an expedited rate if I managed to find a photo of what I wanted. She actually offered to draw it as well, and she obviously knocked it out of the park!"

Maddie was always taking new classes and trying new things, and she was so genuinely kind that she often kept up connections with acquaintances she'd made. This wasn't the first time it had benefitted her, and probably wouldn't be the last. It didn't hurt that she was adamant about paying for people's work and time when things like this came up, so people were usually happy to help if they could.

"Truly a work of art. I wonder if she'd be willing to draw out a tattoo design for me."

"I can ask her, and if she's up for it get you two connected," Maddie said as she got herself settled back into her seat. "Did you end up finding something festive?"

"Nothing ridiculous, I'm afraid. I was so zonked after a busy week, that I just needed to lounge, but I did have this beauty in my closet." Sita shrugged off her coat to display a gorgeous white sweater with delicate silver and cyan snowflakes seeming to fall from the shoulders.

"It's stunning," Anna said, Maddie and I murmuring our agreement. "I knew when I suggested adding the theme that most of us would just grab whatever we had already available, but I wasn't expecting something so gorgeous."

"Wait, how come you didn't let me sleep in this morning then," I joked.

"I'd hazard a guess that you had nothing available to pick from," Sita supplied.

"That all changes today," Anna added happily, "our girl finally caved. Check out mine first so that I can have a moment of glory before Hales makes her big reveal." Anna turned and hung her coat off of her chair before turning around with a flourish. Maddie and Sita each pointed out the different dances on Anna's sweaters, doing a seated version of the dance in their chairs between ordering drinks from a waiter who arrived shortly after we sat down. We all had tears in our eyes from laughing so hard when, ten minutes later, Maddie was attempting to twerk from her chair without realizing that the waiter had walked up behind her and was trying not to spill the tray of drinks in his hands as he shook with silent laughter.

"I didn't know we were having a dance party, but count me in."

"Ari!" All four of us exclaimed as one.

She beamed, walking around the table to give everyone hugs. "Sorry I'm late, I had to help a lost parrot find its owners. Thankfully, its vocabulary was spectacular!"

"What an odd morning," the waiter said, eyes glued to Ari, "but you're just in time for the show." She turned to face our waiter and her smile shifted from friendly to slightly seductive. "I'm Bradley, and I'll be doing my very best to take care of you today." His expression started to mirror Ari's, taking a long pause before continuing. "What can I grab you to drink?"

"Surprise me," she purred, and he started turning around, taking the tray full of our drinks with him. He only made it a few seven steps before stopping, turning around, and handing out the drinks with a sheepish look. Recovering quickly, he laughed at himself before telling us he'd be back in a few minutes.

Ari shrugged her coat off as we all settled back in. Apparently, she'd had a hectic morning that started with spilling coffee all over her snowman-covered sweater when her dog jumped and startled her.

Bradley, predictably, showed back up with Ari's drink when she was mentioning having to whip her shirt off and find something else to wear. The waggling eyebrows he directed her way should have been somewhere between lecherous and lame, but he was doing it so exaggeratedly that it was clear that even he wasn't taking himself seriously. The rest of us were all trying not to laugh at his attempts at flirting, while Ari responded in kind, flustering him.

The rest of brunch went similarly, with Bradley stopping by far more often than necessary, but we were all benefiting from the little bonuses he brought to the table in an attempt to woo Ari. After forcing myself to get over my embarrassment and fear of being laughed at, I showed off my sweater and Anna and I tag-teamed an animated recounting of my morning with the Knittie Bitties. I kept silently reminding myself that my friends were laughing with me, and eventually I forgot to be self-conscious and enjoyed recounting the tale.

We moved on to hyping Sita up for an upcoming job interview, brainstorming different things for Maddie to cover in her blog and social media accounts over the next month, and explaining my parents' change in holiday plans. It didn't sting quite so much today, having wrapped myself in the fun of the first two dares and especially the understanding and support from my friends.

Maddie and Sita didn't celebrate Christmas, but they could tell I was bummed, and they nominated themselves as my date to do different holiday activities if we had time in between the dares. No doubt they'd go all in for them, glad to celebrate for the sake of celebrating. After Anna explained our twelve dares of Christmas list, Sita and Ari demanded a re-do of the today's dare, arguing that they would have given us more competition if they'd known, but Maddie shut them down, apparently now invested in winning today's dare for bragging rights and liking her odds.

"Should we have Bradley pick a winner for your dare," Sita asked later as we were all sipping on the last of our drinks as we waited for our cards to be run for our respective portions of the bill, "or do we think he's going to be unable to be impartial with Ari here?"

Ari snorted, gesturing at the black sweater dress she was wearing. "I don't think I'm even in the running."

"In the running for what?" Bradley really had impeccable timing. He set down each of our checks, with something that looked suspiciously like a phone number scrawled on the bottom of Ari's.

"Well," Anna started, "obviously, we've all donned our absolutely best festive apparel, but who blew the others out of the park?"

"Hmmm," he said, his expression turning studious, "let me see the contenders." Maggie, Anna, and I leaned back in our chairs to show off our sweaters, and Sita held out her arms to show off hers. Bradley laughed at each sweater in turn, pointing out unique elements and compliment-ing my adornments. "While there are three unhinged options, and one elegant one, my preference is always going to be something more subtle." He smiled over at Ari, leaning in slightly, as we all tried to puzzle out what he meant. "There's really no other option for a winner than the woman with green eyes the color of a grove of Christmas trees." He straightened back up, pointing at the writing on the bottom of her check, "give me a call and I'll take you out to celebrate your win." He shot her a wink before he turned around and headed back towards the kitchens.

"Wait, *what*?" Anna said after a few seconds of silence. "Did that just happen?"

"You've got to admit, that was pretty smooth," I said, chuckling and pointing to Ari. "You should probably give him a call later."

"So, what does that mean for your dares?" Sita asked. "Obviously, there was more likely chance that Maggie would steal the win from one of you two if anyone, but either way it's a loss for both of you, right?"

"I guess this means neither of us gets a point for today," Anna shrugged.

DAY 3: COLLECT THREE KISSES UNDER THE MISTLETOE

There was something truly maddening about a Monday before any type of holiday. Everyone was trying to get work done quickly so that they could coast through the rest of the week and maybe even sneak out early, but no one was actually in the mood to do any work.

My day so far had been waves of allegedly urgent emails and projects that were supposedly going to destroy the company if not given immediate attention, interspersed with long periods of absolutely nothing. I could already tell that it was going to be one of those days where plenty of people miraculously all finished work and needed me to weigh in on something right as the day was ending.

Sitting on work until the end of the day to ensure you yourself weren't going to get responses that needed action right at the end of your day was, admittedly, something I'd done before, but it was obnoxious to be on the receiving end. Double standard? Sure, but I tried not to do it often. Only for my problem-child counterparts in other teams.

Since I was usually required to give sign-off on final documents used to place orders at the small sales company I worked at, if something came back to me at the end of the day, the sales teams seemed to think that they could just continue to email and call me all night, sometimes even texting my personal cell phone, though that got them blocked immediately. It was just better for my sanity if the ball was in their court at the end of the day. Luckily, I was ditching work early to meet Anna at a bar with an amazing happy hour deal. I only needed my inbox to remain empty for another ten minutes before I could sneak out.

Our plan for the night evolved as we texted back and forth throughout the day, needing to find a way to give one of us the chance to win today's dare: kissing three people under mistletoe. We had established a few ground rules: kisses had to be with human people (rudely, Anna would not agree to let me count the kisses I got from a coworker's dog who came into the office today), the other person had to witness it, only the first person kissed got to count the smooch towards their goal if the other person got a kiss by the same person, and no leading anyone on.

Our original plan was to wander around the city, stopping into places like stores, bars, and the downtown holiday market until we found some mistletoe. We wanted things to unfold organically—wandering the streets under the city lights, finding mistletoe in a doorway, willing partners magically appearing.

In an attempt to get an advantage, I walked to the nearby holiday market during lunch to scope out any spots where mistletoe hung, but there was none to be found. If a holiday market catering to the magic of the holidays, and reasonably also the romance of that magic, didn't have mistletoe, I didn't have high hopes for us just wandering around the city until we found some. Neither of us could come up with a decent alternative, so we opted to meet up at our favorite local bar to figure things out.

My patience only kept me at my desk for another three minutes before I called it a day and shut my computer down. The few extra minutes of freedom felt like I was getting away with something as I packed up my things and tried to escape without notice. Silently celebrating my success, I pushed open the doors, took a deep breath of fresh air, and started walking over to the bar.

I loved the place we were meeting. The bar took up half of what would have otherwise been one huge space, with a restaurant in the other half, separated by a soundproof, black glass wall. The owners wanted to have a bar space that was a more trendy, young adult vibe (as opposed to the very family-friendly restaurant on the other side) but without needing bar patrons to give up access to great food, even if there was a far more limited menu.

I had a theory that the owners just didn't want people drinking without having anything in their stomachs to ensure no one got too drunk too quickly and became a problem. Whatever the reason, it meant that when I arrived early and grabbed Anna and I a couple seats at the bar in the center of the space, I immediately ordered a few appetizers. Anna plopped down on the seat next to me only a few sips of my old fashioned later.

"I've been thinking about today's dare," Anna said as she sat down. "It's a little weird that we set this one on a Monday night. Somehow, it seems even more awkward."

"We could always switch out today's dare with whatever is set for Friday."

"And have to kiss seven people? I'll pass."

"We could just skip this one. No points for either of us."

Anna considered this for a minute before shaking her head. "That doesn't feel right either. Then it's just eleven dares of Christmas spread across twelve days. I'm dedicated to the bit."

"I guess we'll just see where the night takes us."

"I fully intend on finding my dream man tonight," Anna said as the bartender walked up. He raised an eyebrow at her statement. Anna pointed a finger at one of the bottles on the shelf behind him and continued, "And that man is Johnny Walker. Neat."

"You'll need to get in line; that's my man," the bartender replied, pouring her drink before passing it over, "but I guess I can share." Anna took a sip of her drink, watching as the bartender left to help other patrons.

"I know he's paid to be nice to customers, but do we think I could convince him to help me meet the kiss quota?"

"Of all men that are attracted to women, I'd bet that very few would need to be paid to be nice to you, so who knows."

"Hmmm." She thought it over for a few seconds before exclaiming, "Oh! Look what I made us!" A poster got pulled out of a cylindrical tube from her bag and unrolled. It was a list of our twelve dares, with boxes for who won each day. "Also, I made candy cane stickers to mark which of us, if either or both, wins each dare." The whole thing was reminiscent of a chore chart, but Anna was a graphic designer and an excellent one at that, so it was incredibly detailed, balanced, and visually stunning.

"Now let me just..." Anna added a candy cane sticker next to her name for day one.

"What do we do about yesterday? Neither of us won. Maybe we need some coal stickers."

"Good idea. I'll make some tomorrow." Having gently pulled the poster back from me, it got rolled back up and stored safely in its tube. "Oh, I also grabbed these earlier when I was taking a mental health break from the office," Anna said, pulling two red headbands with mistletoe dangling from plastic sticks out of her bag.

"Do you have any idea how jealous I am of your boss's outlook on work, breaks, and productivity?"

"Honestly, I was really surprised at how chill he was at first, but my team has generated better quality work and brought in a handful of new clients, so it seems like it's not just good for me and the rest of the underlings but also the company as a whole." Anna's old boss had quit unexpectedly, and her boss's boss needed to fill the spot quickly. They ended up bringing in someone who was much younger and more relaxed than his predecessor, who no one thought would last, given the stubborn adherence to a "that's how things are done here" mindset by the higher-ups. Turns out, when they tried to make him fall in line, he refused and told them he'd prove them wrong, and he had. "Being able to walk away from emails and requests when you need a break from it has made being at work so much nicer."

"I take those breaks too. I just put a fake meeting on my calendar and leave when I need them to avoid sending emails that might get me fired."

"Sneaky—I love it. Anyway, a walk turned into some light window shopping, and I couldn't pass these up once I'd spotted them." We put them on, laughing at each other and taking a few silly photos until the appetizers arrived. "Oh, now we're talking." Anna rubbed her hands together while looking over the spring rolls, papaya salad, and ginger-soy chicken wings now in front of us.

Having similar tastes worked well for us at restaurants. We often ended up planning to order the same cocktail off of a specialty menu and the same few dishes with a few backups before we inevitably ended up ordering each of the items we were stuck between and splitting everything.

We made plates for ourselves and drifted into silence during our first and second bites of each dish. Anna laughed when she looked up at me doing a happy little good-food dance in my seat, something that I was constantly doing without noticing.

The mistletoe dangling from my headband had a bad habit of hitting my forehead as I moved and was getting tangled in my bangs, so it had to go. Anna gave mine a look before pulling hers off and sighing. "The headbands also would have been better on a weekend night out," she said. "On a Monday night in a well-lit bar, they're just a little too weird."

"I'm not opposed to reprising them this weekend, but I agree with you on them not fitting the current vibe," I replied in between bites. "Today might be another wash on the dares." I looked up in time to see Anna's expression rapidly change from displeasure to hopeful to sly. She took out her phone, started typing something, waited a beat as she kept eating in silence with her eyes glued to her phone, and then put the phone face-down on the bar and smiled. Huh.

"Hmmm," she replied noncommittally. "Who knows? Maybe the holiday spirit will work some magic." Again, huh. Whatever, I was fine with letting tonight just be a normal happy hour. No points for either of us was really my best outcome, but something about Anna's quick attitude change made me think she was up to something.

Anna and I spent the next thirty minutes chatting about projects we had going on at work, brainstorming holiday gifts for family and friends, and trying to decide on our next TV series to watch together since our current series was coming to a close. In the middle of a heated discussion about the pros and cons of reality television, we both swiveled at the sound of Anna's name being shouted across the bar.

"Anna! My darling! I've found you at last!" A man about our age was weaving through tables to get to us, trailed by another slightly younger man.

"Henry, my love! I've waited years for you to return to me," Anna replied in a fake British accent, gesturing dramatically.

"In fairness," he replied, now sounding much less like the showman he'd just been, "it's barely been half an hour." They hugged before the person behind him gave us a small wave.

"Haley, this is Henry, and this is Daniel. We all work together," Anna introduced us, gesturing at the new arrivals before shifting their way and waving to me, "this is my best friend, Haley."

"I thought you looked familiar," I said to Henry. We'd met previously at Anna's office, but usually just for a passing hello as she and I were heading out for one thing or another.

"You too! I'm glad for the introduction, though. I'd forgotten your name."

"No worries." I had forgotten his name, too, but I remembered how friendly and fun he was when we'd met briefly. "Obviously, that's a sign that you need to join us out more often! Let's grab a few seats."

"First, the reason we're really here," Henry said, turning to Anna, once again adopting the theatrical persona he entered with and wrapping an arm around Daniel's shoulders. "Madame, may we each steal a kiss?"

"You'd better," she joked as she put her headband back on. They each leaned in and kissed her cheek. "Just one more until I claim another win," she said as they settled into the seats next to us.

"We invited Jess as well, but she had other happy hour plans that she had to get to," Daniel added.

"Wait just a minute, you recruited people? I knew you were being cagey about something on your phone earlier!" I had to give her credit; I hadn't even considered it.

"Even so, I still need one more kiss before I get my candy cane sticker."

"The headbands make so much more sense now," the bartender laughed, clearly having been eavesdropping as he wiped off bottles.

"I don't suppose you'd be down for a quick peck?" Anna asked.

"No can do. The only kissing I'm interested in doing is with a gorgeous woman back home. Plus, my girlfriend would kick my ass to the curb so fast I wouldn't even know what happened."

"Fair enough. I am still hungry, though. Do we still have time to put in another order before happy hour ends?"

"You've got about ten minutes," he replied after a quick check of the register's clock.

"Surprise pick?" Anna asked, looking over at me.

"Sounds good to me." Anna looked back at the bartender, ordered another round of drinks for us, and asked him to surprise us with another happy hour dish of his choosing.

A few years ago, when we both started getting paid enough that we had some extra money to play with after our bills were paid, we went out for lunch and were both hungry after eating our entrees. Neither of us felt like looking back through the menu, so we asked our waiter to surprise us with something to split. They sent us something that we likely never would have chosen on our own, but it was delicious. Ever since, when we were in a similar position and just needed a top-off dish, we asked for our waiter or bartender to surprise us. It had mixed results, but it was fun, and we usually liked what we got since the waiter or bartender had a sense of what we liked from what we'd previously ordered.

"What happens if you don't like the item he rings in?" Daniel asked as the bartender turned away.

"We pack it up to-go and give it away if we see anyone homeless on our way home. If we don't, we take it back and try to rework it into something we like."

"What if that doesn't taste good either?"

"We admit defeat."

"That actually sounds like a lot of fun. It would be fun with a group where everything you ordered was a surprise. Hopefully, someone would like each thing."

Henry and Daniel stuck around for about another hour before heading out. They were both so friendly, and I found out that we had a number of common interests. Anna and I opted to stay and order another round of drinks. Henry and Daniel's seats got taken pretty quickly by another group – two guys who needed a few more seats if the almost-subtle looks they were shooting our empty plates and glasses were any indication. They stopped trying to gauge how much longer we were sticking around when our drinks were replaced.

"Anna?" Anna and I must have both assumed that someone else nearby was named Anna as well because the questioning voice barely registered until it came again, closer this time. "Anna, hey, this is a nice surprise."

"Oh my gosh, Jason," Anna said after swiveling on her barstool so abruptly that she almost fell off. There stood her tree-farm hunk. "What are you doing here?"

"Grabbing a drink with some friends," he responded, gesturing to the guys who were sitting on the barstools next to us.

"We'd been trying to steal your seats when you got up. I didn't realize you were part of the group," the guy sitting next to Anna added sheepishly.

"Oh, no, we came here separately."

"Plus," I chimed in, "we absolutely would have been doing the same if the roles were reversed."

"Guys," Jason got their attention, "this is Anna and her roommate, uh, umm…"

"Haley," I offered, taking pity on him. He'd really only had eyes for Anna when we'd met, so I wasn't surprised that he'd forgotten, even if I had hoped his dreamy brother had been talking about me since we'd met.

"Johnny," one of the guys said, waving.

"Levi," said the other. "I'm glad we've been introduced because I have a question for you. I didn't want to seem like I was interrupting or creepy before, but what's with the headbands." He nodded to the bar where our mistletoe-laden headbands were still lying.

"Let me guess," Jason said, reaching for one and putting it on, "this is another one of your dares? Does it count if you're not actually wearing it?"

"Maybe we already completed the dare," Anna said, flicking the mistletoe so that it smacked him in the forehead. "Now that we're under the mistletoe, though, I think you might need to be kissed."

"After being so viciously attached?" Jason held a hand up to his forehead, looking appalled, before winking at her. "I think I do need a kiss to make it better." Anna popped up from her seat, pulled Jason down by his shirt, and then skipped his lips to kiss his forehead.

"Wait, does it count if I kiss him?" She looked at me for confirmation.

"Given the disappointed look on his face, I'll give that one to you." I couldn't help laughing at Jason all but pouting over missing out on a less chaste kiss from Anna.

"Yes!" She shimmied in her chair before turning and kissing Jason on the cheek. "Thank you for securing my win today."

"So, yes on this being tied to the dare?" Jason asked, chuckling. "Do you need a judge again because he's walking in now." Jason nodded at the door where, sure enough, his brother was looking around for him. Adam must have caught sight of Jason because he started weaving through the crowd. He greeted his friends before flicking the mistletoe back into Jason's face. "Why do people keep doing that?" Jason grumbled.

"It is my duty as your brother to annoy you whenever possible," Adam said before turning to see me and Anna. "Wait, aren't you two the tree competitors from this weekend? I didn't realize you would be here." Guess he hadn't been daydreaming of me.

We re-introduced ourselves before explaining to the group about the twelve dares of Christmas, how we met Jason and Adam, and today's dare. I gave a small concession speech while Anna got out a candy cane sticker to hold in the air like a trophy. Leaning into the ridiculousness of it made it so much more fun.

The guys briefly debated whether they were allowed to help me also secure a win for the night, but I brushed them off, joking that I couldn't have seconds from Jason, and since I certainly wouldn't agree to a kiss from a man who couldn't even be trusted with picking out a Christmas tree, I'd still only end up with two kisses, and I didn't want to then feel pressure to track down a third. Instead, I would simply remain kiss-free.

The conversation moved on and was easy and lighthearted enough that we were happy to all hang out together. When it came to deciding whether to order another drink, though, I had to call it a night. Anna was clearly feeling the same because she asked for our bill after the bartender popped over to see how we were doing. We started wrapping things up, saying goodbye to everyone and starting to bundle back up to brave the cold. I finished up with everything first while Anna lingered while she said goodbye to Jason.

"You know, I feel a little bad that you're going home to an apartment with someone else's tree and another loss today," Adam said, softly enough that only I could hear him. "May I?" He was holding out his hand, seemingly waiting for me to put mine in his. When I did, he gave the back of my hand a quick kiss. "There. Now at least you were in the game tonight. I'm going to tell myself that I've been redeemed a bit."

"Perhaps, but maybe we'll run into each other again, and I can put you to work on other dares."

"Based on the way Jason is making googly eyes at your friend, I'd say that's a safe bet."

I turned to check whether he was reading things correctly when Anna turned towards me, zipping up her coat. "Ready?" she asked me, a little breathlessly.

"Ready." We both said one last goodbye to the group, waving as we turned and headed home.

DAY 4: SNEAK HOLIDAY SONG NAMES INTO CONVERSATIONS

The next morning, armed with scrambled eggs and an English muffin slathered in peanut butter, I decided to take the reins of the day's dare. I was determined to win one, especially now that the dare tracking poster Anna made at work was hung up and displayed my 0-3 record.

Earlier, as I was lazily waking up and making breakfast, I'd started to brainstorm a handful of rules for the day's dare. We needed to sneak the names of holiday songs into conversations all day until someone called us out on it.

Anna and I were going to check in when one of us got called out, and the first of us to be called out would lose the dare. To make it fair, I'd decided to propose that we couldn't actively avoid conversations. Anna's company was very flexible about where and how she worked, so I wouldn't have put it past her to just work from home and reschedule calls for later days. As an extension of that, we couldn't be purposefully silent during conversations under the guise of not having anything to add to avoid needing to make a song name reference.

While I was thinking things over, Anna joined me in the kitchen and started making herself coffee. Floating my ideas to her, she added a rule of no repeating any song name more than twice, and any repeats had to be with different people. We also both agreed that we didn't need to keep up the bit with each other. Lastly, when one of us got called out, the other person still had to sneak in at least one more song title successfully in order to win.

Satisfied that I wasn't leaving a giant loophole available to exploit, I grabbed my bag and headed in to work for the day. I popped my headphones in and started searching for lists of holiday songs that I could use throughout the day, justifying not starting up any conversations with strangers as not violating the dare rules because I was following my normal commute routine. Plus, if someone came up to me at 7:30 a.m. to let me know that all they wanted was me for Christmas, I'd immediately start creating distance between us. Save the corny flirting until after at least 10:00 a.m.

Once I got downtown, I turned the corner and nearly ran into a person dressed up in a Santa costume next to a book drive donation box.

"Good morning! Any chance you have some new or lightly used books at home that you'd like to donate," the Santa asked after I stepped back and apologized for nearly running them over.

"Santa, baby," I said, immensely glad I looked up popular holiday song names already, "I don't have any on me, but I think I can maybe rustle some up later. Will you be here all week?"

"Every weekday morning before Christmas Eve. The more you donate, the more likely you are to end up on the nice list."

"In that case, I'll definitely find a few things to donate." I waved and headed inside before texting Anna that I had successfully snuck in my first song title without being caught.

4.2

"I don't mean to alarm you," one of my favorite coworkers, Jordan, said quietly, rushing up to my desk just as I got my coat off, "but there are donuts in the breakroom. I just saw Jeanine arrive, so you know the good ones are going to be gone in the next five minutes."

"Let's go, quick!" I dropped my things haphazardly on my desk, and we speed-walked to the communal breakroom. Jeanine had a gross habit of taking a little bit of every donut, which wouldn't have been too bad on its own, but she didn't cut them. She just grabbed a donut, not bothering to try and limit contact, and just ripped small sections off. It ended with most of the remaining donuts—only the ones that Jeanine liked, of course—all being covered in her fingerprints and half-squished. Anyone who rolled in after her was left deciding between whichever donuts Jeanine hadn't touched or being willing to eat the ones that she ripped pieces from. What a surprise that, a few hours later, Jeanine always returned to package up the remaining donuts because she didn't want them to go to waste. I'd be impressed with her scheming if it wasn't so rude and if she didn't always try to beat me to the chocolate-covered donuts with sprinkles.

"I swear, if she gets her grubby little hands on the bear claws before I get one, we're going to have beef," Jordan said, her voice underscored with a growl.

"Do you think she'd rip pieces off the beef too?" As Jordan chuckled, I remembered the dare rules, so I added, "She probably lies in wait up on the housetop, or, uh, under her desk, for the donuts to arrive." I was pretty proud of that one, even if I did stumble over it. Jordan was so focused on getting to the breakroom quickly without flat-out jogging that she probably wouldn't have noticed if I'd started singing a whole song.

We walked into a thankfully empty breakroom, joined a few minutes later by Nel, a coworker that Jordan knew well but I hadn't worked with much. Jordan had told me in confidence that some colleagues seemed to treat Nel as a dumping ground for work they didn't want to do, and her patience was obviously growing thinner by the day. After her attempts to reprimand those colleagues hadn't worked, Jordan had started making guesses about how long it would take before Nel quit, and she had confided in me that she thought there might be a dramatic exit.

I managed to grab the last donut covered in chocolate and dusted with sprinkles and tuned in to Jordan and Nel's conversation. As it turned out, there wasn't going to be any dramatic exit because Nel had already turned in her resignation and was leaving the company at the end of the week.

She was piling her plate high with donuts, telling us how she had decided not to put up with absolutely anything from anyone for the remainder of her time. When she was done, anyone coming in for a donut would think that Jeanine had already come and gone, this time taking full donuts based on the ones that were left.

I exchanged a look with Jordan, realizing what was happening as Nel continued to happily tell us about the people she had refused extra work from, pointed out inaccuracies in data provided by others, cc'ing the manager on responses to rude emails, etc. Everything that she used to just politely correct was now someone else's problem, with subtle nods to whose fault it actually was. Nel was facing the doorway that Jordan and I had our backs to, and she suddenly switched to talking about the weather as her expression morphed into a picture of innocence.

"Hi, Jeanine," she said, her voice syrupy sweet.

Jeanine didn't reply. Her donut behavior wasn't the only reason she wasn't well-liked by her peers. She was followed into the room by a few other people who each looked between Jeanine and the nearly empty donut box, sighing before realizing that it wasn't Jeanine who had taken them. Jeanine glared at Nel, and I grudgingly but silently gave her credit for being smart enough to know she had no standing for calling her out on taking them all. Nel, on the other hand, was clearly enjoying this too much to let it go.

"Oh, this?" Nel motioned to her heaping plate of donuts. "I'm just really hungry this morning."

"Maybe you should have had breakfast this morning before coming in instead of just assuming you could take everything." Never mind then; Jeanine apparently didn't have any sense of self-preservation. "It's not like you'll even be able to eat all of those."

"Hmmm, it looks like you have one there for each of the remaining twelve days of Christmas," I interjected, mentally checking off my dare requirement for this conversation.

Nel nodded at me before looking back at Jeanine. "You know, Jeanine, you're right. I probably don't need *all* of these." Jeanine looked triumphant, grabbing a plate and taking a step toward Nel, but Nel side-stepped her and held the plate out to the others in the room. "Would any of you like one of these? I used a napkin to load them onto my plate. I wouldn't be so unhygienic as to grab them all with my hands and expect you to still want them." Based on Jeanine's sneer, the dig landed. Someone subtly waved in a few people, and by the time everyone had chosen a donut from Nel's stash, there were only about three left.

"I'll take mine now," Jeanine demanded, entitlement dripping off her words.

"Yours?" Nel asked as she pointedly looked into the box on the table at the remaining donuts. "Which are you going to have today?"

"No, I want—" Jeanine was cut off as Nel took a giant bite of one of her donuts, turned on her heels, and walked out of the room.

Jeanine huffed before storming out as Jordan and I used absolutely all of our self-control to stop from laughing. As soon as we could see her turn down the hall, we both hit our breaking point.

"That was exceptional," Jordan wheezed, wiping tears from her eyes.

"I thought smoke was going to come out of her ears!"

"I love already-quit Nel. I wonder if I can find a reason to cc her on an email with a few people who have been bugging me lately and use her to respond the way I can't."

"You may as well. Nel will be our office vigilante. Maybe Jeanine will even clean up her act on donut days from now on," I said, settling into a chair at the table to eat my donut.

"Doubtful, but I like your optimism."

Jordan and I hung out and chatted for a while longer, both of us having considered and passed on a second donut. I headed back to my desk with a bounce in my step, still with the ever-present mixed feelings about my job, but having a few coworkers that I really liked, with the extra bonus of someone I wasn't a fan of getting their comeuppance, made it so easy to start the day on a high note. As I was settling in, I got a handful of text messages from Anna in quick succession.

Anna: I'm already out for today's dare

Anna: I ran into Henry as I was walking from the metro station and managed to sneak "O, Holy Night" in when I was telling him about seeing Jason and his friends at the bar after he and Daniel left. I think he thought I was just being weird at first, but I had a meeting a little while ago and figured I'd get a song title in before the actual meeting started since my boss wasn't on the call yet. Someone was droning on about the weather, so I said that it was beginning to look a lot like Christmas

Anna: I thought that was pretty smooth, but of course Henry had just joined the call and asked why I kept saying the names of songs before apparently having a mini epiphany and outright asking whether it was for today's dare

Anna: Rude

Anna: Anyway, now my whole team knows about the dares because Henry told them after I tried to deflect. A few of them thought it would be fun to help out, but Henry convinced half of them that it would be fun to try and sabotage me to make me really earn my dare wins

Anna: RUDE

I could picture Anna getting riled up while texting me, so I decided to fan the flames and asked her to send me Henry's number so that we could be properly in cahoots. She sent back a string of angry emojis.

Clearing out my emails, most of which were requests for secondary review of documents or coordination of resources covering holiday hours and backups for people out on vacation, I silently thanked my past self for preparing for needing to switch people in and out on active projects as I easily assigned new resources.

My calm evaporated in a puff of smoke as a new meeting invite popped up from my boss. No agenda, no subject line, just a block of time thirty minutes later with a note to come to her office then or earlier if I had time. I mentally went over everything I had been involved in over the last few weeks and whether I had done anything that might warrant the meeting. Unfortunately, since Anna was done with the dare for the day, I had to work a song title into the conversation with my boss. No amount of staring at the bookmarked list of song titles would help.

Brushing non-existent lint off of my pants, I walked to the wall of windows that my boss had an office along and knocked lightly on her door. People walked across the bridges below, just outside the window, some stopping to enjoy the view, others pulling coats tighter around themselves as they speed-walked to wherever they were headed.

"Come in," came from the other side of the door, and I let myself inside. My boss, Erin, was younger than you'd expect. Early forties, and she was already leading an entire department. She vacillated between being sterner than she needed to be, seemingly in an attempt to establish herself as The Boss, and being more in tune with and on the side of the teams she was supervising rather than her own bosses as a result. She raised a finger before continuing to type something on her computer, leaning back and letting her eyes close for a few seconds.

"Okay," she said, mostly to herself, before looking up at me. Just as she was about to speak, her phone rang, but she scowled down at it before declining the call. "Oh, no, I can't believe I missed that call for the fourth time in the last twenty minutes." Cue the eye roll. "Someone decided that, rather than actually looking for solutions to their problems, they would just jump over everyone involved and make it my problem." She must have seen a brief flicker of panic on my face because she softened her annoyed tone. "Don't worry, you're not in trouble. It's not even something happening on one of your projects. It's actually kind of funny."

As it turned out, one of the lead engineers we'd sent out to replace someone who needed a few days off unexpectedly was the ex-girlfriend of the person overseeing the project from the client end. It couldn't have ended amicably because the client was apparently trying to claim we'd breached our contracts by replacing the prior resource. Erin had already confirmed with someone in legal that we hadn't, so this was definitely just a result of hurt feelings.

I was there so she could ask whether she could pull anyone that I had earmarked for upcoming work that had the specific niche experience the client needed since she didn't have enough candidates to present to the client from her backup list. Conveniently, I had brought my laptop with me, so I pulled up my own resource spreadsheet, and we went through the options. The client had apparently been very particular about not allowing any holiday time off or absences, which we originally had someone offer to accommodate, but now we were looking for a needle in the haystack of someone who hadn't taken PTO.

"You know," I said, a plan forming once I scanned over the list and spotted someone in particular, "last Christmas, Jimmy mentioned that he would be willing to work Christmas Eve and Christmas Day, provided that he got double pay for those hours. I can check with him if he'd be up for the same this year. We'd be incurring some additional internal costs, but Jimmy works quickly, even more so when he's left alone to work, so we would likely shave off enough time to minimize that hit."

"Plus, I'm less likely to get constant calls and emails from them if he's working when they're running a skeleton crew," Erin replied, still focused on my laptop screen. That may have been the smoothest song name-drop of the day. I tried to tamp down the smile that was fighting to break free, knowing I finally won a dare while also scoring some brownie points with my boss. "Okay, yeah, I like this. Go talk to Jimmy and see if he's up for it. Let him know that we'll also give him double the normal per diem for meals we'd provide if he'd been traveling even though this is local to try and sweeten the deal, and then let me know what he says so I can let the client know."

Sensing the dismissal, I left, dropping my laptop at my desk before I went to find Jimmy. The elevators were notoriously slow, so I pulled out my phone to update Anna.

Haley: Guess I just won today's dare then

Anna: Already? You didn't forget that you have to get one more song name in after I got called out, did you?

Haley: Not only did I manage another one already, it was with my boss!

Haley: I might just keep this up all day

Originally, it was a joke, but I ended up actually continuing the dare all day. The next time wasn't even intentional—my coworker and I were talking about ways to make getting emails more fun, and I joked that we should switch the annoying little ding that the email service had as a default to jingle bells. That coworker smiled indulgently at me, not realizing that when I started laughing after I suggested it, I was actually laughing about managing to fit a song title in without even meaning to.

Maybe knowing that I didn't actually *have* to be successful took the pressure off and made it easier, or maybe this was just my superpower.

Eventually, I changed tactics and decided to slowly get more and more obvious, to the point of barely making sense, until I got called out.

Admittedly, I skipped doing it during an impromptu meeting with a client's representative who stopped by the office unexpectedly. He had deep pockets but seemingly even deeper disdain for anyone near him having fun. I'd worked on several projects that his company engaged us for over the years, and I had long since learned to make my voice more monotone and stick to concise, documented facts when speaking to him.

Someone made a suggestion in a meeting last month, a genuinely creative solution that, while not likely to actually work in the long run, might have helped mitigate some delays while we tried to find long-term solutions to a problem we were running into. The client's representative stared at the person who made the suggestion in silence for so long that we finally just ended the meeting. I treated our interactions like being in an acting class. My role: woman who believed that communicating in a way that suggested exclamation points were present was akin to blowing bubbles at a funeral. I hated every minute of it.

By the end of the workday, I still hadn't been called out about the song names, despite them crossing over from a little clunky to truly unhinged. At one point, I told someone, to whom I was explaining that I wouldn't be seeing my family this year for Christmas and in response to whether I had extended family in the area, that I unfortunately did not because my grandma got run over by a reindeer. She was appalled. I thought it was hilarious. There was a chance she told some people to avoid me, though, seeing as no one passing by did more than give me a quick nod before zipping away for the rest of the afternoon.

Maybe it was the repeated review and research into festive winter holiday songs around the world, but at some point, my whole vocabulary started skewing festive. Notably, I found out (from someone pointing it out; I didn't even notice myself) that I'd been saying, "Ah, gumdrops" in the place of cursing or voicing frustration. I didn't normally curse at work, but apparently, my subconscious decided to go all in. That felt like a good time to go home.

4.3

Walking into the apartment, I was greeted by the image of Anna's bare feet sticking up from the back of the couch, the apartment smelling strongly of nail polish. Anna loved trying out different hacks that she found on the internet, so I figured that this is somehow related to one.

"Do toenails dry quicker upside down?" I hung over the back of the couch next to her legs.

"They're just not supposed to be on the floor. Something about creating circular airflow."

"Couldn't you just prop them up on the couch then?"

"Probably, but I felt like being upside down."

"You're a nut, and I love you."

"How was the rest of your day?"

I told Anna the office tea—the donut incident—and gave a handful of examples of my song title references that somehow everyone just took at face value. I wasn't sure what that said about me, that everyone just went along with it, but I decided that it just meant that I was quirky and fun enough on a daily basis that people gave me a long leash of silliness.

I had a passing thought that maybe it was something less kind, like people just thought I was the office weirdo and were tolerating me, but I dismissed it. Normally, I would have started overthinking as soon as that possibility crossed my mind. I wasn't sure why I was able to just dispel it today, not even certain that it wasn't true but instead just considering it irrelevant. I decided to stick with the theme and try to not overthink that realization.

Anna and I laughed as she told me about her whole team and a handful of people from other teams getting on board with the dares. Apparently, there were now smaller groups that were each in cahoots to either help or hinder Anna, and they had decided not to tell her which side they fell on.

"It's not funny, Hales!" Anna said when I couldn't stop giggling. "It'd be one thing if I knew which groups were on my side, but instead, I have to either forego any help to avoid a Hinder," yes, they had given themselves names: the Hinders and the Helpers, "derailing me with the information they find, or risk that I'm giving information to the wrong group!"

"At least you know Henry's allegiance."

"Are you kidding? He was the one to suggest that they keep it a secret to make things more interesting for them, so there's a good chance he switched sides just to mess with me." She threw her hands up in exasperation, which just made me laugh more since now her arms were up in the air, flailing her legs around.

"Maybe he would tell me instead..." I let that hang in the air while I looked through the menu of a nearby restaurant on my phone. "I don't feel like cooking. Do you want anything from Clancy's? I'm going to order and then walk over to grab food to go."

Clancy's was a dive bar with incredible food a few blocks away that was half-hidden. Their sign was just their name on a mailbox, and you let yourself in through what looked like a door to a ground-floor apartment.

The owners had finally bent to pressure from neighborhood patrons to put menus online since they liked to change things up more regularly than a normal dive bar, but they still refused to take online orders. According to them, you'd call if you wanted it badly enough. Anna decided to cook at home, and she started prepping while I sat on a barstool and called in the order.

"Sounds amazing, like it's the most wonderful time of the year," I said to the person taking my phone order when they told me when the order would be ready. Anna rolled her eyes and huffed dramatically as I hung up the phone. "Okay, now I'm done for today. Where are the candy cane stickers?"

Anna just pointed to the dare chart she made, now sporting two little envelopes: a red envelope filled with a bunch of little stickers that looked like pieces of coal and a green envelope filled with candy cane stickers. I took out one of the latter and added it under my name for day four. I was finally in the game.

DAY 5: FIVE RANDOM ACTS OF KINDNESS

Fresh off yesterday's win and the deep and satisfying sleep of an early bedtime in a perfectly temperate room, I woke up refreshed and excited to start the day and the dare. Anna and I spent the morning brainstorming ideas on how to do five random acts of kindness, having decided that we wanted to make sure we both completed today's dare. Dare wins were great, but we wanted to have a day focused on doing something good for those around us.

At the beginning of the week, Anna had asked her boss and gotten approval to take a few hours off in the middle of the day so that she could volunteer somewhere, preferring to help out at either a domestic violence shelter or a food bank. Instead of setting something up in advance, she left getting a volunteer slot set up until today, and as she called around to places, she struggled to find anywhere that needed or could accept her help.

The shelters she'd called had an extensive onboarding and background check process to ensure the safety and confidentiality of the people staying there, so that wasn't an option. Each food bank and soup kitchen she called said that they were full and had no need for more volunteers. The last person she called was must have been at the end of her rope because

Anna was frustratedly told to call back after the feelings of obligation during the holiday season wore off. Even the local hospitals didn't want more volunteers coming in this week; too many people were offering to read to kids or wrap toy drive donations already, and they didn't have enough staff to supervise.

Finally, around lunchtime, someone at her office (one of the "Helpers" that had overheard her calling around) suggested that she check in to see whether there were any nursing homes nearby that might appreciate the extra help. The woman who picked up at the first place she called agreed almost instantly before Anna had even finished the pitch she'd been giving.

Meanwhile, I decided to try and do a handful of small random acts of kindness. Among the crush of buildings downtown, a handful of the buildings near where I worked had been built out so that the open area in front of the buildings were green spaces that mimicked the courtyards of the residential buildings further from downtown.

One in particular had tons of grassy areas (at least in the summer) and lots of seating for people to take their breaks and be able to step outside to get some fresh air without having to leave the area completely. There were coverings throughout the space, providing shade year-round and creating areas that were less snow-covered in the winter.

I walked by the building on my way to my office and sometimes took my lunch over to sit out in the grass and have a little picnic on warm summer days. I didn't go often when I had to bundle up just to go outside, but I'd been noticing that a coffee cart was out in the morning and often saw it there through the afternoon if I happened to head home a bit early. I figured that I could start at lunch by buying someone coffee, and then, hopefully, more opportunities to help would naturally arise. I could have just bought coffee for five people, but that felt a little lazy. I wanted to find five unique ways that I could make someone's life a little easier.

When lunchtime rolled around, I was glad to see that the coffee cart was there, already set up with a line that was getting longer by the minute. That, I had expected—a product of a December day that was unseasonably temperate and sunny. Figuring it would be weird to just randomly cut to the front of the line, pay for someone's drink, and leave, I walked to the back of the line and tried to formulate a plan.

Two people in their early twenties joined the line behind me. Offering to buy their drinks would have gone much more smoothly if I had at least said hello, right? Shifting slightly, I eavesdropped and realized they were talking about a new TV show I enjoyed, so I turned and asked them something about it.

We ended up spending the ten minutes that we waited in line debating the pros and cons of the casting choices. By the time we made it to the front of the line, I requested a hot chocolate and then gestured to my two new acquaintances with an "and whatever they're having" signal.

Clearly taken by surprise, I told them that I was trying to treat people with unexpected kindness today. I hadn't really considered that they'd take advantage of the situation, though I should have, and I found my happiness at being able to do something nice for someone souring slightly when they both started ordering the largest, most elaborate drinks possible, along with multiple pre-packaged snacks the cart sold as well.

After ordering, they went to wait for their drinks as I paid, and then they took their items and left without so much as a quick "thanks" before turning their back to me and walking away. They didn't owe me anything, I knew that, but my shock must have shown clearly on my face because the woman working gave me a pitying look as she told me that she saw it happen a lot around the holidays.

I should still have felt good about doing something kind. Those two were going to be pleased with themselves and their drinks, even if, to them, it would be a story about managing to get free drinks and snacks from some naïve woman. Still, it didn't give me the hit of dopamine I was (admittedly, selfishly) hoping to get. I took a five-dollar bill out of my wallet and added it to the tip jar. I'd tipped earlier when I paid, but the double tip did make me feel better. Maybe I could count that as one act of kindness done because I wasn't counting buying those people's drinks and snacks.

Originally, I'd planned to hang around, warm cup in hand, lying in wait for changes to do something nice, but I was ready to go back to the office. I needed a palate cleanser before trying to do more good deeds for the people around me. I started brainstorming other possibilities and continued through the afternoon with no luck.

5.2

By four o'clock, I was too antsy to actually get any work done. I wanted to do something to benefit someone. At some point, I convinced myself that I needed to go back to the coffee cart and redeem myself. It felt oddly calming in the chaos of the city, and it had a great vantage point of people coming from all directions. I was going to help people, and I was going to do it there. I locked my laptop into a drawer in my desk. I wasn't sure how long this would take, so I didn't want to be lugging around my bag while I was out.

"So, you're back for more," a voice said, pulling my attention up from my phone as I walked back into the building courtyard. "Unfortunately, I'm about to head out."

"No more caffeine for me today," I said, turning towards the woman who made the coffee cart drinks earlier. "Do you need any help getting things cleaned up?"

"I appreciate the offer, but I can't let you help even if I had enough left to do to make it worth it. Health, safety, liability, blah blah blah."

"Ahh, those pesky regulations." I chuckled. "At least you get to head out before the end-of-the-day rush and before it starts getting colder."

"True," she said, locking the cart and pocketing a small key. "You snuck out a little early, too. What're you sticking around here for?"

"I've been trying to find a way to do some random acts of kindness. I figured this block would have enough foot traffic that it should be a breeze."

"Oh, that explains why you offered to help me shut down the cart."

"What? Oh, no! I wasn't even thinking about that. I really just wanted to—"

"Stop, stop," she said, laughing at me. "I was just giving you a hard time."

"Oh."

"Any ideas what you're going to try to do next?"

"Not a clue. I really thought things would just jump out at me." I looked around at the people milling around, most on their phones, walking quickly, likely headed home for the day.

"Well, there's a flower shop around the corner that discounts flowers at the end of the day. Sometimes, they have someone come around during lunch in the summer to try and sell flowers, but I've always thought it would be nice if they brought a bunch over to just hand out for free. Maybe that would be a nice way to start."

"That's brilliant! I love getting flowers; I bet a lot of people would be glad to get a free bouquet."

"It's a block that way," she replied, pointing down the street. "If you do it, try to stop by the cart soon and let me know how it goes."

"I will. Thanks for the suggestion." We each waved before walking in opposite directions.

I'd never noticed the flower shop despite it being just a block off a route that I walked all the time. A portly man was leaning on a counter inside in the middle of an animated discussion with the young man behind the counter. As I stepped inside, the young man gave me a quick hello, but the two continued chatting. It wasn't difficult to locate the buckets filled with water and discounted bouquets. A sign set out the discounted prices and further discounts for buying multiple bouquets. I considered getting just one bouquet, but there were six miniature bouquets in shorter buckets. They were too cute to leave to be discarded.

Arms full of flowers, I made my way out of the store. Someone opened the door for me, and I grabbed the chance to start giving away the bouquets. Confused, the couple heading into the shop politely refused; they were heading in for a consultation. I didn't see why free flowers would impact that, but okay.

It was harder to give away free flowers than one might expect. Back in the courtyard, I approached no less than four people before I was even able to give away one of the bouquets. Most people started speed walking as I got close, and many waved me off immediately as I walked up, saying that they didn't want any, probably assuming that I was selling them.

It took about thirty minutes to get rid of four of the six bouquets. Two of those four went to confused, somewhat reluctant people, but the other two seemed genuinely pleased. Despite those latter two, I had tried to give the flowers away to dozens of people at that point. It was getting increasingly frustrating trying to do something nice but not having anyone receptive to it.

I couldn't fault anyone; I probably would have been just as reluctant to a stranger approaching when I wasn't expecting it. At one point, after being grumpily dismissed by someone, I sharply turned around and ended up slamming my shoulder into a woman whose bag fell to the ground. Sure, I helped her pick up the mess of items that tumbled out around her on the ground, but I was also the cause of them being dropped in the first place, so no counting that towards the dare.

Another fifteen minutes later, still holding the last two bouquets, I heard distant shouting and barking. Both were rapidly getting closer. As I turned to look behind me, what could only be described as a gigantic toasted marshmallow with legs came barreling towards me.

I realized what was happening just as the marshmallow passed by me, and its owner ran into the courtyard. Thankfully, the dog seemed to think he was part of a fun game and, rather than just making a straight shot for escape, ran a circle around the courtyard, weaving through people and benches. Its owner was clearly losing steam, and everyone around us was just staring at them both. I started running at an angle to catch the dog as it veered off to one side. The flowers were getting cumbersome, preventing me from grabbing the dog as it reached me again, so I threw the loathsome things to the ground while continuing to run after the pup.

Managing to snag the end of the dog's trailing lease, I brought us both to a stop and waved to its owner as I sat down on the nearest bench, embarrassingly out of breath from the short sprint. The owner, visibly relieved, slowed considerably. When he got to me, he collapsed onto the bench beside me and thanked me profusely in between deep breaths.

It turned out that the dog's name was Daisy, and she was somehow still a puppy despite her size. She was ninety percent fluffy white and golden-brown fur, the remaining ten percent a floppy tongue that she happily let hang from the side of her open mouth. Her owner took her leash back and held it with a white-knuckled grip.

We exchanged goodbyes before I walked over to the flowers I'd discarded. They weren't in the greatest shape. Between holding and trying to give them away for an hour, being thrown on the ground, and looking as if they'd been walked over in the time since I dropped them, it was obviously time to let them go. I couldn't quite bring myself to throw them away, so I put them on a bench for someone to hopefully find and enjoy.

I had all but given up hope of actually being able to accomplish my goal for the day (who knew how hard it would be to intentionally do nice things for people) until I saw an elderly woman exiting the building that the courtyard sat outside. She was hobbling a bit, looking unsteady, so I figured she would appreciate being helped across the street. I could help!

"Hi, there. How are you today, ma'am? Do you need any help?" The woman stopped walking and abruptly took a step back away from me. Too enthusiastic, got it. I tried again, calming my voice and trying to come off as helpful instead of desperate. "Where are you headed?"

"No, thank you." She started shaking her head furiously.

"No, what? I'm just trying to help you get where you need to go."

"How do you know where I'm going?"

"Well, I don't. You could tell me, and then I can help you."

"But I don't know you."

"My name is Haley. I saw you walking and wanted to help you get you to where you need to go."

"I'm going to the bus, but I don't know you." Her voice raised in volume as she spoke, the last few words nearly shouted.

"Well, you know me now, so how about I help you get to the bus?" I put my arm out, waiting to see if she would take it. I realized that I was coming on too strong, and I didn't want to just grab her to steady her, but she did look like she was about a minute away from toppling over with her tiny frame drowning in a large coat. Just as she nodded at me and reached out to take my arm, a loud, angry voice startled us both. The woman started tipping, so I reached for her arm to steady her.

"Miss! Let her go right this instant." I pulled my arm away instantly before extending it again as the woman swayed. A security officer jogged over, glaring at me the whole way. "Step away from her." I took a step to the side, and then he set his gaze on the old woman. "Are you okay, ma'am? I'll make sure this woman doesn't keep bothering you." My mouth fell open as he looked back at me. "I'll need you to come with me inside."

I followed the security guard, assuming that he just wanted to pull me aside and ask why I'd been pacing around the courtyard for the last ninety minutes or so. Imagine my surprise when he ushered me towards a door near the reception desk as he asked, rather loudly and rudely, for the other security officer, sitting behind the desk, to unlock the "holding room" door.

My brain caught up with my current circumstances and decided, in no uncertain terms, that I would not be entering a holding room of any kind. My feet cemented in place three feet from the open door. It was a close call, but thankfully, the security guard was paying enough attention to not slam into my back when I defied Newton's first law of motion.

"Miss, you need to move."

"So that you can lock me in this room and forget about me? No way! I'd be trapped."

"I'm not going to lock you in and forget about you. We're going to go in and have a conversation where you explain what you've been doing outside the building."

"Can't I just do that here?"

"No, depending on what was going on, we may need you to write a formal statement, and we need somewhere for you to wait without making a scene while I call someone down from the company because someone made a complaint." Apparently, this explanation was acceptable to my subconscious because my feet were moving again. "Take a seat," the officer said as we entered, gesturing at a small table and chairs.

The security guard made me walk through why I was approaching people, my relationship with the woman I was talking to when he showed up, why I was in the area in the first place and all kinds of related follow-up questions. I decided that explaining the dares wouldn't be beneficial to my case, so I just told him that I wanted to try to be a good person and figured that I would come to the courtyard park around end-of-work hours to see if anyone needed help.

It wasn't really a lie. Thirty minutes of asking me the same questions with different phrasing later, the guard made a call from a phone in the corner and told me to stay put before he left the room.

Immediately, I got up to check whether the door was locked. In part to make sure I wasn't stuck in here if he did forget about me (regardless of my cell phone in my pocket and the phone he'd called out on), but also in part because if I was locked in, I was probably in more trouble than if they were trusting me to stay put. The door opened without issue, and I closed it again after a quick "just checking" to the exasperated security guard now sitting at the desk next to the door.

Fifteen minutes later, I heard the security guard's muffled voice talking to someone outside the door. From what I could tell with my ear pressed to the door, he was providing a very brief overview of what I'd told him. The other voice was quieter, too quiet for me to understand anything they were saying. The door handle turned, so I rushed back to my seat as the security guard, now looking even more bored than before, walked inside, followed by another man. A familiar man.

"Adam?"

Adam skipped a step, righting himself just before toppling over and returning his gaze to mine. Recognition and the start of a smile lit his face before shifting to amusement with a touch of exasperation.

"This was a dare, wasn't it?"

"A dare?" The guard asked, looking questioningly at Adam before turning an accusatory glance at me.

"Thanks for calling me, Jon. I can take care of this from here." Adam was still standing close enough to the door that he opened it, waited until the security guard left, and shut it again. He leaned against the wall and looked back at me. "I got called down after a complaint about a woman harassing people coming out of the building. Care to explain?"

According to Adam, someone had called security after watching me approach people with flowers, chase someone's dog, and then allegedly harass an elderly woman. Sure, it seemed like she couldn't hear too well and was half-shouting her replies, and sure, she did keep shout-talking about how she didn't know me, but, well, I, uh...yeah, okay, I might have looked like I was a problem. I told Adam about the day's dare and a general overview of what I'd been trying to do.

"So, you're telling me," Adam began, "that your dare for the day was to simply be a nice person, and instead, you ended up locked in a security holding room?"

"It wasn't locked," I exclaimed before adding with a harumph, "I checked." Adam struggled to hold back laughter but couldn't quite manage. The man had a great laugh. That was all there was to the interrogation, instead moving on to my catching Adam up on the previous dares. We chatted about our relationships with Anna and Jason, what we liked most about the holiday season, and went on a dozen more tangents. The conversation felt easier and flowed more naturally than most I'd had with any new friends and strangers lately, not that I'd really made an effort until the last few days.

At some point, at least forty-five minutes later, Adam's phone started vibrating on the table that we were sitting around. He looked down at it, frowned slightly, and hit a button to stop the buzzing.

"I wish I didn't have to cut this off, but that was a fifteen-minute warning alarm before a call that I need to be on."

"Oh," I replied slowly. "Wait, why were you who got called down here anyway? Obviously, you work here, but do you oversee security or something?"

"No. Well, sort of?" He seemed unsure how to continue, looking around awkwardly. "I'm one of the senior VPs for the company that owns the building. We lease out a few floors, but since we own it, we're responsible for any complaints made."

"Okay, but why you," I paused before I added on, "not that I'm complaining."

"I happened to be walking by the receptionist's desk on my floor when she got the call from security. Thanks for only being a mild threat, by the way. I would have really hated the extra paperwork if you'd turned out to be a real problem." He smiled down at me while he held the door open, and we both shuffled our feet in the lobby, knowing we needed to wrap things up, but neither of us was willing to walk away.

"So, do you think I could get your n—" Adam was cut off mid-sentence by his phone going off. "Crap, that's the three-minute alarm. I really have to go." He looked reluctantly towards the elevator bank behind him before giving me a quick goodbye and rushing over to head back up to his office.

I stood watching the elevator doors close with Adam inside. Were we really just going to leave it at that? In a brief moment of courage, I turned towards the reception desk, where the security guard and other receptionist were staring at me.

"So," I started, "would it be possible to leave a note for someone who's upstairs?"

"Let me guess," the security guard responded with a raised eyebrow, "Adam?"

I shrugged, not caring that it was that obvious. Adam seemed like he was about to ask for my phone number before he had to leave, so it wouldn't be weird if I left it for him, right? If he didn't want to use it, he could just toss it in the trash. That thought was almost enough to make me walk out without leaving a note, but I forced myself to stay put. I finally made myself move and walked over to the desk as the guard was putting a small pad of paper and a pen out for me.

It took a few minutes, in which time the guard and receptionist both offered suggestions on what to write before we collectively decided that I should opt for silly. I handed over the note that read, "In case you need to check my alibi in the future," with my name and number listed below.

"I'll make sure he gets this on his way out," the security guard said as he took the note and his pen back.

"Thanks. And sorry about causing a scene earlier." The guard waved me away, so I put my jacket on and headed home.

I expected to hear Anna singing along with music as I got to the door of our apartment. She liked to sing while she cooked, and it was often the start of dinner dance parties. Instead, when I opened the door, I saw her serving herself a bowl of pasta from a pan of something that looked and smelled delicious with a contemplative look on her face. She looked up and gave me a half smile when I entered, gesturing in invitation at the pan in front of her. Sat on the couch with a bowl of pasta in hand, I told Anna about the last couple hours as we ate.

"How is it possible that I wasn't able to complete today's dare," I lamented, "it was literally just doing nice things for people. What is wrong with me that I can't do five nice things throughout the day?"

"Maybe you were just trying too hard," Anna shrugged, "realistically, you probably did more nice things than that, and they just didn't register because they were second nature. Did you help anyone out at work? Were you patient with anyone who was overwhelmed?"

"Maybe? But those are just normal things. Those aren't intentional."

"That might be the case, but you're a generally kind person, so a lot of kindness is going to just feel like normal human decency."

"Even so, today's dare wasn't one that I wanted to lose."

"The day isn't over, Hales. What can you still do?"

"The dishes!"

"Nice try, but they're mostly done already."

I took our bowls to the kitchen and put them in the dishwasher, regardless. A lightbulb went off in my brain as I looked over at a stack of mail sitting on the counter. "There were tons of packages in the lobby. I could bring them to their recipients' doors."

"Great idea. Let's go do it now while we're thinking about it."

"But you're done for the day."

"With the dare, sure, but I can still help. That doesn't take away from you having the idea and doing something nice as well. We'll just get it done more quickly."

"Okay, I appreciate it."

Anna just nodded, and we got our shoes on and headed down to the lobby. Thankfully, our building only had four floors because it didn't have an elevator, and there really were a lot of packages. We loaded our arms up and started with the top two floors. Anna and I lived on the second floor, so after we'd finished with the third and fourth floors, we came back down to the lobby, distributed everything going to first-floor apartments, and then collected the remainder to put outside doors on our floor.

When I'd finished with what I was carrying, I saw Anna quietly stand outside of the door of an older woman, Gloria, who lived diagonally from us. She often baked and brought the treats to apartment meetings or put them outside everyone's doors on holidays or when she just felt like baking with a note saying hello and that she hoped we enjoyed them.

"There haven't been any treats outside our apartment this week," I said, walking up to Anna. She jolted slightly at my voice and put the two packages she was holding down in front of Gloria's door. "Maybe we could return the favor. I've got all the ingredients at home to make my mom's snickerdoodle cookies. That could be a nice thing to do tonight. I'll make them and bring over a plate. She probably doesn't have people bake for her often since she's such an avid baker, so it might be a treat." Anna looked over at me with an odd look. She seemed almost relieved. "Are you okay? You seem a little out of sorts tonight."

"Yeah. Come on, I'll tell you about it as you make cookies." She gave me a more genuine smile than I'd seen from her tonight, and we walked the few steps back to our own apartment, where I pulled ingredients out of the cupboards as Anna slid onto one of the barstools. She waited until I was done rummaging through cupboards and had everything together before beginning.

"I spent a solid hour this morning calling food banks and shelters, asking if they could use an extra hand for a few hours. For the most part, people were polite about turning me away, letting me know that they had more than enough help but to check back in a few weeks if I still wanted to volunteer. I swear I could almost hear defeat and disappointment in their voices when they said that last part. After that, I called every hospital in the city, offering to come read to kids while their parents were at work, to wrap gifts that came in through toy drives, to do anything really, but they told me basically the same thing. I know a lot of people feel a call to volunteer around the holidays, but I guess I didn't really think many people actually followed through with it."

"I bet the percent that follows through is pretty slim, but since it's all happening at about the same time, it makes sense that they might get a wave of having more volunteers than they want or need."

"True. A few places also said that all volunteers have to get a background check done first, so they couldn't accept walk-in volunteers even if they needed help."

"Makes sense. Maybe people had volunteered in the past as a way to get access to steal drugs or supplies or access to people. You said you were out volunteering earlier when we were texting, though. Did you end up going to the nursing home?"

"Yeah. I hadn't even considered it until someone recommended trying. I figured they would be crowded with people coming to spend time with their friends and family. Still, I looked up the closest one, called, and offered to come by and read to residents or play games or just keep them company. They said yes so quickly, I think they were worried about me changing my mind."

I handed Anna a spatula with cookie dough remnants as I started plopping balls of dough onto baking sheets. She picked at it idly, not saying anything as I transferred the baking sheets to the oven. "How did it go while you were there?"

"Honestly?" She set the spatula down and rested her forehead in her hands for a few seconds. "It was pretty sad. I walked into a communal area where residents were sitting in chairs, quietly watching TV, some of them chatting. The woman who walked me in said that they usually had more visitors, but around the holidays, everyone got busy with their own lives and holiday events and celebrations. Regular visitors might come in for an hour or so here and there, but they were there less often and stayed for less time."

Anna sighed deeply before continuing. "I saw a lady with a book in her lap, so I asked her about it, and she said that she hadn't been able to read it in years because of her eyesight deteriorating. I ended up reading some to her; it was poetry. Some of the poems were heartbreaking; some were so hopeful. A few poems in, the woman told me she was ready for a nap and thanked me for reading them to her.

After that, I ended up joining a group of ladies who were chatting. They told me about their favorite holiday memories, and then I got absolutely destroyed at chess by a man who looked to be in his nineties. I tried to just do the rounds and give everyone some company. With the exception of one grump, everyone seemed to be in better spirits afterward. I can't imagine how lonely they must be if just talking to me helped."

"I understand that. Talking to you always makes my day a little better."

"Just a little?" Anna cracked a smile. "I stayed longer than I expected to, and when I left, the woman at the front desk thanked me repeatedly for coming by and said I'd done a really nice thing. It just doesn't seem like it was enough."

"Well, maybe you can do it again sometime."

"Yeah, I think I'm going to try to start going at least once every month, maybe more, depending on my schedule. I just keep seeing the image of all of them sitting in chairs spread out throughout the room, staring at nothing. I know I can't realistically go all the time or commit to anything, but I wish I could do something better than just showing up, you know?"

"I hear you. Showing up is more than most people do, though, so I wouldn't discount that. If you want to do more, focus on what you can do."

"Like what?"

"You said the woman with the poetry book couldn't read the poems, right?"

"Yeah…"

"What if you recorded yourself reading them? Maybe she has access to a laptop or something where she could listen to them whenever she wanted if she had recordings."

"I like that. I'll have to call the facility to see what they have available that she could play them on, but it shouldn't be too hard." Anna walked around the counter and gave me a hug before heading in the direction of her bedroom. "I'm going to go do some research on recordings and see where I can get a copy of the book. Do you want me to come with you to drop off the cookies once they've cooled?"

"Nah, I've got it covered. If you need any help later, let me know."

She stopped at her bedroom door and looked at me seriously. "Thanks, Hales."

Today's dare seemed to be good for both of us. As the first tray of cookies cooled on the counter and the second went in the oven, I grabbed some cute stationery from my room and wrote a note to our neighbor, just in case she was asleep or out when I walked over. I thanked her for baked goods she'd dropped off in the past and told her a little about my mom making snickerdoodles every year when I went home for Christmas and that I wanted to bake for her for a change.

When I eventually walked over, I knocked lightly on the door to make sure she wouldn't be woken up if she was asleep. It was only a little after nine o'clock, but I had no idea what her schedule was like.

Surprisingly, she came to the door. We chatted for a few minutes, and I hadn't known just how bubbly she was. We typically just waved when we saw one another in the hall, exchanging a quick hello here and there. She mentioned that she'd be starting her holiday baking soon and invited me to join her, which somehow turned into plans to bake together the next day after I was done with work.

I walked back to my apartment with a skip in my step, bolstered further when I got to add a candy cane sticker under my name for today on the dare chart, adding one for Anna as well. Tomorrow's dare, eating only cookies and holiday drinks throughout the day, was well-timed since there were snickerdoodles galore for breakfast.

I was lounging on the couch with a book when my phone dinged.

> *Unknown: After leaving me your number, I guess you can tally another act of kindness*

I couldn't keep the smile off my face. It had to be Adam.

> *Haley: I don't think it counts since it was purely out of self interest*

> *Haley: I did end up completing the dare once I got home, though!*

> *Adam: You didn't break down someone's door when they got locked out instead of calling a locksmith or something did you?*

Haley: Only a few :)

I snuggled under a blanket as we exchanged texts, some decidedly flirty. Eventually, I started to doze on the couch and was only woken up by the ding of my phone getting a text. We said goodnight, and I moved to my room, got ready for bed, and eventually, I fell asleep smiling.

DAY 6: EAT ONLY COOKIES AND HOLIDAY DRINKS ALL DAY

When you were a kid, there was really nothing more enticing than the idea of eating cookies all day. As an adult, it was somewhat less enticing.

Still, I could manage for a day. Snickerdoodles were ready for breakfast. Arguably, they weren't a Christmas cookie in the same way that decorated sugar cookies shaped like reindeer were, but they were a holiday tradition for me. Anna should let me get away with that. If she did, maybe she would also let me get away with shaking things up and getting a slice of a yule log cake or roasted chestnuts.

With the amount of loopholes I had already considered, I didn't have high hopes of success. I had a sweet tooth, sure, but was it worth it? Cookies were great, but a breakfast sandwich was calling my name. Maybe I could sandwich some cookies together.

An hour later, when I'd finally forced myself out of bed and gotten ready for the day, I headed into the kitchen to find Anna eating snickerdoodles and reading something on her phone. That answered that on whether we were counting the snickerdoodles. She was sipping on something that looked suspiciously like coffee.

"Ahem. You wouldn't be deviating from our dare requirements already, would you?" I looked pointedly at her cup.

"This is a hot chocolate, thank you very much. If a shot or two of espresso happened to have fallen into the mug when I made it, well, that's just a bonus. Besides, do you really think Santa stays up all night delivering presents without caffeine? No chance."

"I always figured that magic helped him stay awake."

"Coffee is magic, so you're right about that."

I laughed as I made myself a hot chocolate. I added peppermint for a little boost and then broached the subject of how expansive our options were today. We went back and forth, but ultimately, neither of us wanted to strictly limit ourselves to our original list of cookies, milk, cocoa, and eggnog. Instead, any traditional holiday drink or dessert that you could find at a holiday party became an option. Satisfied with the extra options, I packed up a bag of cookies, tossed them in my purse, and headed to the office.

When I left the apartment without breakfast, I figured that being hungry for a while this morning would be a better option than getting gut rot early from all of the sugar I would surely consume today. Unfortunately, my brain hadn't stopped flashing a great big sign with neon lights and a picture of a bacon-egg-and-cheese sandwich in my head, so when I got off the train near my office, I pulled out a cookie to distract myself.

A second cookie was in order, and I was pleased that they'd turned out so well. I hoped that Gloria enjoyed them. I was just about caught up on morning emails when a calendar invite came in for lunch later today with an important client of the company, though not a client I was currently on a project for. I had worked with the client a few times in the past, though, before my regional assignments changed, and apparently, she'd asked about me after a recent meeting when chatting with my boss. The client was back in the area today and had reached out about an informal lunch, not so much a meeting but more a means to keep up a positive relationship.

This particular client loved to get to know her team, internal and external, beyond solely status updates and was both kind and interesting. On a previous lunch, I learned that she'd taken a three-month sabbatical from work a few years ago in order to enroll in a condensed culinary school program in Italy because she loved throwing dinner parties and cooking and wanted to make sure she was experiencing life outside of work beyond just a week or two throughout the year. Maybe one day, that could be me.

I considered whether I wanted to forego a dare this early in the day. I knew my boss wouldn't be upset if I wasn't able to join, but I didn't actually have anything over lunch that would prevent me from going. Plus, I might be able to get away with dipping out of work early since my lunch break was personal time, not company time, and it was being taken over by work. I checked the location and saw that the client had made a reservation at a trendy new restaurant, somewhere Maggie had been talking about a lot recently because of how difficult it was to get in. After I checked the menu—phenomenal—and the prices—out of my budget—my decision was made. I clicked "accept."

Knowing that I was taking a loss for today's dare, I decided to spend some time getting things sorted for the next few. First order of business, though, was breakfast. I nearly skipped my way to the elevators and headed to my favorite local breakfast sandwich spot.

By the time lunch rolled around, I had handled the small amount of work that was actually getting submitted for review and had been using downtime to look into what I needed to do to start winning some dares.

With a gingerbread house contest on the horizon, I texted Anna to see if she knew of anywhere hosting one or if we were going to host one. I got a cheeky reply thanking me for the idea of a new type of cookie she could seek out for lunch. Anna didn't know of anywhere that was holding a gingerbread house contest, and hosting one felt like a lot of work amidst the rest of the dares, so I went online and surprisingly found a few taking place on the day of that dare. Unfortunately, all of them required registration by deadlines that had already passed or were too far away to be feasible for us to join.

Eventually, I found one that was open to the public and would accommodate as many people as they had supplies for, with a note that the participants could also bring their own supplies to ensure entry. The only problem was that it was the night after the day that dare was currently scheduled.

Anna agreed easily to swap that dare with the one the next day and asked whether I wanted her to print out a new dare chart. We decided against it. This morning, we added the extra rules for today's dare to the chart. We'd been adding doodles here and there, and I didn't want to lose the history of how things had evolved. It felt like a cookbook filled with notes and specks of splattered ingredients: well loved. That's how I wanted to feel in the days leading up to Christmas.

When lunchtime rolled around, I headed to the elevators. My boss was going to be in a meeting on a different floor until it was time to leave, so I was meeting her and two colleagues that the client was currently working with in the lobby. I was over-prepared and ended up in the lobby about ten minutes early, but I snagged one of the surprisingly cozy chairs set out for guests around small tables. I was scrolling through a food blog when a text notification popped up.

> *Adam: I've been thinking, and I think it might be a good idea for you to have an alibi on Saturday. You know, just in case there's another incident and we need to clear your name*

> *Haley: Is this your way of telling me that you have inside knowledge of coming shenanigans?*

> *Adam: Shenanigans? SHENANIGANS? No. No, ma'am. I have no knowledge of any such tomfoolery*

Adam: But we should probably make sure everything is in order just in case

Haley: I want to say yes, but before I can, I need to figure out where and how to become Santa or an elf for the day and then see how that all plays out.

Haley: I did a quick search online earlier, and did you know there are whole schools devoted to training people to be Santa for the holidays? I'm guessing I'm going to end up an elf.

Adam: Or Mrs. Claus

Haley: I would make a kick-butt Mrs. Claus

Adam: This is another dare, yeah? I was walking through that big Christmas market downtown and they had signs about Santa being there each day starting tomorrow. Not sure about elves.

Haley: Maybe if I just get an elf costume and show up no one would question it

Adam: You're not helping your troublemaker reputation

Haley: It's fun trouble!

Adam: Santa, please help us all

"Who's giving you that goofy smile?" My boss smirked at me knowingly as I jolted, almost dropping my phone. "Ready to go?" I looked behind her, saw my other colleagues chatting quietly, and stood up.

"Yup, all set. Are we meeting Ms. Johnson at the restaurant?" I didn't see the client in the lobby, thankfully. I wouldn't have been thrilled to be caught by her making goo-goo eyes at my phone, though she'd probably find it hilarious.

There was very little left in the work day after lunch. The client was one that everyone both respected and genuinely liked being around, and we ended up staying for several hours.

After an hour at the office handling the few requests that had come in while we were gone, I packed up and headed over to the holiday market to check Adam's intel about a Santa being around over the next few days to take pictures with kids. It was a short walk, but it felt even shorter as the scents of spiced nuts, mulled wine, and incense from market vendors traveled far enough to entice anyone nearby. I bee-lined for the hot chocolate station and ended up with a soft pretzel.

The market started up in late November and ran through the end of the year, and since it wasn't my first time visiting this season, I felt less of an urge to stop by every stall. I still lingered by my favorites, admiring the glass-blown ornaments hung to reflect the lights above, carved luminaries, and incense smokers portraying Santa in different attire. My favorite was a Santa in a fishing hat and vest, complete with a pole and the tiniest little fish hanging from the hook. He looked just like my dad did when he tried to teach me and Jake to fish one weekend that we spent at a cabin on a lake as kids. Neither of us really got the hang of things, instead spending most of the day good-naturedly ribbing our dad for his outfit.

After a bit of wandering, a good deal of people-watching, and a cup of mulled wine, I found the sign that Adam must have seen. There was a small area of the market sectioned off by a thick velvet rope; a throne-like chair sat within, next to a giant sack of presents that a woman was in the process of adjusting to sit just so. A large sign detailed Santa's arrival and when he would be there each day, including a six-hour block listed for Saturday. Six hours, though... Maybe I could get away with not having to stay the whole time.

"Excuse me, are you involved with getting things set up for the Santa visits," I asked the woman inside the ropes.

"That's me," she said, turning just enough to point to the sign beside Santa's throne, "the schedule is right there, and it's first come, first served. You should expect a line."

"I was wondering about Saturday and whether there would be any elves here with Santa."

"Nope, no elves." She stood up and stretched a bit before turning towards me. "That would be a nice addition, and we have in the past, but we just don't have the budget for it this year. The committee decided to have Santa here for longer each day instead."

"Would you be interested in an elf? A free elf for the day?" I crossed my fingers inside my mittens.

"You want to dress up as an elf and spend hours dealing with a bunch of bored kids and their impatient parents waiting in line to see Santa?"

"Well, when you put it that way, how could I not?" The woman just kept staring at me, so I figured I had to give her something, but maybe something truth-adjacent, not wanting to fully explain the dares. "Here's the thing: I have to be Santa's elf for a while on Saturday, or I'll lose a bet. I told a guy about the challenge, and he suggested checking here. If you let me come and keep the kids and parents a little bit entertained and take pictures with them with Santa, I can both not lose a bet and make the guy feel useful. It's a win-win for me and a win-win for you."

"Okay," she conceded after a moment of consideration, "but we don't have an elf costume, and I expect you to dress up. Do you have a family-friendly costume?"

"Not yet, but I will!"

"Okay, but if you show up here without one, don't expect to stay."

"It'll be sorted by Saturday. Worst case scenario is that there isn't an elf, and you're just in the same position you would have been if I hadn't walked up."

"Fair enough. Santa starts Saturday at 10:00 a.m. Get here a little bit before that, and we'll have a spot for you to change. If you're not in enough layers to stay warm, make sure your coat still matches the theme. I'll be at that booth." She pointed at a booth set up with an array of whimsical winter and holiday-themed jewelry. "So just check in with me when you get here, and I'll point you in the right direction."

"Sounds great. I'll see you Saturday!" I started walking backward and waving as I bid her goodbye before turning and speed-walking away. I had to get clear of her before she changed her mind. I couldn't believe how easy that was, but I guess offering free labor wasn't a hard sell.

Once on a bus headed towards my apartment, I opened the text thread I had going with Adam.

Haley: Thanks for the tip about Santa at the Christmas market. Guess who's going to be an elf on Saturday?

Adam: Did they give you a funny hat to wear?

Haley: No, they didn't have an outfit. I'm going to have to figure that part out on my own and cobble something together

Adam: Hmmm, maybe you can convince some elf friends to help you

Haley: I'll have to make a few elf friends first

A text came through moments later with a link to a map. A route was outlined from our general location to the North Pole. A burst of laughter escaped me before I was able to rein it in. Adam made a good point, though. I actually did have some new friends who might be able to help with a costume.

<h1 style="text-align:center">6.4</h1>

The first thing I heard when I opened the door to the craft store was Bernie animatedly telling a story. She didn't stop for even a moment as the bells chimed as the door opened.

"—and then, just when he was about to sit down, smug as can be, we each squeezed the whoopie cushions that we had with us in our hiding places! You should have seen his face! He even looked down at his behind. Of course, we had Georgia ready, and she walked in and said, as he was checking out his caboose, 'hope it wasn't a wet one!'" Bernie nearly fell out of her seat as she laughed. Raquel was staring, open-mouthed, looking at Bernie with fear and awe. Dale and two others that I hadn't met in my previous visit were laughing so hard that they were wheezing and trying to catch their breath.

"I don't know what I walked into, but I'm sure glad I did," I said, coming into view and smiling at everyone.

"Starfish!" Bernie threw up her arms, motioning me over.

"Starfish?"

"Bernie has been testing out new nicknames for everyone. Today's nicknames are sea creature themed," Raquel explained. "Dale is now 'anemone.'"

"I was going to resist, but I find it somewhat endearing." Dave smiled indulgently at Bernie before looking back over at me. "How did the holiday sweater contest go? Are you here to show off a trophy?"

"I didn't win."

Bernie, Raquel, and Dale all immediately responded with variations of "How could they?" and "are they daft?" as I shrugged and sat down. The others got a quick rundown of the sweater that they helped me with, and I explained that I was up against tough competition, but ultimately, the waiter, who was our judge, chose to try for a date instead.

"Did he and your friend end up going out?" From the few interactions we'd had so far, it was already clear that Raquel was a romantic. She must have been hoping for a meet-cute.

"I don't actually know. I'll have to ask and let you know."

"So, dear, to what do we owe the pleasure?" Bernie had gone back to knitting but was looking at me even as her fingers raced through the motions.

"I thought you might be interested in knowing the silliness I've gotten myself into for Saturday, and you might have some ideas of where I could start for looking for an elf costume."

"Don't tell me that we're going to have to teach you to sew in just a few hours this time."

"Definitely not. I'm planning on pulling one together with things I have or can find at the thrift store, but now that I'm a certified crafter, maybe I'll jazz it up in your honor."

Bernie nodded at me with a hint of a smile. Something about Bernie's approval made me feel like I won a marathon, and the friendly nature of the others was so welcoming and relaxing. I had been worried initially that the Knittie Bitties were just humoring me before and wouldn't welcome me back, but that was clearly all in my head.

I silently re-dedicated myself to making more time to get back here for things that weren't related to needing help with the dares, though that might have to wait until after Christmas. I started explaining about trying to plan out some advantages for the next few days of dares.

Bernie shrugged off my relief on so easily being able to volunteer as an elf, suggesting that I could have just shown up and acted like I was meant to be there without asking. Raquel pointed out that a random woman coming in costume to herd children in a line and take pictures of them would be considered creepy, but Bernie just doubled down that with enough confidence I could convince anyone that they just weren't high enough up the event planning food chain to know that I was meant to be there. I didn't bother mentioning that the event planning food chain was just one person. I exchanged a look with Dale, who widened his eyes and mouthed "Yikes" while Bernie wasn't looking.

"An earlier problem I'm trying to solve," I said, trying to change the subject, "is where there might be reindeer near the city. Tomorrow, I need to take a picture with a live reindeer." One of the new-to-me women in the group suggested checking if the nearby zoo had any, but when I did, there were none mentioned on the zoo's website where the other animals and seasonal exhibits were listed.

"Remember how I told you my wife and I kind of hopped between hobbies for a while," Dave asked, "one of those hobbies was gardening at a community garden plot. The guy that runs it has a cousin with a farm a few hours outside of the city with an odd assortment of animals. I think he might actually have a few reindeer that he brings around for events each holiday season."

"Seriously? You know a guy who knows a guy who has reindeer?"

"I know a guy who knows a guy who *might* have a reindeer. They could also be moose or normal deer that he just tells people are reindeer."

"I'd like to say that I wouldn't be fooled by that, but it would be a lie."

"I can ask the guy about it if you want. If his cousin has them and is doing an event somewhere, you might be able to go, or you might be able to just go out to the farm, but that would be a lot of driving for one picture."

"I don't actually have a car. My roommate has one that we often use together or that I use for quick errands, but driving out to the farm might be a bit much. If you don't mind asking if he's doing any events, though, that would be great."

"I don't mind at all. Program your number in, and I'll text you when I hear back." Dale handed me his phone to add myself as a contact. I sent myself a text message so that I could add him to my own contacts list.

Happy to have a lead for tomorrow's dare, I asked everyone in the group about their week. Raquel mentioned that she baked with her mother and sister every year, usually for a cookie exchange, but apparently, this year, the ladies who ran the exchange decided to make it more of a full-meal potluck rather than solely desserts. Some groups were bringing appetizers that could be frozen and reheated; others were bringing soups; Raquel and her family were in charge of breads. She said she was happy to still have a baking day but was clearly bummed that it wasn't the usual cookie-fest.

When I mentioned that I was going to be heading over to my neighbor's house to bake cookies, her eyes lit up. I couldn't invite her without talking to Gloria first—I didn't even know if Gloria's kitchen would accommodate all three of us—but we exchanged numbers so that I could ask Gloria if it would be alright to invite her over.

If tonight didn't work, we agreed to pick a day and have our own cookie fest. Anna would love it too; she cooked frequently but always liked the role of taste-tester best for baked goods. When I said goodbye to everyone, promising to come back soon to update them on the next few days of dares, Bernie yelled out that she expected me to pick a craft I'd like to try and learn first for my next visit. I pretended not to hear her.

Back at the apartment building, I stopped to check in with Gloria, who was thrilled by the idea of Raquel joining us. She told me to come over whenever I was ready, so I headed back to my apartment to drop off my things, texting Raquel along the way to let her know that she was welcome to join.

She replied almost immediately, first in a string of excited emojis and then asking whether she should pick anything up. I had asked the same when I spoke to Gloria, and she seemed almost offended, so I let Raquel know and sent her my apartment's address and number, figuring that she'd be more comfortable coming to my apartment first and going over together.

"Anna?" I was met with groaning from the couch. Anna was sprawled out with an arm over her eyes. "Are you okay?"

"Too much sugar," she mumbled, "cookies have betrayed me." Anna and I both had a flare for the dramatic when we didn't feel well and memories of her patience with me when I'd eaten salsa so hot it rivaled the fires of hell had me empathizing instead of laughing. "I should have stopped, Hales. I wasn't even hungry. Someone brought in an apple pie, and no one was eating it, but I thought, 'hey, apple pie is often at holiday parties,' so I thought I had a loophole! I figured I'd just eat the filling—basically just apple sauce, right? Wrong! It was basically an apple sugar sauce. And then I thought that since cookies are more doughy, they might soak up some of the gelatinous, sugary mixture, but *no!*"

"Okay, well, how about I make you a sandwich or some soup or—"

"No! No soup! It will slosh around too much. And no sandwich—I'm too close to victory over the cookies."

"I think the cookies might have already won, but for now, let's call it a win and get you something more substantial." I walked over to the dare chart and added a coal sticker under my name and a candy cane sticker under Anna's. "See, you're victorious. Honestly, I can't believe you managed this long. I folded before 9:00 a.m. after the breakfast sandwich cravings got to me, and a lunch invite came through."

I started pulling together the ingredients for grilled cheese to make for Anna and me before I headed back to Gloria's when the front door buzzer sounded. I let her in and waited with the door open for Raquel to top the stairs. The three of us ate grilled cheese sandwiches as Anna told us about her harrowing day of desserts. By the time we were all done eating, Anna had perked up considerably.

Anna sighed and laid back on the couch theatrically while scrolling through streaming movie options as Raquel and I put on our shoes and said goodbye. After a warm greeting from Gloria and being ushered inside, it was clear that I didn't need to worry about there not being room for all of us in the kitchen. It was huge, approximately the size of mine and Anna's kitchen and living room combined, and, as Gloria gave us a tour through her home, we found out that it used to be two separate two-bedroom condos that she bought from their respective owners and completely renovated to make one luxurious, three-bedroom condo with giant shared spaces, though Gloria lived alone currently.

"I guess that explains why I've never seen anyone coming out of the front door one down from you. I just thought the unit was empty."

Gloria flashed me a smile as we ended up in her office. She tilted a book on her shelf down, triggering the bookshelf to open. A hidden door! "I didn't want the extra door to go into any of my main rooms, but I also didn't want to have to have a layout structured around making a second entryway. Instead, I added this mini room."

We walked into a room that had just enough space for two plush armchairs snugly situated with a tiny table between them. A TV the size of the wall was mounted across from them, and an assortment of pillows and blankets were stacked on high shelves. There were fairy lights strung up that Gloria switched on, and, yep, a door that looked like the second door to the hallway. "I come in here to have little movie nights or sometimes to read. When I was renovating, I was writing a lot of suspense and mystery, so I was intrigued by the idea of having a panic room. Though, since the door opens up right to the hall, it's not terribly effective."

"When you were writing? Are you an author?" Raquel inspected the space as she asked.

"A screenwriter. Mostly made-for-TV, but some larger projects as well."

"So cool."

Gloria lived such a cool life. As we headed back to her kitchen, she told us about trips and classes she'd taken and research she'd done in pursuit of her scripts being authentic. She'd talked her way into a job on a lobster fishing boat only to be fired at the end of the first day when she'd been caught trying to free the lobsters. She'd spent a year learning to forge metal weapons, and she'd lived almost completely off-grid for a month in Alaska.

She told us about her adventures while directing Raquel and me through the different steps of making and decorating several types of cookies. We made cut-out sugar cookies first so that they would cool and eventually all sat down to decorate.

The cookies Gloria made looked as if they belonged in a bakery. It shouldn't have come as a surprise when I jokingly asked if that's where she'd learned how to bake and she had, in fact, worked at a boulangerie in a small town outside of Paris for a year while writing abroad. Raquel's cookies looked almost as good and even better after Gloria gave her a few tips. The same could not be said for mine, but they tasted delicious regardless.

I was really only dedicating half of my time to decorating cookies. The other half I spent chattering away. I always enjoyed baking, but I almost always baked alone. Sometimes, Anna would sit at the barstools, and we would talk while I worked, but baking together with Raquel and Gloria brought a new level of enjoyment to the process. Eventually, all of the cookies were decorated, and we moved on to sipping glasses of wine while snacking on fresh focaccia that Gloria had made earlier in the week.

We all jumped a bit as a cell phone started going off. It was an alarm I'd set to remind myself to take evening meds.

"Oh my gosh, it's 10:00 p.m. already," Raquel said as she jumped out of her chair when I turned my phone screen to show that it was just an alarm. "I didn't realize it had gotten so late. I'm really sorry to cut this short, but I need to get going."

"Time moves quickly with good company," Gloria replied. I couldn't disagree. Now that my alarm had gone off and our rhythm shifted a bit, though, I noticed that I was actually a bit tired.

"I had a really good time tonight. Thanks for hosting us, Gloria," I said. Gloria reached out her hand to me, so I took it, and she gave my hand a squeeze.

"And thanks for letting me come as well," Raquel added. "I'd really like to get together and bake again soon."

"I definitely need to know your secrets for bread, Gloria." I picked up and gazed longingly at the small piece of focaccia left on my plate before popping it into my mouth.

"Anytime, darlings, you're always welcome!" Raquel and I each gave Gloria a hug goodbye before heading down the hall.

"I appreciate you inviting me along tonight, Haley," Raquel said as I walked her out to the bike she had ridden over and locked up outside. "It's been difficult finding new friends since I moved here last winter. The Knittie Bitties are wonderful, obviously, but I love meeting new people, especially people my age."

"Of course! I was so glad you could come. The next week is going to be a bit of a chaotic mess, but if you get some time during and definitely after the holiday, let's make some plans to hang out. Anna's normally not so close to a sugar crash as she was tonight, but I'm sure she'd love to see you again as well."

"Sounds great to me. Keep me updated on the dares in the meantime, and make sure you figure out what craft you want Bernie to teach you." She winked before hopping on her bike, waving goodbye, and pedaling away. I headed back into the apartment, quietly entering and finding the television still on but Anna asleep on the couch. I pulled the blanket that was half-fallen on the floor back over her before turning off the television. She didn't even stir. After retreating to my bedroom, I quickly got ready for bed before shutting my eyes, able to feel the smile etched onto my face.

The dares were silly, sure, but they were opening up my life to new people, and I had been having so much fun. Maybe Anna would go for monthly dares in the future, just something to spice up our routines. I bet I could rile Bernie up into agreeing to some silly dares. Although, I couldn't confidently say that I'd be able to keep up with Bernie. It didn't really matter. I was just happy. I'd find ways to carry this fun approach into my life beyond Christmas later. For now, sleep.

DAY 7: GET A PICTURE WITH A LIVE REINDEER

I woke up feeling refreshed and ready for the day. Anna and I usually spent Friday nights on our couch, loafing around after the work week and ordered in from a restaurant neither of us had tried previously. We typically decided on a few possible places to order from a day or two in advance and then had fun going through menus together and drooling over photos of food people had posted with reviews.

This week, though, we'd had so much going on that we hadn't even discussed it. I'd have to look through my list of places that were on deck later and send over some suggestions. First, I needed to sit down and make a to-do list; there were all kinds of tasks floating around that I needed to address. I went to grab one of the cookies that I brought home last night, only to find a note taped to the bag.

BEWARE: Seems sweet but will betray you!

Anna clearly wasn't over her stomachache from yesterday. I laughed, taking a picture of the note before grabbing a cookie and taking a bite. I'd heard Anna leave shortly after I'd woken up, so I assumed that she had an early meeting, but I was curious to see what she would come up with for today's dare. She could use her car to venture out further if needed. I hadn't heard back from Dale yesterday, and the likelihood of his friend's cousin being in the city somewhere seemed so slim that it wasn't worth relying on.

I filled a thermos with hot chocolate (I wasn't a fan of coffee) and added a few to-do items to a running list on my phone, including researching places to find a reindeer. Looking over at the dare chart, I was pleased for a moment that tomorrow's dare was all set up before my adrenaline shot up at remembering that I hadn't figured out a costume. If I didn't look like an elf, I couldn't volunteer.

That needed immediate attention, so I switched out of my notes app and started searching online for anywhere that I might be able to get an elf costume same-day. Most nearby thrift stores weren't open yet, though I expected that any elf costumes that they had were already gone. Still, I made a list of their names, locations, and numbers to call in a few hours.

Thankfully, the city was big enough that there were also a few year-round costume shops. One was already open, so I called right away, only to be told that they were out of elf costumes. I headed out of the apartment, now feeling slightly anxious. I couldn't do anything for now, so I forced myself to take a few deep breaths to calm my nerves. I shook out my hands and boarded the train, finding an unlikely spot to sit. I used the commute on more reindeer research.

7.2

Dale: I have half-good news for you about the reindeer

I looked at my phone as it vibrated to alert me to incoming text messages. Seeing the first of the messages on the lock screen, I was tempted to drop what I was working on to look at the update. Unfortunately, I was nearing the end of a deadline that was already tight, so I forced myself to re-focus.

After about twenty minutes, I finalized a few documents and sent them off in an email to a client. I was glad the requests had come in early, as they were the only thing that I anticipated coming in today that needed my involvement.

Originally planning to be with my parents for the week of Christmas, I'd taken next week off work, so this was my last day before a week of vacation, and I'd organized most things to have already wrapped up and had blocked my calendar as a catch-up day to make sure I was able to dedicate time to anything urgent that came in.

Based on where all of my projects were at process- and implementation-wise, I was almost certainly going to have a mostly free afternoon. It had taken longer to complete everything than I expected; I looked at the clock and noticed nearly three hours had passed since I had gotten to work. I needed to call around about the elf costumes, but first, I was bouncing in my chair with anticipation of what Dale's "half" good news was.

Dale: I have half-good news for you about the reindeer

Dale: My friend's cousin does have reindeer

Dale: Even better, he has BABY reindeer

Dale: LOOK AT THE BABY REINDEER

Dale's messages were followed by a photo of a tiny reindeer. It looked like a mix of a baby cow and a baby deer. I wanted to pet it so badly.

Dale: Apparently, one of his reindeer got pregnant later
than the usual breeding season. That baby is a few months
old but still so little!

Dale: Anyway, he's taking a different (adult, boo) reindeer
to a private school that has classes on sustainable livestock

and agriculture practices and giving a lecture in the after-noon and then staying to let other classes come out and see the reindeer

Dale: It's on the outskirts of the city, though, so it'll probably be a pain to get to

Dale: No idea if you can just show up, but he'll be there from 1:00 p.m. until 4:00 p.m. if you want to try

His last message was followed by the name and address of the school. One internet search later, I learned that it was a specialized high school for students who excelled in math and science. From my apartment building, it wouldn't actually be that bad of a walk to a train station whose route stopped quite close to the school. It was going to be a long train ride out and back, but my phone had a hotspot that I could use with my laptop, and I could monitor my emails on my phone. If anything urgent came up, I could work from the train.

I wondered if I could get away with telling my boss I was going to work from home for the afternoon, considering I'd ducked out early yesterday, too. I meant to do some work yesterday evening but never got around to it.

Thankfully, there wasn't any new, urgent work either, and nothing that I wasn't able to get handled right away. Completing the new request that took up the last few hours was a priority project, and I'd managed to close it out without any remaining open items, so I was hoping I could use that as leverage. I'd update her to let her know that it had been closed and then ask about working from home later. I sent Dale a text back, thanking him profusely for asking his friend and gushing about the baby reindeer.

After talking with my boss and getting the go-ahead to work remotely for the afternoon, I found an empty conference room and called around about an elf costume. Of seven different thrift stores, all but one were out of holiday costumes. The only place that did have one in stock checked on the size and, unfortunately, I didn't think the parents of kids coming to see Santa would appreciate the unintentionally sexy elf version, assuming I managed to squeeze myself into it.

Thankfully, the costume shop left on my list had a few available. They had my size and walked me through how to find their inventory on the website. As an added bonus, they allowed rentals. The price for a weekend rental was more than the cost of buying a cheap costume online, but at least this one I could be sure was available, appeared to be good quality, and I wouldn't be stuck with an elf costume afterward.

The person helping me agreed to put one of the costumes on hold for an hour so that I could stop by and pick them up on my way back to my apartment. I let out a sigh of relief as we hung up and then went back to my desk to continue clearing out emails and requests as quickly as I could competently handle them.

Just over an hour later, I had picked up a dress, belt, hat, and shoe covers from the costume shop, dropped the costume off in my closet at home, and was speed walking to the train station eight blocks away. My laptop was zipped away in a backpack that would hopefully help me blend on school grounds.

As soon as I was on the train, I pulled out my phone and checked my email; nothing had come in that needed my input. I switched over to an internet browser and searched Gloria's name, looking through some of the movies and television shows she'd been involved with. As it turned out, she was seriously underselling herself last night.

I took a few screenshots of her credits (there are so many it took multiple to fit them all in) before texting them to Anna and Raquel on a group chat and suggesting Raquel join for a Friday movie night soon, and we check out something Gloria wrote. We exchanged messages over the course of the train ride, debating which to start with and speculating on whether she had enough interaction with the various casts to have had a romantic dalliance with anyone famous. The girls took a united front and insisted that I be the one to ask her about it.

As the robotic, recorded voice on the train announced my stop, I pulled up directions on my phone from the train station to the school—it looked to only be about a ten-minute walk. I was assuming that the lecture and reindeer would be held outside, likely in a back field of some kind, and that I could just walk the perimeter of the school until I found it. I needed to come up with a believable story for why I was there and why I was late because, if I could swing it, I wanted to pet that reindeer.

The school was visible from several blocks away, sprawling across what looked like four city blocks just in one direction. It resembled a college campus more than it did a high school. The entrance boasted a large sign for the main entrance and office building, but I skirted to the left and continued walking, heading towards the back of the complex where I assumed the reindeer would be.

When I was nearing what appeared to be the furthest back building, I heard light voices and peered across the space between the last two buildings. I could see a trailer as well as a crowd of students. The reindeer wasn't visible, so it must have been behind the trailer.

Debating whether to try and just walk across the courtyard that separated me from where the lecture was being held or continuing to walk around the buildings, I decided to go through. I straightened my posture and stared unwaveringly ahead, sure that anyone looking at me would assume I belonged there. I silently wished that I'd brought a notebook or something that might make me look less like I was a grown adult skulking around a school.

I only got about four steps in before I saw a security guard exit one of the nearby buildings and start walking across the courtyard. When she spotted me, she changed direction slightly to bring her more directly into my path.

"Ma'am," she said as we neared each other, "where are you headed?"

"Over to the courtyard to retrieve something, and then I'll be on my way." This was the best option that I'd come up with earlier: pretending I'd been here earlier, forgotten something, and just needed to pop over to get it back.

"The courtyard is currently being used for a guest lecture, so you won't be able to go there now. Why don't you come with me, and we'll see if anything was dropped off at the office."

"Oh, well, I doubt anyone would have even noticed my tools. I intentionally put them out of the way to avoid damage, and I won't intrude on the lecture at all."

"Ma'am. We'll go to the office." She was looking at me as if this was a test, so I nodded and walked in the direction she was indicating with her arm. Why did I mention specifically what I left? What tools was I talking about?

I had my phone in my hand, and I opened the camera app and tried to inconspicuously gauge whether I might be able to sneak a quick photo on the way if walking in this direction meant that the reindeer became visible. No luck, unfortunately. We got to the main office building, and I was dropped off at the front desk. Though the security officer walked to the far side of the room and started chatting with someone at a different desk, I could see her looking back over at me regularly out of my periphery.

"Hi. What can I help you with?" I looked down at the boy who greeted me. He couldn't have been more than sixteen years old, but I glanced at the book he closed as I walked up. It was a textbook on something called chaos mathematics, so he must be a student here.

"Umm, hi. I was here earlier, and I left something in the back courtyard. I was hoping to just go grab it."

"It looks like that space is currently occupied," he said, after checking something on the computer in front of him, "and I can't authorize access when there is a class out there, but I can check the lost and found for you. What did you leave there?" He pulled out a large box from a shelf behind the desk and started moving objects around inside of it.

"I, uh, left a few small tools."

"Okay..." The kid looked at me like he was waiting for more information. When I didn't say anything more, he continued, "What kind of tools?"

"They're, uh, for measuring different elements of... bee habitats." I saw an article on bees on the school's website earlier. There was a page on the site about recent school news, and one piece mentioned that they'd brought in specialists to check the space and suitability of a certain space at the school to allow the students to house bees for a new research project. I had no idea where that space was, but logically, anyone checking the environment would need to review surrounding areas as well, right?

"I don't know what those would look like, but the only things in here are clothes, a watch, and some pens."

"You keep pens in the lost and found? What's the point?"

"You'd be surprised how serious some people are about their pens."

I shrugged. "Alright, umm, well, thanks for looking. I guess I'll just call my, uh, my contact and ask them to look for them."

"Do you want to leave some contact information in case they get turned in? Because of how many people are out there, the odds are good that someone might find them and bring them here later."

"Sure, yeah. Obviously I need those tools, so that would be a normal thing to do." The kid pushed a pen and some paper toward me, and I hesitated before putting down a fake name and number. No one was going to be turning in missing bee habitat testing tools, and when someone realized that I'd been lying, I didn't want them to have my information.

As I stood back up, I remembered spotting a sign for a restroom down the hall and asked if I could use it before heading out. It was back in the direction I came through with the security guard, so maybe I could check for a window or something that I could spot the reindeer through. The kid at the desk was already sitting back down and opening his book back up and just shrugged at me and said to go ahead.

I walked towards the bathroom and hesitated at the door until I saw the security guard looking my way, so I went in. There was a small, very high window in the wall, but I couldn't see anything from it. I figured that the guard would wait a few minutes and then start watching the door, so I peeked back out. Thankfully, her head was turned, so I exited and pulled the door closed behind me quickly and quietly.

I darted to the other side of the hall, out of view, and speed-walked as lightly as I could down the hall to where I could see light flooding in. There were two large glass doors exiting out closer to the courtyard where the reindeer was, and *I could see the reindeer*! I took out my phone quickly and switched the front-facing camera on. I took a few quick shots of me in front of the door with the reindeer in the background. I was considering trying to go out when the security guard came storming down the hall.

"Ma'am! You have no reason to be down here. You need to leave." I almost dropped my phone when I turned toward her, but the screen was visible when I lowered the phone, and it was clearly still in camera mode. "Are you taking photos? You can't just—"

"Oh, you know," I said quickly, cutting her off, "it's just such good lighting here. Can't pass that up. My information is at the front desk, though, so I'm sure someone will call if my things turn up." I quickly turned and walked as fast as I could without outright jogging to the front door. I didn't stop until I was a few blocks away from the school, certain I was completely clear of the entrance. I leaned over and put my hands on my knees, breathing heavily from the adrenaline, and laughed out loud. Back at the train station, I pulled out my phone to confirm that I did actually get the photo I needed.

I couldn't help but laugh to myself; this was the second time this week that a security guard had to escort me somewhere due to my suspicious behavior. A week ago, I was boring. Actually, maybe I had just been in a bit of a rut. Not that I was looking for another security guard interaction to add to the tally, but I didn't hate that I was being a little more open lately.

Usually, going home to lounge on the couch always sounded so good that I had dismissed a number of plans and potential opportunities to meet new people and try new things. I was glad these dares were shaking things back up. With that in mind, I opened my text thread with Adam and sent off a message.

Hales: can you pass along a message to security guards working at your building?

Adam: do I even want to know?

Haley: let him know that if he needs a support group for security guards who have had to deal with me this week, he won't be the only member

Adam: I'm a little concerned that I'm not enough of a bad boy to keep up with you

Hales: stick with me, kid, and I'll teach you everything I know

Adam and I texted back and forth for a bit before I got on a train heading towards home and took out my laptop. I managed to get everything that had come in completed and returned in the forty-ish minutes before the train reached my stop. The streets were slushy from the top layer of snow on the sidewalks melting in the unexpected but welcome afternoon sun. I stepped to the side to let someone get by using the thin patch of sidewalk that wasn't a mini puddle, just as a door opened two feet in front of me.

The most incredible scents of garlic and fresh bread wafted out of an Italian restaurant. By the time I got through looking at the appetizers listed on the menu in a glass case by the door, I was nearly drooling. I took a quick photo of the name on the door to ask Anna about when I got home since I never got around to researching dinner places for our movie night, but I was hopeful that she hadn't ever been to this place so that I could lobby for ordering everything on the menu. Or, you know, just six or seven things; I could be reasonable.

7.3

Anna arrived home around 8:00 p.m., shortly before our food was delivered. She had texted earlier that she'd be getting home late, and because she hadn't been to the Italian place I passed earlier, I ordered us a spread to share. She came out of her room after changing into pajamas as I was taking the tops off of various to-go containers. Two pastas, arancini, fresh bread with an assortment of spreads, and tiramisu had our apartment smelling divine.

"Good find on this place, Hales. If it tastes half as good as it smells, I'm sold." Anna took the plate I handed her, and we both started serving ourselves a bit of everything.

I laughed as Anna started dancing in place in her spot on the couch after a few bites of pasta. "How was work? Did you get everything wrapped up that you needed to before the break?" While I had to take time off work, Anna's company shut down the week of Christmas through the new year. Anytime my boss wanted to follow suit, I was here for it.

"Yeah. It was actually a pretty light day. I just had to head back in for a while to finish up. I meant to drive out to the suburbs around lunchtime and be back with enough of the regular workday left to finish up at my normal time, but I ended up staying out there for a lot longer than I expected."

"Does this mean that you found a reindeer?"

"That kind of depends on who you ask." Confusion stopped my fork a few inches from my still-open mouth, and Anna shot me a grin before continuing. "A few days ago, I was searching all over online for somewhere that had a reindeer, and I found all of these articles about today being the first day that a supposedly famous reindeer would be returning to some tree lot in the suburbs. The place looked pretty legit, and there were all kinds of comments from people about how excited they were, and they couldn't wait to bring carrots for the reindeer and play reindeer games. There were photos of the tree lot and of people in their adjoining market; there were even a bunch of photos of some guy dressed like a reindeer, so I figured this was clearly *a thing* there."

"Oh, wow. That's cool. So, did you go see it? Did you get to pet it? Was it soft?"

"Well, this is one of those 'hindsight is 50/50' situations. I should have realized that there weren't any photos of an actual reindeer...just the guy dressed as one." My eyes widened, and I waited as Anna held her hand up while she stopped to take a sip of water. "Lo and behold, the reindeer *was* the guy. There was no actual reindeer. It was just a guy in a reindeer suit walking around."

"Was he just on all fours the whole time? That must have been obnoxious."

"Nope. This reindeer was a species native only to that specific tree farm." Anna rolled her eyes, but her smile gave away how amused she was. "The guy was standing up in the front two legs, and there was something connected to his waist that formed the body and back legs of the reindeer. The back legs had wheels, so it rolled around with him."

I couldn't hold back my laughter at this point. "Please tell me you got a photo with this guy."

"Oh, just wait, it gets better."

"How?"

"Apparently, this guy works at the tree farm, and a few years back, he dressed up as a reindeer for just an hour or so when some kids were disappointed when they were supposed to have a reindeer visit, but it fell through. Everyone had so much fun with it that this guy dressing up like a reindeer has become a beloved local tradition. They actually have reindeer-themed games for kids and adults to play and a surprisingly great little farm stand, so I got something to eat and hot cider and watched the reindeer-man play reindeer games.

There was a cart selling carrots, which I didn't think much of when I still thought there was a real reindeer, but I was a little confused by people buying carrots and bringing them over to the reindeer guy. I figured he'd pretend to eat them and then put them in a pocket or something, but he refused them all. Weirdly, everyone seemed to find this hilarious.

A woman told me all of this while her kids were running around, and we ended up sitting down together at one of the big picnic tables. Turns out that the guy in the reindeer suit hates carrots, so it's become a running joke to try and get him to eat one. Anyone who manages it has a lucky year the following year, so people try to trick him into eating one.

As we were sitting there chatting, someone came up with three cups of what I assumed were hot chocolate or cider. The person handed one to the reindeer—who, it turns out, had little hidden slots where his arms could come out when needed—and one to the other person the reindeer guy was talking to.

The reindeer guy took a sip of his drink and then did an actual spit-take like in the movies. The guy who'd given the drink to him yelled out 'carrots,' and everyone started cheering while the reindeer guy started grumbling loudly about carrot juice. It was incredible. The woman I was sitting with told me that, while lots of people bought a carrot at the carrot stall as a joke because they were cheap and the proceeds went to local projects and helping local businesses and families in need, there were always people trying to trick the reindeer into eating or drinking something with carrots."

"Hmm, how much does he need to consume? If he spit out the carrot juice, does it even count?"

"No clue. I suspect he swallowed some before realizing it, or maybe just getting him to take a bite or drink is enough. I heard that last year, only one person managed to trick him with chocolate-covered pretzel sticks that had carrot ribbons around the part of the pretzel that was covered in chocolate. Someone brought a tray of them and passed them out."

"How did they make sure that the reindeer guy got the one with carrot, though? Wouldn't it have been suspicious if he got handed one particular one and wasn't allowed to swap?"

"That's the best part! Apparently, the person made them all like that. They made sure to pass a bunch out on the way and let the reindeer guy choose his own. Other people were eating them already but either didn't notice or were playing along because as soon as he took a bite, people started celebrating. There's a bell hung up that gets rung every time he gets tricked, and the woman who told me said he hadn't even realized that he had been tricked until someone rang the bell."

"Amazing. Please, please tell me you got a picture with this guy."

"I sure did!" Anna pulled out her phone and turned it to face me.

"Wait!"

"Yup."

"Anna!"

"I know."

"He's got a carrot in his mouth!" The photo on the phone was a selfie of Anna and a guy in a reindeer costume, but he had a large carrot between his teeth and was grimacing.

"He only bit down on it for the photo because I asked him to put his hands back in the costume. I couldn't let the illusion be shattered. He spit it out immediately after I took the photo, but I looked, and it had bite marks on it."

"I bet he ingested a tiny bit of carrot. Oh, maybe you're about to have a lucky year!"

"Someone did actually ring the bell as I took the photo, so I guess they counted it. You know what that means, don't you?" Anna got up and refilled her water.

"What?"

"I'm going to have an edge for the next few dares."

"I don't know. I got a picture with an actual reindeer—that's just a guy." I took out my phone and passed it to Anna with the picture I'd taken earlier pulled up. "Honestly, though, I'd give you this one. You met a reindeer legend!"

"I like the days we both win." Anna smiled at me as she sat back down on the couch. "Now, why is this photo of a bunch of kids with a reindeer and your giant eyeball in the corner?"

I gave Anna a play-by-play of my attempts to sneak into the high school earlier and then to try and evade the security guard. Afterward, we finished eating while scrolling through movie options. Once our plates were out of the way and we were snuggled into little blanket nests, we started the first movie. Hopefully this week, unlike the last, we wouldn't end up planning any schemes.

DAY 8: BE SANTA OR AN ELF FOR THE DAY

You know that feeling when you wake up feeling more refreshed than you ought to be, given how late you stayed up the night before? It surprised me every time it happened.

My eyes blinked open, though my alarm hadn't gone off, so I grabbed my phone from the end table to check the time. I beat my alarm by four minutes. Waking up to an alarm was abrupt and loud and just not the vibe I was looking for on a Saturday morning, even one where I didn't have the luxury of sleeping in.

Anna and I ended up only watching one movie before we headed to bed, and we opted not to drink, so I slept well and felt good. I bicycled my legs until they'd pushed the comforter to the end of the bed before doing some stretches.

Still in my pajamas, I headed into the kitchen and collected pancake batter ingredients as well as an assortment of berries to make into a quick compote for a topping. Putting on some music—quietly so as to not wake Anna—I danced around the kitchen while I mixed, poured, and flipped. With a baking sheet loaded with pancakes warming in the oven, I served myself a plate, drowning the pancakes in the blackberry and raspberry sauce I made.

"Goooood morning!" Anna looked up blearily at my enthusiastic greeting as she shuffled into the kitchen. "Want me to make you a plate?"

"Sure. We still have syrup somewhere, right?" I swiveled around and pulled the syrup out of the fridge.

"Did you not sleep well? You're usually the earlier bird of the two of us."

"Yeah, I just went down the rabbit hole of random videos online and stayed up way later than I meant to."

"Find out anything interesting?"

"Lots of gardening tips. Board game recommendations."

"I look forward to us keeping a plant alive for more than a few weeks. Honestly, any plant will do. Maybe we should try to grow some herbs this summer. This sauce," I said, gesturing with my fork to the container I transferred the extra compote into, "would be heavenly with a little fresh basil, but I wasn't about to go to the store for it."

"That sounds like a summer-us decision."

"I'll put it on the agenda for May." I sat down with Anna at the barstools after grabbing us each a glass of water. "At least it's Saturday, and we're officially done with work for a while. You can eat and then nap the day away to catch up."

"Eh, I need to get ready for later."

"What've you got going on later?"

"Umm, you know, weekend errands and things." Anna shoved a giant forkful of pancakes into her mouth and then nodded. Odd. I wondered whether she was going to be an elf somewhere. Was it a secret? Were we actually competing today, rather than just the normal joking competition as we both worked on dares? I didn't love it, but maybe she just didn't want to be seen dressed up like an elf. That, I could empathize with. I was hopeful that no one I knew would show up at the market today. "What've you got planned for the day?"

I wasn't sure why, other than Anna herself not being forthcoming, but I decided to skirt the issue. "I'm helping out a friend with something this morning," I started, hoping my exaggeration wasn't noticeable given that Pam, the woman coordinating the Santa at the market today, was barely an acquaintance, "and then I have some tentative plans to see Adam." She didn't need to know that, at most, I was hoping he might stop by, given that I told him I'd be there today.

"Adam? Jason's brother Adam? Picked my tree, Adam? The guy who prevented you from maybe being arrested?"

"Okay, I definitely wasn't getting arrested, just questioned by a security guard."

"So it is that Adam."

"Yup. We've been texting regularly, and we might meet up later today."

"He seemed like a really cool guy. What are you two doing?"

"We might go to the holiday market downtown for a bit." Anna froze for a moment before trying a bit too hard to act casual. Interesting. "Then I guess we'll just see where it goes."

"He knows he'll always be second fiddle to me in your life, right?" Anna's teasing, coupled with her stern expression, broke the ball of tension in my chest put there by my exaggerating to the point of basically lying. I didn't even know why I was doing it. As I finished eating and started cleaning up the kitchen, Anna got up and said that she was going to go back to bed for a bit, so I quickly got dressed in something neutral that I could wear as a base layer before stuffing the elf costume into a backpack. Surprisingly, I was running ahead of schedule, and it wasn't completely frigid outside, so I decided to walk along the bus route until one was getting close rather than just waiting.

I walked into the market twenty minutes before Santa was due to start greeting people. The market itself was already open, so I wandered around for a few minutes before heading over to find Pam. She was sitting at her table with a display of delicate pieces of jewelry in front of her.

The other day, she had a large amount of very on-theme pieces like Christmas trees, candy canes, and snowflake-shaped jewelry. One or two still remained, but they were outliers amongst the rest of the items. When I asked about the change, she told me that she'd made those pieces specifically for this market because people always wanted them but that her normal style was more abstract.

As I looked at her work again, I could see that they did evoke the feeling of winter and nature, but you had to look long enough to appreciate them. A passing glance wouldn't do it, though they were beautiful enough to draw passersby to a halt, giving them time.

Pam took me to a small building the size of two booths combined, but that was fully enclosed. I recognized this building. Whereas the booths were all temporary structures that got removed after the market, this small building was always in this space. I never knew what was inside of it, though, and the windows were too high to see inside. As it turned out, it was a small office, an even smaller bathroom, and a seating area with a tiny table and a few chairs. The area that the market was occupying was often used to host events, and having a small base of operations made sense, but they rarely went on for longer than a day or two.

"This is Bert," Pam said as she gestured to an older man sitting in one of the chairs by the table, dressed as Santa. He looked up from the phone in his hand to say hello. "Bert, this is..." Pam trailed off, clearly having forgotten my name.

"Haley," I offered, smiling and raising a hand to wave.

"Yes, Haley. She'll be joining as an elf assistant this morning." She turned back towards me. "Make sure you're dressed and ready in the next ten minutes. Please try to stay in character with the kids." With that, she turned and started to leave. In the few steps it took before she reached the door, something she said registered.

"Wait, Pam."

"Hmm?" Pam had her hand on the door, clearly ready to get back to her booth and her friend.

"You said 'this morning.' I thought that Santa would be here until 4:00 p.m. today."

"Oh, right. We have someone else for the second half of the shift, so you'll only need to stay until 1:00 p.m. today." I must have looked disappointed, though I was really just surprised, because Pam continued, "If you want to stay, I guess you could work it out with the afternoon person, but there isn't going to be a ton of room blocked off."

"Oh, no, it's fine. I just suddenly have more free time today than I expected." If I didn't actually have to spend my entire afternoon as an elf, I wasn't complaining. "I'm going to change. See you in a bit."

I headed into the bathroom, despite just tossing the costume on over my black leggings and top. The dress was long-sleeved, but thankfully, the sleeves of the dress weren't so tight that they were uncomfortable layered over my thermal long-sleeved shirt. I had worn a green coat that I'd gotten a few years ago for when I inevitably got cold, along with mittens, a hat for underneath my decorative elf hat, and bright red leg warmers above the shoe covers the costume came with. I pulled out my phone and took a photo showing my outfit while making a silly face. I'd show Anna my outfit later, but for now, I texted the photo to Adam.

Haley: [photo]

Haley: Guess who just arrived from the North Pole and has an in with Santa

Adam: You look great! Are elves resistant to the cold, though?

Haley: I have a coat and extra layers, but I'm mostly kept warm by the holiday spirit

Adam: Whiskey?

Haley: Only if it's added to hot chocolate

Adam: Noted. Maybe someone will show up with some cocoa later to warm you up

Haley: Just so long as they arrive before 1:00 p.m.

I heard Bert and his chair groaning as he got up in the main area, and a quick check of my phone showed that it was time to head out to start greeting kids and their parents.

Haley: Santa is calling. I'll try to put a good word in for you
:)

I turned my phone on do-not-disturb, tucking it into the pocket of my leggings beneath the skirt of my elf costume. I did the same with the cards from my wallet and my apartment key in the pocket on the other leg, just in case. I didn't expect that anyone would actually come into this building and steal my stuff, but why risk it when I had the pockets available.

Bert transformed from quiet to jubilant the instant we stepped outside and fell into the character, even for the short walk to the area where families were lined up. He spoke loudly to me about needing to check "The List" and wanting to make sure the elves had time to check the sleigh, responding to my slightly bemused look with a pointed look and head nod towards the kids that we were passing that weren't yet in line. As soon as the kids saw us, they turned and stared, so they were probably listening, and they all certainly got excited as Santa passed and gave small waves to many of them.

I was determined to have fun with this. Was I a little embarrassed to be out in public as an elf? Sure, but the last week of dares had started to erode my self-consciousness. I crafted a persona for my role as an elf. First up, a name: Ellie. Ellie the Elf. And Ellie the Elf would be very excited to see that there were already over a dozen kids in line to meet Santa, even if Haley suspected it was going to be a long couple of hours.

After Bert got settled on his chair and gave a small introductory speech about how Santa especially liked when little boys and girls were patient and kind to those around them (surprisingly, it seemed to make even the kids on the cusp of a tantrum calm down a bit), I waved the first child forward to see Santa.

When I stepped away and turned back out toward the other kids, asking the nearest child whether they were excited to see Santa, I saw Pam looking over in my periphery. She watched Bert for a minute before checking on me. We met each other's gaze, and she nodded approvingly before turning back to her friend to chat.

The next couple hours passed while I made small talk with parents and answered questions from kids in line about what the North Pole and Santa's workshop were like. I kept adding new traits to Ellie the Elf's personality, and as time went by, I became more animated rather than steadily becoming exhausted of the act as I'd expected.

Ellie the Elf's favorite color was any color in glitter form, and her favorite food was marshmallows. Sometimes, Ellie the Elf would bring toys from the workshop out to the reindeer to see if they'd like them. Once, she brought roller skates, and the reindeer all nearly fell on their butts, but luckily, they remembered that they could fly and went into the air instead!

I was in the middle of telling a very detailed account of the reindeer versus roller skate story when I heard a young girl say, "Uncle Adam, is that your elf friend?" Glancing over my shoulder, I saw Adam holding a girl who looked to be about six years old, smiling at her as she pointed and waved when she noticed I was looking back at her. I quickly said goodbye to the kids I had been talking to and walked over to Adam.

"Well, well, well. If it isn't my favorite person on the naughty list." I smirked at Adam.

I was about to say hello to the little girl he was holding, but she gasped, and her eyes went so wide it was almost comical as she looked at Adam and whispered, "No."

"Come on now. You know I haven't been on the naughty list since I started eating all my vegetables and cleaning up my toys every night," Adam responded seriously. He looked at the girl in his arms and continued, "Those things are very important if you want to get on the nice list, Gracie."

"Is that true?" she asked me as she put her hands on her head in worry.

I cleared the smirk off my face before looking at her and replying as solemnly as I could manage. "It is. Not only is it important to be healthy and tidy, but if there are toys all over, Santa might step on something and hurt himself. We don't want that!"

She considered me for a few seconds before sticking her hand out to me. "Okay, I'll do my best."

Barely keeping a straight face, I shook her hand before looking back to Adam. "So, 'Uncle Adam,' is it? Jason's kid? Or do you have more siblings?"

"Neither," another voice said from my left. "Hey, I'm Chris. This is my wife, Leila." The woman beside him said hello with a friendly smile. "We've just known each other the majority of our lives."

"They're best bugs," Gracie said happily.

"We're best *buds*," Adam corrected. "You're the only little bug around here." She was wearing a jacket covered in little cartoon butterflies and ladybugs that Adam pointed to before looking back up at me to explain further, "Chris and I met in first grade. We decided to draw mustaches on our faces with permanent markers we pilfered from the teacher's desk, and we've been friends ever since."

"Much to the dismay of our mothers, who had already become rivals a year prior. Jason and my older sister were also in the same class, and something happened with a glue stick and a frog. We keep trying to get them to explain what happened, but everyone has a different story." Chris chuckled. "Adam and I sometimes use it to our advantage these days."

"In our defense," Adam said, "we tried getting them to mend fences dozens of times over. Now we just harmlessly mention that, say, Chris's mom has perfected her lemon bread recipe and that I had some when I visited, and it was delicious. If that spurs my mom into making lemon bread that she insists I bring to enjoy with Chris, so be it."

"I'm not entirely convinced that it isn't a rivalry rooted in begrudging respect and maybe even friendship at this point. They do always seem to have fun with it."

"I thought it was ridiculous until Gracie started at preschool," Leila said with a grimace. "One of the other kids has an absolutely vile parent, always talking about how she deigns to keep her son there when he's so obviously advanced compared to the other kids and making snide remarks like belittling the themes the other kids have for their birthday parties." Leila shook her head. "I've been trying not to react and just ignore her, but secretly, I'm always thinking up snarky replies. Getting stuck in a feud for the next three decades isn't worth saying them out loud, though."

"It's almost time for Santa!" Gracie squealed, wiggling around in Adam's arms. We'd moved into the line-up of kids and parents and had been slowly moving further towards the front of the line. Bert clearly didn't need the help of an elf assistant, given how smoothly the line had continued to flow. When it was Gracie's turn, Adam put her down, and her parents started taking pictures as Gracie decisively told Santa about the toys she wanted and the backup toys that she would accept if her first choices were unavailable.

"So, any chance you're going to get a break soon," Adam asked as we watched Gracie start summing up her requests to ensure Santa had understood. "And if so, any interest in going to go grab a coffee nearby?"

"What time is it?" I didn't want to take my phone out of my pocket around all the kids. I was ignoring my elf duties already; I didn't want to ruin the magic of Ellie the Elf by whipping out a phone when I'd decided that elves in the North Pole had reindeer deliver messages as a means of communication. Not that any of the kids I'd told that to were nearby still.

"Umm," Adam pulled out his phone and checked. "12:40 p.m."

"I was going to have a break, but apparently, there's someone coming in later to be the elf helper, so if you don't mind waiting about twenty minutes, I'll be done then."

"Chris, Leila, Gracie, and I were going to walk around the market after Gracie got to see Santa, so that works out perfectly. I'll head back over here around then."

"Sounds good." I saw Chris, Leila, and Gracie standing and chatting behind Adam, a different toddler now in deep conversation with Santa.

"Looks like you should get back to uncle duties, and I need to get back to being Ellie the Elf." Adam checked over his shoulder and then smiled at me before heading back to his friends.

"Now," I said, turning back to the line of kids, "who can name all of Santa's reindeer? Do you want to guess their favorite reindeer games?"

8.2

The next twenty minutes passed in the blink of an eye. I didn't even notice it was almost over until I heard Pam's voice telling someone that she would show them where to change. I looked around but was too late to see who it was before they were lost in the afternoon crowd of market-goers.

Pam stopped by me on her way back to her booth, letting me know that my replacement was just changing and would take over shortly. Ten minutes later, I saw my best friend in striped tights, a green dress, and a small red apron with a pocket that she was dumping mini candy canes from a box into before tossing the empty box into a nearby recycling can. Her hair was in two braids tied at the ends with tinsel.

"Anna!" She looked up when I yelled out, confused at first until she spotted me and immediately started laughing. She skipped, actually skipped, over to me, and I tugged on one of her braids.

"Did we seriously have the exact same idea?"

"I guess so! Although, I got the idea originally from Adam."

"The same Adam that you're supposedly out meeting up with right now?" She gave me a pointed look, and I held both hands up in front of myself.

"Hey, he's here now, walking around somewhere with a friend and his wife and kid."

"He's married?"

"No, sorry, his friend's wife and their kid." Anna's outrage dissipated immediately. "We're going to go grab something to drink once I'm done here."

"So, you weren't just trying to throw me off this morning."

"You were being suspicious, and it made me suspicious! For some reason, I thought you might be up to something."

"I thought the same! We were both just being weird, clearly."

"Our silliness matches our outfits. But, come on, no hat?"

"I was working with what I had available!"

"You had striped tights at home?"

"Weirdly, yes. There's a hole on the butt, but no one needs to know that."

"It was nice to meet you, Haley." Anna and I both looked over at Leila's farewell as she, Chris, and Gracie separated from Adam and headed toward the exit. Adam stopped as he got to us but turned and waved back at Gracie, who was still waving at us from her place atop Chris's shoulders.

"Hey," Adam said to me as he turned back to us before shifting towards Anna. "Hey, Anna. Nice to see you again."

"How much did you hear?" she asked immediately.

"I have no idea what you could possibly mean. I am *hole-y* unaware of what you were saying as I walked up." He seemed to be trying very hard not to laugh.

"Give me just a few minutes. I've got a change of clothes in my bag in the office. I'll be ready to go after that."

"Before you change, do either of you have your phone on you?" Adam looked between us and continued when neither of us said anything. "Come on, you're not really going to change before you get some pictures of you both together as elves, are you?"

"Ah! I didn't even think of that," Anna said. "My phone is back in the office. Do you have yours?" Anna looked at me and let out a whoop when I pulled it from the pocket under my skirt. "That's my girl!"

Adam spent the next ten minutes taking pictures of us. Cute ones, silly ones, and action shots where we walked up to a few booths pretending to shop. There was a rare break in the line of kids coming to see Santa, so Bert even humored us and took a few with us as well.

After we'd taken dozens of photos, Anna grabbed my phone from Adam and took a few of us together. She wasn't too embarrassing about it. Adam had me take a photo of him on Bert's lap on his phone as well. Finally, I gave Anna some tips on how best to entertain the kids and mollify the parents before we hugged goodbye. I went back to the office to change, though my hat got left with Anna to complete her costume.

Adam was at a booth a few steps away, admiring the glass ornaments strung up and asking the vendor about them. As I was walking up, he checked his phone and laughed, stepping out of the way of a few other patrons and seemingly typing out a text to someone. I walked up as he was finishing, and he turned the phone to show me the screen.

"I sent my mom the photo of me and Santa. She wants to know whether I'll have enough coal to fuel the grill come summer." I laughed, reading her text on his phone. "I told her I had an elf connection to get me onto the nice list, though, so here's to hoping that I have to buy charcoal for the grill." Adam put his phone away and clapped his gloved hands together, making a soft smack. "Now," he said, "have you gotten a chance to walk around the market yet? We could get a coffee and check out the booths first if you'd like."

"Didn't you just go around to see everything?"

"Yeah, but I was mostly hoisting Gracie up to look at things and entertaining her while Chris and Leila got a chance to look around without worrying about her behaving."

"You're a good friend." Adam shrugged but otherwise didn't reply. "Well, I did come walk through last week, but I didn't have time to go check out the fancy ornaments tents. I'd love to go see what's new this year."

"Sounds good. Interested in a coffee, cocoa, or mulled wine to warm our fingers before heading that way?"

"Cocoa for me."

Adam and I chatted about our drink preferences and an array of other casual things. At one point in line for the ornament tent, we were in a fierce debate about the best toy from the nineties and ultimately talked each other out of our initial proposed winners and decided that it was just a golden age for weird toys.

We told each other about our families and how we usually celebrated Christmas. It turned out that Adam's mom grew up celebrating Christmas, and his dad grew up celebrating Hannukah, so now their family celebrated both. He clearly loved the holiday season and noted that he had the most fun on years when Hannukah and Christmas didn't overlap because it meant he got longer to celebrate with his family.

I told him about my parents' tradition of getting me and my brother special ornaments for our trees each year and confessed that I usually ended up buying myself at least three more on top of that.

I ended up buying only one small glass bauble that somehow had an even smaller glass snowflake suspended inside after we went through the ornament tents. The person working at the register wrapped the delicate glass orb and put it snugly inside a box that was small enough to slip into my backpack. Once we got outside, I moved things around so that the ornament was surrounded by the soft fabric of the elf costume and hopefully cushioned enough to prevent any damage.

We were getting to the end of the market when Adam mentioned that an ice rink was set up a few miles away at a big park. I was glad to have an excuse to continue our time together, and we hopped on a bus headed in the direction of the park. We still had to walk the remaining four blocks once we left the bus, but it was a nice day, and we weren't in a rush.

People of all ages were skating in large circles around the ice rink with twinkling lights strung above. Adam and I considered getting in line to skate, but as we watched, there was almost no movement, and we didn't want to wait endlessly. Someone nearby was dragging what looked to be a heavy-duty inflatable tube, similar to the kind you might drag behind a power boat on a lake, except that it had a mesh interior floor to sit on instead of being a true open-middle donut tube. Curious, we got out of line and followed the person carrying the tube.

If either of us had just skimmed over the signs not related to ice skating, we would have seen that there was a tube sledding hill on the other side of the rink. Even knowing it existed, we couldn't see a hill big enough to sled down. Still, we carried on and eventually realized that what we thought was just a large mound of snow half-hidden behind a bunch of trees was actually the top half of the sledding hill. It used the natural slope of the land next to the ice rink to its advantage, extending further down beyond the trees. You had to get all the way around it to really see what was going on.

"This looks fun! Are you up for it," I asked Adam as we watched people climb to the top and then cheer out and laugh all the way down.

"Definitely."

We walked to a small wooden booth that people were lined up in front of, presuming that they were lining up to enter. When we got to the front, Adam paid for us both before I even had a chance to offer to pay my share. We got our hands stamped with a smudged star and were directed to another line.

At the front of that line, we were let into the sledding area and told that we could go up and down as many times as we'd like and that we could exit and reenter as much as we'd like but that we wouldn't have priority over people who were already inside if they were at capacity. Though there were a few dozen people sliding and racing back up to the top via a set of stairs on either side of the hill, we were allowed to enter immediately after being given a quick set of rules and safety precautions.

About halfway up the stairs to the top, I looked out and realized that we were actually decently high up, certainly higher than I expected, though the grade of the hill was much gentler than it looked originally. Instead of a short but very steep hill, the structure was set up to be a longer ride to the bottom, with waves of short bursts of steep inclines that gave way to nearly flat areas to slow riders down. I almost tripped over one of the stairs as I looked out to the tubes sliding down the hill, but Adam was paying enough attention that he managed to wrap an arm around my waist and steady me.

"I think we're supposed to wait until we get to the top and get into the tubes before we start falling," he said, grinning at me. I almost made a joke about how I just couldn't help falling for him before I realized that this was essentially a first date, and despite my love of romance novels, I wasn't about to fall in love in a week. Although, between the daily texts and the time we'd spent together so far, I was fairly certain he'd just roll with it or start pretending to swoon. That just made me like him more.

"Then let's get up there!" At this point, we were actually only a few steps from the top, so we arrived quickly. We were each handed an inner tube to drag along with us to wherever we wanted to take off. The tubes were deceptively heavy, and I was glad that we weren't responsible for dragging them all the way up the hill; I probably would have just opted to be done after one trip down the hill if that were the case.

There were handholds at short intervals all the way around the tube, and Adam grabbed one of mine and helped me drag it along with his. A few kids around us were pushing their tubes across the top section of the hill instead of pulling them.

What seemed like a smart idea at first turned into one of the kids pushing a little too hard, losing a grip on his tube, and then watching as the tube went over the edge without him. Thankfully, the kid didn't get pulled along behind it and have to navigate his way to the side or bottom without getting hit by a different rider, but he did hang his head in defeat as he turned around to get another tube.

When we got past the halfway mark, there was more space to get set up and ready. The first half of the space on the platform was filled with people who stopped at the first open spot, jumped into their tube, and zipped down the hill.

If you wanted to get seated first, on the mesh lining inside the tube, you could do so further back and then get a push to start by employees scattered throughout the platform. We opted to do that, at least for our first run down, so that we could test things out. Adam held my tube as I hopped in before getting into his next to me. We looked around for someone to give us a push, to no avail. Instead, we started trying to wiggle ourselves closer to the edge of the platform, hoping that once we were over the edge slightly, gravity would do its job. We were getting pretty close when a few kids ran by and stopped long enough to shove our tubes forward.

The initial drop wasn't very steep, but the sudden dip and the quick uptick in speed made it seem more extreme. I looked over and saw Adam laughing; he turned his megawatt smile toward me as he let out a loud whoop. As we came to the first slight plateau, our tubes slowed down, but not enough to stop our forward motion.

Someone must have jumped into their tube with much more force behind us because a tube bounced roughly against my own, which then bounced against Adam's tube. It was jarring but in a fun way that was reminiscent of bumper cars. After a few more slopes and plateaus and running into a handful of other tubes, we both made it to the bottom of the hill. Off to the side, there was a pile-up of tubes and kids trying to get out before falling back over when another tube bounced into them.

"That was incredible!" Adam's joy was palpable and infectious; I couldn't seem to stop smiling. We walked to the bottom of the stairs, this time on the opposite side we'd entered, where a conveyor belt was set up, constantly moving and half-filled with tubes from people who had also just gotten to the bottom of the hill.

There were ledges running throughout to keep the tubes from just sliding back down on their way up the hill as they rode the conveyor belt up. We waited to push our tubes onto the conveyor belt at the bottom and then headed back up the stairs.

Two more rides down the hill later, we saw a few people zooming down the hill with two people riding together. "Want to try going on one tube," I asked Adam.

"I absolutely do."

This time, when we got back to the top of the hill, we got a single tube to share and pulled it back further from the ledge so that we could sort out how we were both going to fit. The people we saw doing it before must have been tiny because they were sitting side-by-side. There was no way Adam and I were going to fit that way.

"How about this," Adam said as he lowered himself onto the tube, "if I put my knees out towards the edges, you could sit in between them."

"With my back on the other side or..."

"I think with your back to my chest would be best." Music to my ears. I tossed my leg over one side of the tube and half-fell in the rest of the way, adjusting until I was leaning comfortably against Adam. He had his hands along the outside of the tube, gripping the handholds, so I reached out to do the same. I could only reach the ones he was already holding. Oh, darn. I looked up at him over my shoulder and felt my cheeks heat slightly. "You ready?"

"Ready or not, here you go," someone yelled as they pushed our tube forward and over the edge. I leaned forward slightly from the sudden shift, and one of Adam's arms came down around my waist to hold me in place. As we got to the first plateau, he shifted as if he was about to move his arm back, but I put my hand on his to keep it in place. We were each holding opposite handholds on the tube, and I leaned back a bit further. Adam dipped his head forward slightly, his cheek pressing against mine.

Secretly thinking that this would be a cute way to have a first kiss, I moved slightly to the side in order to turn my head enough to look up at him. Adam's face was a picture of happiness, and when he shifted his gaze to meet my eyes, his happiness was layered with something softer, something more intimate.

We just stared at each other for a few seconds before Adam shut his eyes, mine quickly following as he leaned towards me. I felt the tip of his nose brush my cheek, and I tilted my head slightly. There couldn't have been more than an inch between our lips, but neither of us was in a hurry. My eyes fluttered open for a moment, wondering whether I should close the distance between—*BAM*!

Our foreheads separated before knocking back into each other hard, jarring us both and ruining the moment. We bounced enough that Adam pressed me back into him, cheek-to-cheek again to prevent more damage. I groaned, using my free hand, the one not white-knuckling the tube's nearest handhold, to rub at my forehead.

"Get a room," a kid shouted from nearby as another few yelled cat-calls our way. Based on the trajectory of two of them, it looked like they might have been who slammed into us.

When we got to the bottom of the hill, Adam eased out of the tube and pushed it, with me still sitting in the middle, to the back of what we'd dubbed the "landing zone." Once there, he held his hand out to help me stand. "Are you okay?" He looked guilty, as if this was somehow his fault, despite riding together being my idea and me having turned to initiate the almost-kiss.

"Sore, but I'll be fine. My mother always told me I was hard-headed, so I think I'll keep this collision to myself to avoid giving her proof." One side of his mouth tilted up the tiniest bit, but he was still looking over my face for any signs of hurt. The area around his left eyebrow was already slightly swollen and had to hurt.

Despite the throbbing in my head, I didn't want this to be how our afternoon together ended. Instead, I looked around and saw a booth selling snacks and drinks behind a handful of picnic tables with heating lamps interspersed between them. "I think I know what will make me feel better," I said, trying to be coy but unsure if I was pulling it off.

"Oh?" Adam's eyes darted down to my lips before meeting my gaze again. As much as I wanted to continue where we got interrupted, I decided to bring some levity to the moment instead. Mostly because I could really use some ice and pain relievers.

"A pretzel," I said, evoking a laugh from Adam. "And some ice. I think we both might need some ice." Adam looked at my forehead again, and I was hoping that it wasn't already swollen or bruised. He touched the bump on his eyebrow, now a bit bigger than just a few moments ago, and winced slightly.

A few minutes later, we were at a picnic table with our haul in a coveted spot just under one of the heaters. We had decided to split a pretzel with warm cheese dipping sauce, and we each had our own little baggie of ice and a cup of hot cider. I pulled a few pain relievers from a pocket in my backpack for us both. "So," I said, breaking the silence, "do you participate in any other extreme sports?"

"I've played a few games of wiffle ball in my time."

"No Olympic dreams?"

"Unfortunately, with sports, they want you to follow sets of rules rather than just whacking the ball as hard as you can towards your brother's head."

"Oh, no!"

"In my defense, he had ruined a truly breathtaking block tower that I'd made earlier in the day."

"Ah, so just last week then?"

"More like thirty years ago. I've been blacklisted from all professional wiffle ball opportunities since."

"Their loss."

"More recently, Jason, a few friends, and I joined a hockey league so that we could get space on a rink to play once a week. It wasn't supposed to be too competitive, but there are games set up through the league season, and some of the other teams are pretty intense about it. I prefer the practice nights where it's just me and my friends playing casually."

"Is it at an indoor rink, or is there an outdoor rink somewhere nearby?"

"Indoor. There actually are a few outdoor rinks, and people play out on the lake, but when we were kids, Jason had a close call and almost fell through the ice. We were out on a lake in our neighborhood. I was eleven years old at the time, and Jason slammed his stick down on the ice after missing a shot on our makeshift goal zone. It was more of an 'aw shucks' smack than having any actual anger or strength behind it, and I'm still surprised that it created the small crack that formed.

Once it did, though, the break started spreading, and Jason skated as fast as he could back to the shore, yelling the whole time for me to get back as well. I was a lot closer, so I was back on land, just watching the fear on my brother's face. The crack spread out pretty wide, breaking even further and creating a large hole with chunks of nearby ice breaking off where he had been skating when it started. The cracks spidered out and broke off even more in the opposite direction, closer to the deeper water."

"Did Jason fall through?" I couldn't help the tinge of panic in my voice, especially given the stricken look on Adam's face as he relived the memory.

"No, he was fine. He's always been a fast skater, thankfully, but watching my brother try to outrun ice cracking behind him, even if it stopped well before it ever reached the shore and he was probably quickly out of any real danger of falling through, was terrifying. I just had to watch as ice cracked behind him as he screamed at me to stay back. We never ended up going to get the buckets that we had put out to serve as our goalposts. Neither of us was willing to step back on the ice, and we didn't want our parents going out either, so we lied and said they broke, so we threw them out. The buckets might still be in the lake, for all we know.

"The idea of skating on ice on a deep lake still makes me so anxious that it isn't worth it. Jason has done it since, though not often, and he always seems on edge when he does. The rest of our friends are just happy to play on a well-maintained rink." Adam looked down at the table and took a few deep breaths before cutting off another piece of our shared pretzel.

"Did you stop playing hockey for a while?" I asked hesitantly, not sure if I should have changed the subject instead.

"No. Or at least, not long enough to be meaningful. We didn't play for a few weeks until we found somewhere else to skate. There was a rink near our school that was close enough to walk to after school if we were together and close enough that our parents were happy to take us there in our free time. It was a flooded field, so even if all the ice melted, we would only be in a few inches of water.

The parking lot was close enough that our mom could keep an eye on us from the car, so she used to stay in the heat of the car, chatting on the phone with her friends while we skated. On rare occasions, the rink would be empty, and we could play one-on-one games, but mostly, we just raced around the rink, weaving in between all the other kids that were there." Adam's expression had shifted to one of fondness and nostalgia rather than the palpable fear of a few minutes ago. "What about you? Do you play any sports?"

"I tried out a ton growing up, but now not so much. I like being active, but I don't enjoy any specific sport enough to want to do it regularly.

Like, I love swimming, but I mainly want to just swim around for a bit, float in the water, and then lounge in the sun when I want to get out."

"I get that. As much as I enjoy hockey, it's really just an excuse to get together with my friends and do something we all enjoy. It's more a social thing than it is about the hockey."

"I know what you mean. I spent a night recently baking with a new friend and a neighbor of mine and ended up feeling the same way. Sure, there were cookies at the end, and I'm a fan of cookies, but it felt very much like something that was just keeping our hands busy while we got to know each other better and spent the night chatting."

I told Adam about my night with Raquel and Gloria. He was a great listener, engaged and asking questions, but not so many that I couldn't get the story out. He laughed along as I told him about Gloria having a panic room that she'd made into a mini movie room and the eccentricities of my neighbor before asking about how I knew Raquel and whether she had any hidden rooms as well. I didn't know enough to confirm since I hadn't been to her place, but I told him about the Knittie Bitties and that I needed to come up with a craft to learn before I saw Bernie next. He suggested basket weaving and jokingly asked to commission a picnic basket once I'd gotten good at it.

An hour later, long after we had devoured our pretzel while slowly sipping our ciders to make them last, Adam's phone started buzzing. He took it out of his pocket, checked his screen, and dismissed whatever came through. It buzzed again once, then twice more, shorter bursts this time.

"Sorry, I just dismissed a call from my mom, and it sounds like she might have sent a few texts. I just want to make sure nothing's wrong."

"No problem." I took the last sip of my cider while I watched Adam read something on his phone and then smiled softly as he typed out a reply.

"I'm having dinner at my parents' house tonight," he said as he put his phone back in his pocket, "and my mom wants me to pick up a few things on the way. My aunt and cousin are getting into town in time for dinner and staying the next few days too, so she keeps remembering more things she wants to have on hand, thus the multiple messages."

"I was going to ask if you wanted to brave another ride down the hill, but do you have enough time?"

"For another separate ride, I do. As much as I want an excuse to wrap my arms around you again, I just don't have time for another go down the hill and an emergency room visit when we both end up with concussions."

"Oh, I was definitely ditching you at the top for my own tube."

We disposed of our trash before heading back to the slide area. I popped my mitten off to show the stamp I got earlier, and Adam did the same with his glove. My legs started to protest a bit as we walked up the stairs again after having cooled back down at the picnic table, but I got to the top and started dragging a tube over towards where we'd been taking off down the hill earlier.

"Should we do a running start and jump in at the last minute," Adam asked while watching a few people do just that.

"I think I'm going to stick with what I know."

"I'll give you a push once you're settled, and then I think I'm going to try it." I got seated in my tube and let Adam know that I was ready. He pulled back the tube a bit before taking a few running steps forward before letting me go. I took off faster than I had before when other people were just giving us an easy shove forward, but it was exhilarating. I looked back as soon as I was at the first plateau and saw Adam's tube racing down towards me. His legs were out for a bit before he wiggled around to try and get fully inside the tube.

"What's the verdict," I asked as we met at the bottom.

"Fun, much faster, but I almost overshot it and landed outside of the tube. I managed to stay in it, but barely."

"The extra speed from your running push for me was fun too. Good to know for our future inner tube sledding adventures." I was hoping there would be more, and Adam's smile gave me hope he wanted that, too.

We returned our tubes to the conveyor belt and turned towards the exit instead of going back up the stairs. Adam offered to get us a ride-share with two stops, but I waved off the offer since we were so close to one of the train stations that ran toward my apartment. Plus, he was headed to Jason's townhouse so that they could drive out to their parents' house together after he picked up what his mom needed, and it was in the opposite direction of my apartment. Adam walked me to the train station, where we said goodbye and exchanged a hug. His hand shifted from my back, grazed down my arm, and he squeezed my hand before stepping away.

I got to the train platform and shut my eyes while I waited. "Oh, I know that look. What's their name?" A woman that looked about five years younger than me was turned toward me, smirking and looking like she'd just learned a secret. I couldn't help grinning back at her, though it was really just a stretch of the smile that already covered my face.

"Adam," I said quietly, the name mostly lost in the noise of the train's arrival. I repeated it as the doors opened, even quieter this time, but she nodded.

"Get it, girl," she laughed, heading off to find a seat. I trailed behind before finding my own seat. I watched as the city flew by, stop after stop, and smiled the whole ride home.

DAY 9: WIN A SNOWBALL FIGHT

I slept in on Sunday. It was nearly ten o'clock in the morning before I woke, and then I stayed in bed playing on my phone for another hour. By the time I finally rolled out of bed and wandered into our living room, Anna was prepping ingredients to make lunch, some kind of soup by the look of things.

"Well, hello, sleepy head," Anna greeted me, looking up long enough to smile before going back to cutting onions. "If you want soup, it'll be ready in about an hour, but there are also pastries if you want one in the meantime." Anna, goddess that she is, put a box of pastries on the bar counter. In response to my clear indecision, stuck between grabbing the apple turnover or a chocolate croissant, Anna put a knife down next to the box. There were definite perks to living with a friend who'd known you for a decade. I cut both pastries in half and alternated as I ate them both.

"Thanks," I said after a few bites. "How was the rest of your night?" Anna had gone out as soon as she was done at the market, not bothering to stop home and change but rather embracing her elf outfit. I'd heard her come in late but was watching a movie in bed and fell asleep soon after.

"Fun! We went to a holiday pop-up bar. I was, of course, an absolute hit. Too bad there wasn't a costume contest. Julie and I ended up bailing kind of early and went to get pizza, where we stayed for a few hours chatting and drinking, long enough that we ended up ordering another round of food as a late-night snack. Thankfully, the place was pretty empty, so we didn't feel too bad about taking up a table for that long, and the waitress actually came and hung out for a bit."

Julie was a friend of Anna's from college that I'd never really gotten to know well; she was pretty reserved and just had an easier time one-on-one with Anna than she did the few times we all three tried to do something together. They didn't see each other often, but when they did, it always ended up with them talking for several hours. It was a bit hard for me to reconcile knowing that Julie was so chatty with Anna when she was so quiet when I was around (although Anna did say that she was like that with most people), but I had long since come to terms with me and Julie being unlikely to end up as more than acquaintances connected through Anna.

A result of Anna and I having been as close as we were for as long as we'd been friends meant that we often ended up integrating friends we made separately into one collective friend group. Julie always served as a good reminder to me that it was healthy to have separate friendships as well. I made a mental note that, as much as I thought Anna and Raquel would get along, I should make sure I wasn't just inviting Raquel to group things and instead made time for us to get to know each other one-on-one as well.

Anna told me about the things Bert was grumbling under his breath by the time the last hour of Santa and Elf duty rolled around, and I told Anna about my date with Adam. She gasped at the start of my retelling of our almost-kiss before shaking with laughter at it never actually happening and the resulting lump on my forehead. "Glad my embarrassment is entertaining to you," I said, though, admittedly, it would be pretty funny if it hadn't happened to me.

"You have to admit, whether you two end up dating or not, we're going to look back on this and laugh."

"True, and even though it was a disaster in that moment, it didn't ruin the day."

"Do you have plans this afternoon," Anna asked me after we'd both provided a play-by-play of our nights (hers considerably more interesting than my night making breakfast for dinner and watching several movies) and some random gossip from Anna's office while we took out bowls and each ladled ourselves a bowl of soup.

"I need to get over to the costume shop before they close to return the elf costume," I started, stopping when Anna hopped up from her chair, went to her purse, and pulled out the hat she borrowed after I left the market, "oh, I almost forgot about the hat, thanks. After that, I'm not sure. I guess doing whatever today's dare is." I shrugged but looked over my shoulder to try and see what was on the list for the day.

"You don't even know what today's dare is?"

"Honestly, no. The craziness of the last few days of dares was enough to think about. I checked earlier in the week, and I don't remember thinking it needed much preparation, but that's about it."

"Ah, true. The last few days have been a little bit nuts—not to mention we were both being awkward about yesterday's challenge, which was so dumb. This is something we're supposed to be having fun doing with one another, so I think we should go out together today, return your costume, and then find a park and get whoever is there to be part of an epic snowball fight! We can both be team captains."

"Oh, right, one of the dares that switched days."

"Mhmm, and after we're done, I'm going to try to pick up a few things for my mom that I've been waiting for sales on. No sales yet, but I refuse to still be getting gifts on Christmas Eve, so it's time. Do you have anyone left on your list?"

"I didn't, but now that I'm going to your family's Christmas, I want to pick something up for your mom and grandpa. Maybe a few other little things for anyone else there." Anna's family Christmas was always a revolving door of guests. She and her mom and her grandpa all stayed put throughout the day and evening, and everyone else came and went as they could, coordinating around trying to see other family and friends.

"Perfect, we can pop into shops together until we're sick of it."

"Works for me," I replied, though my focus was on the chart. Today and the next two days of challenges we should be able to do together, but the last day was the day we'd set for getting multiple points to try and tip the scales. "Are we doing dare twelve together? The one where we're collecting all the various items of the twelve days of Christmas song?"

"I don't think we can. We'd just end up getting the same things, and it would be a draw. Maybe we should pick an end time when we meet up back here. Also, I don't think we should be able to get anything in advance. So, no starting today and picking up anything if it appeals. No doing research or brainstorming even. Even if we see something perfect, it will be a race to get it, assuming no one else does in the meantime."

"Okay, we can figure out timing later, making it work so that we'll have the whole day, but we also won't both be finishing at midnight." I considered the challenge for a few seconds before adding, "Also, do we want to check in once we finish one of the items so that we can't both use the same thing to win?"

"I like that in theory, but that also means we couldn't change our minds if we found something better, and we might end up giving each other ideas for items on things we're stumped on. The likelihood of us getting the same things probably isn't that high."

"Good point. I think we're set on the last day's rules, then. We can always add more if we think of any." Anna walked to the junk drawer in our kitchen and grabbed a pen before adding the rules to the chart while I cleaned up our dishes and put the rest of the soup in containers in the fridge. Once done, Anna lounged on the couch while I got ready to head out for the day. I showered last night, so I just got dressed and put the elf costume, including the hat, back into the garment bag it left the shop in.

An hour later, the costume was returned, and my arms were glad to be freed up. Thankfully, I checked the store hours because we were originally going to make a few stops along the way, but we managed to get to the store just before they closed. If that had happened, I would have had to carry it around all day, and I'd be charged for another day on the rental. No, thank you. Since one of the shops Anna wanted to stop at was near a big park where people enjoyed the space almost year-round, we hopped on a bus and headed back that way.

"So, where to first," Anna asked as we stepped off the bus. We could either walk a few blocks to the park nearby or start popping into shops lining the street.

"Park," I said, heading that way, "I don't want to end up having to juggle bags during an epic snowball fight victory."

"In your dreams," Anna replied, scoffing. "Fair point about the bags, though."

"Plus, this way, the losing team captain can buy the winning team captain a hot cider to warm up before we start looking for gifts." I loved holiday drink season. I didn't normally drink much more than water and ginger ale, but during winter, all bets were off. What was I supposed to do, *not* consume enough hot chocolate and cider to concern my doctor? Come on now.

"Ooh, I do love coffee that I don't have to pay for. Let's do it!"

When we arrived at the park, there were fewer people than we expected. Normally, there were all kinds of people playing with their dogs, building snowmen, or walking on the trail of packed snow that circled the park. There was a group of people around our age playing catch in one section and a few kids running around like they were powered by sugar cubes on the far side of the park. Their parents were standing together, talking while the kids exhausted themselves.

As much of a sure bet that the kids were for joining a snowball fight, I didn't know if I really wanted to be two adults having a snowball battle with a bunch of pre-teens. There were a handful of smaller groups of people milling around, seemingly at the park just for a change of scenery from the chaos of the city center, that might be willing to join. Benches throughout the park were also occupied, and a handful of decorated pine trees throughout the park were being admired.

"So, uh, how do we do this?" I looked over at Anna, unsure of our next step. Would it be weird to go up to another grown adult and ask if they want to throw fluffy, frozen water at their friends? If someone approached me with that question, I would probably be caught off-guard. I mean, I'd say yes, but still.

"Maybe we start with that group," Anna said, pointing to the now-smaller group of three playing catch. "They're already throwing a ball around, so we can always lie and say we got inspired to have a snowball fight when we saw them."

"And if they offer to just let us join and play catch for a bit instead?"

"We tell them we're trying to connect to our inner child? Or that we're trying to make snowball fights a recognized Olympic sport, and we need to practice to make the future team?"

"How do you come up with these things so easily?"

"It's a gift."

Fortunately, when we approached the people tossing around a softball, most of them thought a snowball fight sounded fun. Unfortunately, one of them was weirdly concerned about having even team sizes when so few people were playing, so we needed to find more participants.

Doubly unfortunate, they weren't planning on sticking around for long, so we needed to find more players quickly. We approached a group of twenty-something women, all holding coffee cups and having a mini photoshoot. Neither of us was shocked when they passed, but two people walking nearby overheard us mentioning it and asked if they could join—score!

We were still uneven, though, and who knows what Stickler Steve considered a big enough group to make uneven teams not matter (I didn't actually know his name, but in my head, he'd become Stickler Steve who loved rules). We walked past an elderly couple sitting on a bench, and the woman asked what we were chatting with people about. They must have watched us approach the first two groups.

"We're trying to organize a snowball fight," Anna told the couple.

"That does sound fun!" The man jumped to his feet, much more spry than I expected. "Honey, let's show these young kids how it's done."

"You go on, dear," the woman said, "I'll be a cheerleader."

"Oh, like it's 1973 all over again. If only it was warm enough for the old skirt." The man winked at his wife, whose cheeks rapidly grew pink in response before he crooked each arm and held each elbow out towards me and Anna. We hooked our arms through his, and he walked us over to the section of the park that we'd directed the other two groups to. On the way over, he told us his name, George, and asked us to make him look good in front of Lottie, his wife.

"Hi, everyone. I'm Haley, and this is Anna," I said, pointing to Anna, who waved to the group. "How about we each captain a team and will pick teams? That way, there's a mix of who's together?" Most of the group shrugged or murmured their agreement, but not George.

"Actually, I think we're missing something," George interjected, putting his hand on my arm. Then, without any notice, George surprised us all by shouting to the whole park, "Hey! We're having a snowball fight! Everyone that wants to join is welcome, so come over here, and we'll pick teams!"

George's voice carried, and the kids on the far side of the park all stopped running around, looked between themselves, and then raced over to us. Their parents yelled to them, but it was no use, so they all reluctantly started walking toward us as well. They stopped before they got close enough to actually join our group and instead seemed content to be close enough to make sure their kids weren't going to run out of the park without them or cause any trouble.

"Welcome, welcome," George said, clapping his hands together. He was obviously already having fun, and his enthusiasm was easy to mirror. Even Stickler Steve was grinning and just gave the kids a brief glance rather than re-running the numbers.

"Okay," I started again, "so Anna and I will pick teams—"

"No way," came from one kid as another complained, "I want to pick!"

"No, I want to be the captain," someone else said, stomping their feet.

"Well, see, we wanted to be on oppos—" My words barely broke through the noise of the bickering kids. The other adults in the group looked to be less interested in sticking around for a snowball fight now, too.

"I think we best let the children pick," George whispered over to me. He turned back to the group, pulled his hand out of his glove, put two fingers in his mouth, and whistled loudly. The kids all stopped arguing and looked at him. "Two of you can be captains. Circle up. There are four of you, so break into groups of two and do rock, paper, scissors." Once each group had a winner, the two new captains assessed those of us standing around.

"You," one said, pointing at Stickler Steve.

"You," the other said, pointing at George. This went on until we were all sorted. Neither Anna nor I got picked last, which meant these kids couldn't tell how abysmal I was during the one year I joined a softball league. Anna and I ended up on the same team.

"I guess we win together or we lose together, huh," she said to me, bumping her shoulder against mine.

"Let's win this thing," I replied. She turned back to the center and addressed the group. "Okay, we'll play the first game dodgeball style. Once you're hit, go off to the side. Last team standing wins."

"What if, instead of going to the side, we have to sit or stand in place where we got hit. That way, we become obstacles for the rest of the game." The suggestion came from one of the girls who asked Anna and me if they could join after we struck out with the selfie crowd.

"That sounds cool. We're doing that," one of the captains decided. Was I that decisive at eleven years old? I certainly wasn't now. "My team, let's go over there and talk strategy!"

We trailed along behind our captain about fifty feet away from the group that stayed put. The "strategy" essentially boiled down to not getting hit and instead getting as many people from the other team out as possible. Truly groundbreaking stuff.

"Ready?" George yelled from the other team's group. The rest of his team was kneeling down and making the start of a teeny tiny wall of snow. None of them would fit behind it when it was that short, but it was funny to watch them all try and race to build a protected area.

"Ready!" We all called back as we scattered and started making small balls of snow to launch as soon as we started.

"Okay!" George shouted though I couldn't see him anymore. "On your marks!" Where was he hiding... "Get set!" Aha! I followed his voice to a tree that hid most of his body, but I could see his face peeking out to get a good look at the playing field. "GO!"

For a few minutes, people were running back and forth, and snowballs were flying everywhere. A member of my team got hit pretty quickly while out in the open space of the park. I was making and tossing snowballs as quickly as I could, never hitting anything but also managing to roll out of the way of the few that were directed at me.

One of the tweens on my team, a girl with braided pigtails and a fierce expression worthy of a warrior despite the ridiculously low stakes, army crawled over to hide behind a collection of snowmen near where I was trying to hide behind a half-destroyed snow fort.

"Hey, you," she whisper-shouted at me, "your aim sucks." Ouch. "See that guy over there who was too big to avoid being hit?" She jerked her head over at the guy who got hit early on, standing about fifteen feet in front of us. "We need a bigger area of protection. Are you ready to sacrifice for your team?"

"Huh?"

"Adults," she said, rolling her eyes at me before continuing, "you need to get up next to him and then stay there. Throw as much as you can while there, but with you two next to each other, you'll be enough of a wall that I can get behind you. I'll be blocked from hits but will be able to stand up and be closer to the other team. I should be able to take them out one by one." Couldn't say that I expected to be made into sacrificial bait today, but I wasn't actually hitting anything when I tried.

"Umm, okay, I guess."

"Good. I'll cover you. Just be ready to run when I tell you to."

Apparently, no one expected me to just get up and run into the open, especially not without holding or throwing any snowballs, because I made it to the guy's side easily. I even had time to bend down and make a few snowballs before standing up with them in my arms.

I didn't get a chance to throw them, though, because, as soon as I stood, I felt a snowball smack into my thigh. It smarted a bit, and when I looked down it seemed to have been slushy snow that somehow got packed tightly enough to throw considering how wet my pant leg was from that one hit. Instead of just dropping the snowballs I was holding, I bent down and put them on the ground gently, trying to keep them from falling apart. Maybe the kid that sent me out here would be able to use them when she used us as a protective wall.

"Hey," the guy beside me said, grinning as he looked around the park, watching the battle rage on. "I'm Mark. First out."

"Haley. The sacrifice." He chuckled, and we went on to swap commentary of people we spotted hiding and on throws, hits, and misses as the battle was waged. The girl that sent me out here ran toward us before ducking and sliding to her hands and knees behind us. She underestimated how fast she was going, though, and Mark and I almost toppled over when she connected with our legs.

"Thanks for the ammo, lady," she said while collecting the snowballs I had set down that were still intact. Mark snorted out a laugh, and we watched as the last few people standing managed to evade snowballs tossed their way. Eventually, we were down only to the girl using me and Mark as a shield on our team, but the other team had at least two people still in the game.

Make that three people. A snowball came hurling towards us, low and from the opposite side of the game field as the rest of the snowballs. It hit her boots that were sticking out from the protective barrier we provided. "NO," she cried out.

One of the people from the other team had apparently gone under the radar long enough that they managed to get to the edge of what we'd marked as the informal line between our team areas, mostly hidden behind a bench. A snowball hadn't come from that area in a long while, and, coupled with the constant snow-fire from the two others on the opposite side of the field, we didn't even know that that person was still in play, lying in wait.

"She's out, she's out," the sneaky third player yelled as he jumped out of hiding, bouncing up and down. "We won!" Their whole team started cheering.

Out of nowhere, a snowball came flying toward the kid who sent the winning throw, connecting with a wet *smack* to his shoulder. He stopped celebrating, looked at the snow now on his shoulder, and looked back up to see George throw another snowball, this time at me.

I dodged out of the way and then dipped down to grab two handfuls of snow, tighten them in my fists, and squish them onto each the head of the kid behind me and Mark's neck where his jacket collar ended. Mark gasped from the cold snow hitting his skin as the girl behind me shouted an affronted, "Hey!"

George grinned and then sprinted toward a tree for cover as he yelled out, "Free for all!" Immediately, everyone began making snowballs and tossing them at whoever was closest to them while running for cover. I ran toward Anna, who was crouched down near a bench, fully intending to drop a snowball on her head, but she turned around and threw an armload of snow, not packed into a ball, just loose snow, up into my face.

I stumbled before coming to a halt as I wiped the snow off my face and tried to get it out of my jacket. Anna made her escape in that time, and I got hit with another snowball, this time from the back. I gave up on getting the snow out of my shirt and whirled around to chase the person that hit me. I found brief cover and made a pile of snowballs that I tossed at everyone who came near before getting up and running for a new spot.

After about fifteen minutes, all of the adults were drooping, clearly exhausted from sprinting continuously and we ended up in a group off to the side. The tweens were still going. We all watched as one of them jumped to avoid a hit and instead ended up tumbling into a snowman. The impact was enough to dislodge the snowman's head. It fell onto the kid as he lay on the ground, catching his breath.

One of his friends stopped long enough to ask if he was okay, which got a thumbs up from the kid, who laughed despite being partially buried in snow. At this point, I was completely soaked through from a mix of snow and sweat. Anna looked to be in the same boat. She took off her hat and shook snow out of it, her hair wet and stuck to her forehead.

"I've got to head out, but that was actually really fun," Stickler Steve said to the group as he put the phone he'd just glanced at back in his coat before zipping the pocket it was in. George raised his eyebrows and shot me a look that said '*well, duh, it was fun,*' before shaking Stickler Steve and his friends waved goodbye.

The other women who joined said a quick goodbye before they walked over to a nearby bench to sit down. Anna and I walked with George back to Lottie. She clapped as we arrived, laughing as George swept her up off the bench and gave her a kiss.

"The only thing sweeter than victory is you, my love." They continued gazing into each other's eyes, Lottie giggling as George pulled one of her hands to the side, and he swayed them back and forth to dance in place.

"I want to be like them when I grow up," Anna said quietly enough that only I could hear her.

"Thanks for letting me join your game, ladies," George said to us, now cheek-to-cheek with Lottie as they both looked at us smiling. "I had a wonderful time, but these old bones need to take my lovely wife home to warm up."

"You're the best, George," I told him, and we waved as he spun Lottie before they started walking out of the park, hand in hand. We watched them until they were all the way out of the park before heading out ourselves. We exited the same way so we could have walked with them, but it was heartwarming watching them go together, swinging their twined hands, laughing, and smiling at each other.

"So," Anna said, bringing my attention to her, "I guess we both lost this one."

"Does this mean we have to buy each other a hot drink?"

"Yes, please. That sounds so good right now."

9.2

Anna and I walked out of the park and made our way back to the nearby street where we'd gotten off the bus. Thankfully, it was a busy enough street of shops that there were a few different cafes, and one we knew and liked was nearby with tables available inside. I bought Anna a latte, and she bought me a hot apple cider with caramel. Mine ended up being ready first, and I took my mittens off to absorb some of the warmth from the cup into my chilled fingers.

Spotting an open table by the window, I nudged Anna and nodded towards it. Her name was called just as I turned away, so I waited, looking over my shoulder, until she took her cup off the counter and followed me to the table. I sat, wincing as I felt my butt and legs press the cold, wet fabric of my jeans between me and the chair.

Steam rose from the small hole in the lid of my cider, and I started at it, trying to focus on anything but how wet my butt was. Trying to shift focus, I took off my jacket to let it hang from the chair and dry out a bit. Promises from the original tags of it being water-resistant were obviously greatly exaggerated.

Anna unzipped her coat without first taking off her scarf, and she grimaced as half-melted slush fell from a fold in her scarf onto her shirt and then to the floor. She shut her eyes and sighed before pulling her coat, only halfway off her arms, back on fully before sitting down.

"Nope!" Anna must have only brushed the seat before she hopped back up to standing. "All of my clothes are soaking wet. I thought sitting down for a bit would dry us out, but I can't do it. Are your pants dry?"

"Not even close."

"Aren't you uncomfortable sitting on them?"

"Yes, but I was hoping I'd get used to it quickly. Or dry out quickly."

"I think I just need to stand." Anna sighed before looking out the window. "Actually, how would you feel about stopping just at the little paper goods and gifts store down the street and then heading home? We're right here, so I'd like to go, but getting into warm clothes and taking a bath sounds so good right now."

"Don't have to ask me twice." I cringed as I got up, knowing that I had to put my jacket back on, now cold and heavy with the water it absorbed, but no longer sitting in a puddle of my own making was too appealing.

Once we were bundled back up, we took our drinks and headed out of the café. The shop that Anna wanted to go to was only about a block down the street, thankfully, and while I was glad to not be sitting in wet clothes, walking in wet clothes out in the cold was its own special form of misery.

My jeans got colder the longer we were outside, and the wet hair against my neck was freezing into stiff clumps. My awareness of how my clothes, hair, and the air felt against my skin was making me feel itchy and overstimulated by the time we got to the shop, so I took off my hat and scarf, tied up my hair, and took off my jacket once inside for good measure. The relief was immediate and, though I still didn't love the soggy texture of my pants, I was no longer zeroed in on and consumed by how they felt.

Anna had already moved to a corner of the shop and was quietly laughing at a line of mugs adorned with snarky phrases. The store was marketed as a paper goods store, but there were small gift items throughout, many of which were sourced from local artists.

My eye caught on a beautiful display of ceramics. The rim of a serving bowl was cut in five places, pulled tighter to overlap the pieces where they'd been cut. The slight layering and indents where the cut pieces were joined gave the impression of flower petals, reminding me of Anna's mom.

She loved growing her own food for as long as I'd known her, and she was well known throughout her neighborhood for the bountiful harvests her garden produced which she shared with the local food bank and shelters in the area. In the summer, she regularly brought or sent Anna back to our apartment with, heirloom tomato tarts, inventive pesto varieties using unique ingredients, and baskets filled with vegetables that somehow tasted better than anything we were able to get from any grocery store. Typically, these edible care packages were supplemented by a handful of wildflowers or other blooms that grew along the edges of her garden.

Mrs. Koyama would joke that she just tossed seeds around the perimeter and let nature take care of the rest, but you were guaranteed to find several books on flowers, and gardening tips peppered throughout the neat stacks of books in each room of her home. Her deliveries were always a treat, and Anna and I always ended up oohing and awing at the beautiful dishes she gave us.

If you watched her, though, if you really paid attention, you'd see that, though she certainly was happy when we complimented the edible items she brought, her eyes lit up in a way that showed how proud she was when you complimented the flowers that accompanied them.

Once, I must have commented more than usual about how stunning the color of a stem of snapdragons was, a deep red that seemed almost purple in the innermost part of the mouth of the flowers, and she told me bashfully that she'd looked into how to create hybrid color blooms a few years prior and that this was her first successful attempt. Her cheeks were rosy as she told me the secret that she'd even given them a name.

She whispered the name then, a few words in her native Japanese that I couldn't translate, but I felt her pride and reverence in the way that she said it. She squeezed my shoulder and walked back to Anna, who had been cutting up a quiche her mom had brought, but many of the mini bouquets that we'd received since included snapdragons, sometimes with colors that I'd never seen before.

I picked the bowl up from the display, knowing that it was the perfect gift. It could hold her garden harvests, sure, but the subtle ode to flowers would be an ever-present reminder and moment of appreciation for the flora that surrounded the garden and brought even more life and beauty throughout the space.

I clutched the bowl to my chest as I walked throughout the rest of the store, picked up some socks covered in cats for Anna's grandpa (the man was obsessed with his cat), and a few extra little items, some silly and some universal and functional, just in case I'd forgotten anyone on my list or in case someone got me something unexpectedly.

I liked having a small cache of gifts for holidays that kept me, and sometimes my friends and family, out of sticky situations. The number of times I'd helped someone come through for Secret Santa or a White Elephant exchange was larger than you'd expect.

As I waited in line to purchase the items, a display of candy with a treat that was meant to look like coal and held in a small sack reminiscent of Santa's bag of presents from the holiday market yesterday made me think of Adam. Normally, I would have taken a photo, sent it with a silly caption, and left it at that, but as I heard a voice call "next" and beckon me up to one of the open registers, I brought the candy with me. Maybe I'd find time to give it to him, or maybe I'd just send a photo and keep it for myself. Time would tell.

After paying for my items, I looked around for Anna, finding her at the end of the line to check out herself. She held a beautiful scarf, wrapping the fingers of one hand around it before sliding the fabric through her fingers. "Is that for your mom," I asked her.

"Well," she said, taking some of the scarf in each hand and holding up what turned out to be two matching scarves, "one of them is. The other is for me. Mom's always commenting on how her new neighbor and the neighbor's daughter wear lots of matching dresses, so obviously we need a mother-daughter day with matching outfits."

"Cute. They're gorgeous, and they look so soft."

"Feel them!" I took one of the scarves from Anna and understood why she was nearly petting them when I found her—it was so silky smooth that it nearly fell from my grasp before I got a better grip. "Really, I found one and was trying to decide whether to keep it or gift it when a woman came by to add a few more to the display and then there were two. This way, I get to give my mom a nice gift, and I get to give myself a little treat. It's a win-win."

I trailed behind Anna, back to the register I left a few minutes ago, where the store clerk joked that I couldn't stay away. Once Anna paid and her scarves were wrapped up, we checked the bus schedule and debated whether it would be worth getting a ride share back to our apartment.

The bus was only a few minutes away, too close to justify the extra expense, so we waited, dancing in place to stay warm until the bus arrived. Thankfully, though we were both still damp from the snowball battle earlier, we weren't soggy messes anymore. Still, neither of us wanted to sit, so we stood for the duration of the trip before getting to our stop and speed-walking home, energized by the promise of warm, dry clothes.

"Would you care if I took over the bathroom for an hour or so to take a bath? I want to soak in bubbles and warmth." Anna had her eyes closed, smiling as she took off her hat, gloves, scarf, coat, and boots. She started walking back to her bedroom without waiting for an answer. and I glanced up to see her pulling her sweater off before she even made it past her door. I snorted out a laugh before calling back a reply.

"If you can wait long enough for me to shower first, then go for it."

"Sounds good. Yell to me when you're out of the bathroom. I'm just going to lay here until then."

Putting my bag of gifts down, I got my coat and winter accessories off and then headed to the bathroom to start the water. I didn't normally take scalding hot showers, but I felt frozen from the inside out, and it was going to take some serious heat to rewarm me.

Grabbing a fresh towel from my room, I headed back into the bathroom, where I put the towel currently hung up on a rack by the shower door onto the floor. I stripped out of my clothes and piled them on the floor towel.

By the time I stepped under the showerhead, the water was heated just above what was probably considered safe for my skin, but it felt like a dream. I lathered my hair with first shampoo and then conditioner, trying to detangle the array of knots. Once my fingers were running through my hair without pulling, I washed the sweat and snow from my body and cleaned my face of running mascara.

I spent some time thawing under the heated spray before stepping out, wrapping myself in a fresh towel, and heading back to my bedroom, bringing my heap of dirty clothes with me. Yelling to Anna to let her know I was done, I flopped down onto my bed face-first. I moved my towel up to my hair and then turned over and shut my eyes.

Something about showers always made me tired, and I genuinely did not understand people who could towel-dry and then immediately put on clothes. I was never fully dry from the towel, and then my clothes stuck to me. I'd tried finding a robe that felt good after showering, but they always felt like they were sticking to my skin, too. Air drying while I took a mini nap sounded perfect.

9.3

I registered voices in the bathroom as the buzzing of my phone on my nightstand brought me back to consciousness. My eyes slowly blinked open, and I realized that Anna must have set up her laptop so that she could watch a movie while she soaked. A quick look at the clock on my phone showed that I'd only been asleep for about twenty minutes. I was glad for the unintended wake-up call because I often ended up napping so long that I couldn't fall asleep that night. While I didn't feel completely awake and refreshed, I did feel better than when we got home. I used to roll my eyes as a kid when my parents said that Jake and I were probably tired because we had gotten so much fresh air on days when we came back from running around out in the neighborhood, but it seemed to be true today.

Moving to the couch, I turned on the television but couldn't decide on something to watch, and I was similarly indecisive when I looked at my bookshelf to try to pick something to read. Instead, I scrolled through news articles on my phone before getting sucked into online quizzes.

After repeated failed attempts to have an online quiz guess my zodiac sign, I dropped my phone on the coffee table and stared at the ceiling. At some point, the noise from the bathroom had stopped, and I had faint recollections of hearing the bathroom door opening and Anna's bedroom door closing. She must have gone back to her room to veg out, maybe take a nap.

Unlike me, Anna was a champion napper. The woman could take a four-hour nap (what I called a "half-sleep"), wake up long enough to have a snack, and then go back to bed for the night and sleep until the morning.

Taking stock of myself, I realized that I still felt a chill in my bones. Blankets would help, but I needed to heat up from the inside. Tea was the answer. I was risking overdoing it on hot chocolate and cider lately, if such a thing could even happen, and I wanted something less sweet for now.

There was a variety box of tea packets in the cupboard, but I didn't have a favorite. I didn't drink tea enough to really have a preference other than "not fruity," so I always just hoped for the best. Rifling through the tea options, I picked one at random, but it still didn't feel like a cup of tea would settle me.

I sat on a barstool and gazed around the apartment, snickering as I looked at our bookshelves, trying to decide what book I would choose to use as an access point to a sometimes panic-room, sometimes movie-room like Gloria had. I was struck by the realization that I had been so enamored with her having a secret room behind a bookcase that I never checked what book she had chosen. I looked down at the tea bag in my hand (a ginger-forward blend, according to the label) and decided to walk over to see if she'd like to join me for a cup of tea and answers.

"Haley, hello," Gloria said after she threw the door open with gusto. "How are you?" I wondered idly whether it was possible to be sad in Gloria's presence. How we had lived so closely but without any real interaction before this week was a mystery to me.

"I'm good. I was about to make myself a cup of tea and was wondering if you'd like to join me."

"Oh! Well, that sounds lovely, but I'm knee-deep in gift wrapping." Gloria gestured behind her where several rolls of wrapping paper were balanced on the arms of a chair, and three wrapped gifts were stacked just beside a much larger pile of boxes and bags that I assumed were gifts that still needed to be wrapped.

"Oh...Okay, maybe another time." I tried to hide my disappointment as it hit me, but Gloria wasn't having any of that.

"Nonsense! Do you have any presents that you need to wrap? Go get them. If you don't have any, come keep me company while I finish. Do you have a special tea, or should I pick something to brew?"

"If you have something that isn't fruity, that would be great. I'll be back in a few minutes."

"Good, good. The door will be unlocked, so just let yourself in." I walked a few steps backward until Gloria's door shut and then spun around to go get the presents that I'd gotten so far for friends and family. Anna was still in her room, so I snuck out the sweater and terrarium kit I got her, along with the rest of the gifts and a few rolls of wrapping paper and ribbon. Without knowing if Anna was asleep in her room, I didn't want to call out and possibly wake her, so I just let myself back out into the hallway quietly and then walked down to Gloria's door.

When I let myself in, Gloria was humming along with music that was playing from a portable speaker set up on her counter while setting out cups of sugar and milk as the water in her kettle heated. "Haley, I'm awfully glad you popped over. I like wrapping gifts as much as the next person, but it's better with company."

"I don't really mind wrapping, but for some reason, I always put it off until the last minute, and then it stresses me out. This will be a nice change." The kettle's whine pulled Gloria's gaze, and she poured us each a cup of water, added a teabag to each cup, and then beckoned me over to finish mine however I'd prefer. I set mine aside to let it steep and cool so that I could taste it before doctoring it to my preferences.

Gloria was taking me on a tour through her wrapping so far, explaining what gifts were already done and noting each that was left along with who was receiving each and why. By the time she was done, I had a cup of tea (now with sugar and a tiny splash of milk added), and all of my own gifts were spread out. I began measuring out how much wrapping paper I needed for the first gift I grabbed as I told Gloria who it was for and why I thought they'd like it. She asked me for the same explanation for each new gift I started wrapping, and I began to notice whose gifts I had put less effort and thought into, which made me feel a bit guilty.

It turned into a conversation about whether gift-giving was a materialistic requirement and whether we should bother with it unless there was a deep and meaningful connection to the gift. We went back and forth on the topic, neither of us really having a clear answer on how we felt and often changing how we were leaning as new points were brought up. I had never liked the materialistic nature of certain holidays, but I also loved giving people gifts, hoping it was something that they would enjoy. Thankfully, no one in my life made me feel like I was obligated to give gifts at all, much less any certain types or monetary levels of gifts, so it made it easier to enjoy the practice.

"What are those for?" Gloria pointed to a little pile I'd made of the bonus or in-case-of-emergency gifts I had bought earlier.

"I like to have a few extra gifts on hand in case I get stuck in a situation where I have to pretend that I've got a gift back out in my car or in my bag that's in another room when someone brings me a gift."

"Does that happen often?"

"Not too often, but more often than you'd expect. It ends up being that I go to a holiday event and find out that there was a small gift exchange or game that the person who invited me forgot to mention. Once, I went to a friend's holiday party and had a Secret Santa gift set, half of which was a bag of dark chocolate-covered caramels, wrapped and ready, only to overhear the person I was Secret Santa for talking about how she hated dark chocolate, so I swapped it out with something else that I'd had in reserve in my bag."

"Bonus, you then had dark chocolate-covered caramels."

"Exactly!" I looked through the small pile of gifts, realizing that many had similar shapes, so I wouldn't be able to feel which was which once they were wrapped. "I need to get some small gift bags for these. That way, I know which is which, but I'm not just handing out unwrapped gifts."

"What about these," Gloria asked, rifling through a small plastic tub of wrapping materials before pulling out a handful of mini drawstring bags decorated with snowflakes.

"Those would be perfect! Are you sure you don't mind my taking them? What if you need them? I could get you some replacements."

"Oh, dear, this is the tip of the iceberg when it comes to gift wrap and gift bags that I have stored away. Please, lighten the load."

Gloria and I kept wrapping until we were both finished, sharing memories of the best and worst gifts we'd received and holiday traditions, old and new. Eventually, we moved to her living room, where I sat in an oversized chair and had the most divinely soft blanket tossed over my legs. Gloria told me about the Christmas lunch feast she was hosting for a handful of local friends.

I learned that she'd been doing this for years, always setting at least two extra places for anyone who didn't have somewhere to spend the holiday that she could invite last-minute without it being an imposition. They always got used, which was both heartwarming (because they weren't left alone when they didn't want to be) and sad (because so many people didn't have family or friends nearby to celebrate with.

According to Gloria, only about half of the group of regulars celebrated Christmas. Some of the rest of the group celebrated other holidays, and some didn't celebrate anything at all. Gloria welcomed everyone, and people often brought dishes that were traditional for their own celebrations or cultures. If not for Anna's family being so close by, maybe I would have been joining Gloria for lunch. Although, without the dares as the catalyst that led me to really talk to Gloria, I never would have even known about it. Funny how that worked.

DAY 10: WIN A GINGERBREAD HOUSE COMPETITION

It was officially the week of Christmas. That was the first thought I had as I started to wake up. My parents only lived a few hours away, so I really could just drive over the day before to celebrate, but every year I took the whole week off work to spend quality time with my parents and, when he was there, my brother. I had already taken the week off before I found out my parents were leaving for the holiday, and when their plans changed, I decided that mine didn't have to.

My body apparently didn't get the memo, though, given that I was awake at 8:00 a.m. despite not having set an alarm. Unlike yesterday, I was actually feeling rested. Normally, even when I'd gotten enough sleep, I was slow to wake up. I considered whether to loaf around, luxuriating in bed because I had the morning free, but ultimately I decided against it. There was too much of a risk that I would end up falling back asleep, which meant that I'd inevitably wake up in two hours somehow tired again.

Waffles were the answer. Honestly, when were they not? I bicycled my legs until my comforter and sheets were in a messy pile at the end of my bed before I rolled over and stood up. Time to switch from my nighttime pajamas to my daytime pajamas that masqueraded as loungewear.

On went soft drawstring pants, slippers, and an oversized hoody. Silky matching sets were cute and all, but they were powerless against the winter chill once I'd left the warm cocoon of my bed.

There was no sign of Anna when I entered the kitchen. I rifled through our cabinets, pulling out ingredients, and remembered that we used the last of the syrup the other day. We also didn't have any berries left (my preferred topping), so a trip to the store was the first order of business. Thankfully, there was a corner market only a block from our building. I brushed off the passing thought that I should have a snack before going to avoid impulse purchases in a misguided attempt to prove to myself that I had self-control.

As a surprise to absolutely no one, including myself, I didn't exercise any self-control. My intent to get the two items I needed was outweighed by my roaming stomach, which decided that waffles were a good start, but a breakfast feast of waffles, eggs, bacon, sausage, and hashbrowns would really start the holiday break off with a bang.

I wandered around the store, caving to my breakfast whims for longer than I cared to admit, and I ended up with a full tote of groceries and an armful of juice bottles because I couldn't decide between orange, pineapple, or mango juice. Anna was awake an hour later when I returned to the apartment, and after an initial short of laughter, she helped me put away the groceries without judgment. It wouldn't be the first time (or the last) that one of us went to the store without supervision or willpower.

Another hour later, Anna and I were sitting on the couch, the meager remnants of our breakfast on our plates on the coffee table. Conservatively, I assumed that my body was currently made up of ninety-seven percent breakfast food and three percent regret. It was just so delicious at the time. Anna and I were in full food coma mode; sitting upright and trying to stay awake seemed futile. Internally, I was trying to talk myself down from wondering whether a stomach could actually burst or if it was stretchy enough to withstand what I'd just put it through; I was breathing through bouts of nausea.

When my phone dinged, and a text from Adam came through asking if I wanted to meet him for lunch, I had to stop myself from throwing the phone away from me because it contained an invitation for more food. The only thing that stopped me was the knowledge that I'd have to get up to retrieve it at some point, and I was not moving anytime soon. I reread the text after tamping down my desire to take up indoor pitching.

> *Adam: Hey, any interest in meeting me for a late lunch today?*

Ugh. Did I want to see him enough to endure lunch in a few hours?

> *Haley: If you'd asked a few hours ago, it would have been an absolutely, but I've eaten my weight in breakfast foods*

> *Haley: It will be a miracle if I'm hungry again before the new year*

> *Adam: So, I should cancel the thirty-seven-course meal I planned for us?*

Haley: Gag

Adam: Raincheck?

*Haley: *looks around* nope, no rain here*

Adam: Cute

Haley: Yes, to the raincheck

Groaning, I turned my head to look at Anna, intent on telling her that I was going to try to sleep off our bad decisions, but her eyes were already closed, her breathing even and slow. I tried to maneuver myself off the couch without jostling her, but it was no use.

"I'm going back to bed," I told her, getting a responsive "hmm" in return as she pulled her feet up on the couch and resituated herself so that she was lying down. Her eyes never even opened, so I couldn't tell if she was already asleep again or not, but there was nothing really left to say.

I stumbled my way into my bedroom and turned on the fan in one corner of my room. I didn't normally use it in the winter, but I wanted the coziness of snuggling under all of my bedcovers despite already feel-ing overheated. I curled up in bed, and my consciousness faded to black almost immediately.

10.2

I woke up for the second time more than two hours later. I didn't feel wonderful, but I also no longer felt like I might implode, so I was calling that a win. Anna was still on the couch when I ventured back out, but she was awake and watching a video on her phone. She looked up at me as I leaned over the back of the couch, checking out the video she was watching of a woman making gingerbread.

"You realize we have to go make gingerbread houses tonight?" She grimaced, clearly still uncomfortable. "I bought the ingredients yesterday to make sheets of gingerbread from scratch so that we could cut out whatever shapes we want, but I don't want to get up."

"I was just planning on getting a kit with the pre-made pieces. They usually come with stuff to decorate with, too."

"Eh, then you're stuck with whatever they give you, and they don't taste good."

"I don't think taste will factor into judging. They're providing a lot of base ingredients, including gingerbread, for the people who registered before the first deadline."

"Still, I think I'm going to try to make gingerbread. It'll look nicer than those stale, shrink-wrapped pieces. Plus, what if they're broken?"

"Then I'll steal some of yours, duh." Anna snorted a laugh in response. "I think the extra stuff they provide is pretty basic, though, so I do want to find some fun decorations."

"There's a new specialty candy store downtown that probably has interesting stuff."

"Seriously?"

"Yeah, Sandy's Candies. It's pretty close to my office. We ordered small mystery bags from them that went into swag bags for a client event last month. I think they do classes too, but they operate like a normal candy shop where you just pick what you want and pay by weight."

"Hmm, maybe I'll head down there and see if they have anything that would be good for our gingerbread houses."

"They definitely would. Would you pick up some for me, too? I don't want to have to rely solely on what the event has available for anyone to use. Who knows if they'll have enough, you know?"

"Sure. I'm going to stop and get a gingerbread house kit or two for the gingerbread, though. Do you want me to get you one, just in case?"

"Nah, I'm going to get up in a few minutes and make my own. I should have enough time to make a second batch if something goes wrong with the first or I need more."

"Okay. Let me know if you change your mind." I wandered back to my bedroom while I searched online to find and map a route to the candy shop Anna mentioned. After getting changed, I put on my winter gear and started the trek to the closest stop for the bus I needed, reopening the text thread with Adam once I got on and was seated. Maybe he'd be open to candy for lunch.

Haley: so, about that rain check

Adam: I'm listening

Haley: I'm still a no-go for lunch, but I've got to stop by Sandy's Candies. Want to come look at buckets of candy with me?

Haley: You could always get a bag for yourself if you still need lunch

Adam: I ended up ordering something and ate while working. I'm ready for a break, though, so I'm in. When are you heading there?

Haley: I'm on the bus now. Should be there in about 15 minutes

Adam: Perfect, I'll finish up what I'm working on and meet you there

A tall drink of water leaned against the window of the candy shop as I walked up. His hands were cupped around his eyes as he peered inside.

"You could go in, you know," I said to Adam as I got closer, and he turned toward me, happy as a, well, an adult at a candy shop.

"I wanted to wait to share the candy magic when we go in. There's a sign on the door advertising potion-making classes. I have no idea what kind of potions you can make with candy, but I'm so intrigued that we might need to go to one." I zeroed in on the "we" of his comment.

"I wonder if they maybe infuse the candy into different liquids."

"I've seen people do that with alcohol, so that could be it." Adam held the door open for me, and we were met with a blast of sweet air. Stepping inside, there was a section dedicated to chocolate, one dedicated to sprinkles, one dedicated to gummies (that one was gigantic), and tons more unspecified space. "This is five-year-old Adam's heaven." His eyes were comically wide as they darted around, trying to take everything in. I finally had to tug on his sleeve to get him out of the way of the door as other patrons tried to maneuver around him to the door.

We went to a station where you could choose a cute little tin or container for your candy, but we both opted for generic bags. According to the sign by the bags, everything was priced by weight, with the exception of one small section of specialty options that had their own designated bags, so we were able to mix together all of the candy we got. I ended up bringing a few bags with me just in case I wanted to keep some things separate for ease of being able to find what I needed tonight.

We walked to the chocolate section first, where I found candy-coated chocolate balls in bright colors. I was worried about them squishing, though, so I made a mental note that they were here in case I couldn't find a suitable alternative.

There wasn't much else in the chocolate section that would work well for a gingerbread house. I turned to tell Adam that I was going to move on, only to find him with a half-full bag already. I watched as he put a small amount of one candy into his bag before moving to the next and doing the same. The third he approached must have been a favorite because it got double the amount before he returned to the same, smaller amount at the next bin. So, Adam liked chocolate. Good to know.

"Are you getting some of each," I asked. Adam's focus never wavered from the candy.

"I wanted to try a little bit of everything that looked good, but, yeah, it's turning out to be everything." I chuckled as he used tongs to sort through what looked like chocolate snowmen to find the best pieces.

"Okay, I'm going to keep wandering. I'll meet you in the candy aisle later." Adam laughed at that, pointedly looking around at the store filled with nothing but candy aisles before shaking his head and going back to the chocolates.

I left him there as I made my way over to the sprinkles section. There should be at least some good filler sprinkles or something to dust over the frosting to look like snow, but I was wholly unprepared for what I found. The sheer number of types and blends of sprinkles blew my mind. There was an entire row of small jars that you could fill with edible glitter. *Edible glitter*! I was an adult with my own bank account, and I was about to be financially irresponsible.

A few jars of edible glitter went into my bag before I moved on to the rows upon rows of what was labeled as "sanding sugar," with dozens of bins of different individual colors and blends. I tried to make good decisions; I tried to only take what I'd realistically use for the gingerbread houses later, but *come on*. I resolved to make cakes and cupcakes soon. Or dessert pancakes and waffles. Or milkshakes! Anything that could use up the extras I inevitably had after tonight.

I did, eventually, make my way through the sprinkle section and onto some of the others. I made myself a separate grab bag of gummy candies that I knew likely wouldn't be used tonight, but I wanted to try them. I ended up with another large bag full of brightly colored ornament candies, snowflake marshmallows, some type of candy "floss" that was reminiscent of tinsel, and a smattering of whatever else caught my eye. Adam found me when I was debating whether to get another bag since the ones I already had were full. He was holding three bags—one large bag that was full to the brim and two smaller, half-full bags.

"You're making out like a bandit. What've you got so far," I asked him.

"This one," he started, holding up the large bag, "is a chocolate extravaganza for myself. This one is taffy for my parents, and this one"—he switched his hand that held the two small bags to indicate one, then the other—"is a mini assortment for Gracie."

"I'd love to tell you that all of this isn't for me, but that would be a lie."

"What is all of this for anyway? You mentioned needing it for tonight. Another dare?"

"Yeah, Anna and I are entering a gingerbread house competition tonight."

"They won't have supplies there?"

"We didn't enter early enough to reserve gingerbread, but there will be some communal building and decorating supplies. Who knows how much, though. I figured that the judges wouldn't want to just keep seeing the same thing over and over, so this might be a way to add a little pizzazz."

"Do you already have gingerbread? I saw some kits up front. The woman working the register told me that they host gingerbread house classes here during the holiday season, so they make extra and sell kits to bring home."

"Oh! I was going to stop somewhere and get a kit, but most of the time, they've been sitting on the shelves for so long and are pretty underwhelming. I bet the ones here are so much better."

"They looked pretty good. I try making a gingerbread house each year, but they always fall apart on me."

"Same. I'm hoping whatever they have available tonight as a binder works well. Anna's at home trying to make gingerbread, but I don't want to risk it. It's usually pretty soft for a while, isn't it?"

"No clue. Do you have to make a house, or can you build whatever you want?"

"I think you have free reign. Which is good because if mine falls apart, I'm just going to call them ancient ruins of a Christmas village."

"Clever. I think I would break the pieces down into smaller pieces and make a little miniature village of gingerbread houses. I'd hazard a guess that smaller structures would stay together more easily. Plus, people love miniature things."

"Hmmm, so you're saying cute would win over the ruins of an abandoned city? Oh! A gingerbread cemetery! It'd be like Halloween and Christmas combined. Spooky and sweet!"

"I would love to see that amidst a sea of little Christmas cottages."

"I'd invite you to see it, but Anna and I are making it a friend date night and going to dinner after."

Adam shrugged. "Send me a picture, especially if you end up making ruins or a graveyard."

"Deal." I checked through my bags of candy, finally able to convince myself that I didn't need to start another bag. "Do you have any more sections to look through here, or are you fully stocked on candy?"

"I think I'm set. The fact that this place is within walking distance of my office is going to become problematic, but I think I can scrounge up some self-control and stick with what I've got for now."

"Yeah, I'm definitely coming back here. Now, where did you see those gingerbread house kits?" Adam walked me up toward the registers where there was a table stacked with sticker-clad boxes boasting that they had everything needed to make a gingerbread house: a base, pre-cut gingerbread pieces, frosting for adhering the pieces together, frosting for attaching decorations, and, obviously, sprinkles and candy decorations. I guess I didn't need to buy extra candy, but this way, I'd get a bonus surprise since they all had different mystery packs of decorations.

I grabbed one of the mid-size boxes of the three size options before grabbing a second, either for backup pieces for myself in case I broke something, or in case Anna ended up needing it. She hadn't texted about how her gingerbread making was going, so hopefully, I'd just have two kits worth of supplies to choose from, but I didn't want her scrambling in case something happened.

"All this talk of gingerbread houses, I obviously need to make one too," Adam said as he picked up one of the small kit boxes before leaving the table to walk the few feet to the registers.

"Ah, so you got one after all," the woman behind the register said to Adam, nodding at the kit box in his hand. "And two for you," she said as I put them both down on the counter alongside my bags of candy and jars of edible glitter. "Are you having a party?"

"My roommate and I are entering a gingerbread house competition tonight," I explained, "and he just loves a good gingerbread house." I glanced over my shoulder at Adam, who nodded. Every time we were together, he was so unapologetically enthusiastic about what made him happy, as simple or silly as it seemed. I had a passing thought that it would be fun to take him to the aquarium or zoo and see his eyes light up. I loved wandering around and seeing the fish and animals, but I always felt rushed when I went with people. I could tell Adam would take his time and enjoy wandering through slowly with me.

I started imagining all of the various activities and potential dates we could go on together, and I must have zoned out a bit because, when I blinked myself out of my daze, all of my items were rung up and bagged. The woman working and Adam were chatting about classes that the store offered while they waited for me to snap out of it and pay. After I had, Adam smiled down at me as he put his items on the counter and asked the clerk about the class schedule. A line had formed behind us as Adam paid, so we took a business card with the store's website listed to check out their classes later.

"Well," Adam said as we exited the sugar-laced air of the shop and stepped back out onto the sidewalk, "that was fun. Potentially more fun than lunch would have been because now I have candy and a project."

"Are you going to make your gingerbread house tonight?"

"Probably. It feels like a good night for building it while tossing a movie on."

"You'll need to send me a picture of yours when you're done."

"I will." He checked his watch before sighing slightly. "Unfortunately, I need to head back to the office to finish up a few things this afternoon."

"No worries. I need to head back home anyway. The competition is early, so we don't want to be rushed."

"I'm glad you texted me about coming with you. I had fun, umm, browsing near you? I mean...do you know what I mean?"

"I do. I had fun browsing near you, too."

"Don't forget to send me a picture of your masterpiece tonight."

"Promise." I headed back towards the bus stop and snuck a taste of some of the candies I'd gotten while I waited. The bus came quickly enough that I hadn't made much of a dent. Still, I had enough that it was lucky I had stuck to the bag of gummy candies not meant for decorations.

10.3

I didn't realize it was possible to step into a made-for-television holiday movie, and yet... Anna and I walked through the doors of the community center's banquet room and into what could only be described as an explosion of cheer.

There were festive backdrops hung up behind more than a dozen tables, each set up with two workspaces. The tables alternated green and red tablecloths, and there were lights strung throughout the space that managed to provide some color and ambiance despite being in a fully lit room. A group of kids played in the far corner while a few others were trying to sneak candy, frosting, and gingerbread off the supply tables. When caught, they were redirected to tables filled with snacks, desserts, and drinks.

Adults of all ages milled around, some chatting, some setting out supplies that they picked up from check-in or brought in themselves. Light music played, and there were three Christmas trees set up, each decorated differently.

One of the trees was decorated with what looked like handmade ornaments, presumably made by kids at the community center; one was filled with tags that listed ages and numbers of children, presumably so that people could sponsor a local family and help with getting presents.

There were already tons of gifts piled at the base of that tree, ready to be picked up by the recipient families, and the remaining tags were few and far between. The last tree had laminated pictures strung with ribbon that hung from the branches. Based on the backgrounds of each, they looked to have been taken at the community center, probably of families that visited and events that had been held.

"It's a lot of Christmas, and only Christmas, decorations for a community center," Anna whispered to me as we approached the front of the line. The woman at the check-in desk still heard her quiet criticism, but she didn't seem offended.

"On years where there's no overlap, like this one, we decorate for Christmas between other winter holidays. On years where holidays do overlap, we put decorations out each at the same time. We want everyone to feel welcome when they're here."

Anna considered this for a moment before nodding and then pointing to the tree with the gift tags. "What's the drop-off deadline for the sponsorship tree?"

"Christmas Eve at noon, but we contact the families as soon as the gifts for their tag are dropped off, so the earlier you drop them off, the more time they have to work with to get here and get them home."

"Can we still take tags?"

"Absolutely! We're going to mention it while the judges are doing their rounds, and we're hoping that we can get the remainder picked up tonight. Since a lot of what is left is for families with multiple kids and more difficult to get sponsorships for, if it's not in your budget, we also will accept more general gifts for kids. We just ask that you add a removable note with what each is or what age range it's for so that everything can be distributed to families that have kids in that age range."

"Thanks. I'll check them out."

"Speaking of checking things out, let's get you checked in." Anna and I got our table assignment, thankfully ending up at the same table as we requested, and headed over to set up.

Earlier, when I got back to the apartment, I walked in to the smell of slightly burnt gingerbread and a very frazzled roommate. Apparently, she spent a lot of time procrastinating before starting baking, and then she was talking to her mom on the phone when the first batch was cooking and didn't hear the timer go off.

The first trays of gingerbread were burnt to a crisp, so she tried to rush through making a second batch but spilled a bowl of dry ingredients on the ground. I found her frantically measuring things out to see if there was enough left to make more when I walked in. Anna nearly cried when I pulled the second gingerbread house kit out of my bag for her. I cleaned up the kitchen after making Anna sit down for a bit to decompress.

I managed to fight off the urge to go through the contents of the kit box before now. I had Anna double-check that there was gingerbread inside, but otherwise, I wanted to be surprised by the frosting colors, sprinkles, and candy. Anna looked through hers to help calm her nerves when she was feeling unprepared, so I saw some of the possibilities, but allegedly, all the boxes were different.

My excitement built as I opened the lid and found a medium bag each of white and silver frosting and a small bag of bright green frosting. There was also a small jar of green edible glitter (one of the colors I hadn't bought earlier), three marshmallows shaped and decorated like snowmen, a slightly deformed snow-dog marshmallow, gumdrops, and a few different blends of sprinkles.

Anna's box was more traditional, with a focus on smaller, uniform candies for decorating. There were a variety of trays and bowls on each table; people at other tables were separating out decorative items in them, so I started doing the same with the candies I bought earlier.

When everyone had arrived and checked in, there was a five-minute warning given for when the competition clock would start counting down the hour that everyone had available to finish. I'd been eavesdropping on nearby conversations and had overheard people talking about the elaborate designs they'd planned. How many people practiced for this? Anna came back to our table and plopped a plate down in front of me filled with hummus, vegetables, crackers, cheese, and a cupcake. She sat down next to me with her own plate, and we watched people as they flitted around us, an odd tension in the air.

"Is it just me, or are people taking this way too seriously for a gingerbread contest?" Anna looked around the room as she considered my question.

"Well, it looks like most people are in the same boat as us—thought this was casual and now are a little unsure because of the four or five people taking this too seriously."

"Alright, everyone," one of the organizers began before clapping her hands loudly, pulling everyone's attention, "are you ready?" There were murmured yeses throughout the room, and a few people clapped or gave a "wooo" in response. "Excellent. Here's your countdown." The woman started at ten and slowly counted down before shouting, "Go!"

Anna and I watched as everyone stood poised for the start at their stations, arms held above the supplies until they were permitted to start, at which point there was a wave of people rushing the three tables spread out in front of the competitors' tables where decorating supplies were available. Since everyone's station was already stocked with two piping bags of white frosting (and gingerbread, for those that registered early), there was really no need to join the fray to fight over the additional, limited supplies.

Anna and I ate the rest of our snacks before I took the plates to the trash. By the time I got back, Anna had cut a hole in the tip of her piping bag of frosting and was lining one of the sides of a gingerbread piece. She squished the frosted side together with another piece to start creating the house structure. I did the same, albeit more impatiently.

A few attempts and re-attempts later, trying to let the pieces dry before moving on to the next piece, I managed to get four sides up and was in the process of adding the roof. The first piece went on without issue. The second seemed to work until, of course, I tried to hold it while also bending forward to pull the tray of sprinkles and candies that I'd started to separate out earlier toward me.

Fun fact: when you're using downward pressure on top of a piece of gingerbread, and then you lean forward and end up putting more pressure on the hand holding the gingerbread in place while it dried, you will have used enough pressure to break, not just your roof tiles, but also at least one of the walls. Maybe more walls if you're an overachiever, but I only broke one.

Anna heard me curse under my breath and looked over before stilling and surveying the damage. I waved her off with my now-free hand while I tried to decide whether I wanted to attempt to glue the pieces of the wall together. This would be an excellent start for my gingerbread ruins or even pivoting to my gingerbread cemetery, but I'd been watching and eavesdropping on the judges earlier and knew they wouldn't be amused by either option.

Shaking my head and chuckling quietly, I looked over each piece of gingerbread, knowing how I was going to pivot. I found a small knife at the shared supplied table and brought it back to my station to start cutting up the pieces of gingerbread into smaller squares and rectangles.

"What are you doing?" Anna asked, looking over as she sorted out red and green gumdrops.

"Salvaging the wreckage," I replied distractedly. Anna just shrugged and went back to decorating her fully assembled and seemingly structurally sound gingerbread house. Thankfully, because Sandy's Candies made fresh gingerbread for their kits, it was actually manageable to cut each of the pieces down into smaller, somewhat uniform pieces. The original two pieces of gingerbread had dried together well enough that I was able to cut them down while keeping them together, so I ended up further along than I expected to be.

Once everything was as close as I was going to get them to being uniform shapes, I started organizing the smaller pieces into groups and then using frosting to attach the sides and make smaller structures. The smaller houses needed a lot less support while they dried and fused together, so I just lined them up in a row and added supports from the kit box and trays on the sides again, but it was now enough that I didn't need to hold each one until they were dry. I plopped down into my chair to wait, took my phone out, and took a quick photo before sending off a text.

Haley: [photo]

Haley: I hope you don't mind, but I stole your idea. Soon, there's going to be a little Christmas village of mini gingerbread houses!

Adam: No graveyard?

Haley: I didn't want to give the judges somewhere to bury me. I overheard a woman talking about her plan to make a gingerbread version of the restaurant she works at and saw one of the judges give her a disapproving scowl from a few feet away

Adam: Ahh, gingerbread traditionalists...

Haley: Fingers crossed they like minis

Adam: In case you need any inspiration, here's what I've been working on

Adam: [photo]

I opened the photo Adam sent, and a burst of laughter escaped me, drawing the eyes of everyone within a few tables' distance. I sunk down lower into my chair and waited for everyone to go back to their work before pulling the phone from where it was pressed against my chest.

The photo was focused on a mostly intact gingerbread house sitting on what looked to be Adam's coffee table with the rest of his supplies spread out to the side. The sides and roof were all attached, but Adam had carved out pieces where the walls met the roof to look like someone had taken a giant bite out of the house. He must have just started because there weren't any decorations yet other than candy outlines of a door and two windows.

Haley: A masterpiece in the making

I nudged Anna and showed her the photo before putting my phone back down and testing out whether my pieces were ready for decorations. It took me a few minutes to actually start, realizing that I should have looked up some decorating ideas, especially now that I had not one but four little houses to transform. I did a quick search on my phone for ideas but decided to just wing it.

Using the silver frosting I got in my kit, I gave each house a little door, some rectangular and some with arched tops, and at least one window. As much as I didn't want to revert back to the attachment and drying stage, I cut out a few teeny pieces of the remaining gingerbread to give two of the houses each a chimney. Amongst the surprise sprinkles that came in my kit, there were a small number of candies shaped like little trees. They were small enough that I was able to add a few to the backs of the houses to make sure they weren't blank.

I realized that I now had much less of a need for frosting, so I spread a small layer of white frosting all over the base that was provided before sticking the little houses on where I wanted them and then sprinkled white sanding sugar over the "snow" on the board. Next step: cover at least one of the rooftops in snow. Because of how small each of my houses was, I was tempted to cover another in snow to avoid the more difficult, precise decorating needed, but their small stature also meant that most of the attention was going to be on the roofs, so I needed to at least try to put some work in. It could always snow on the village again later if things didn't turn out well.

I sat back after twenty minutes and admired the rooftops I'd decorated. The snow-covered one had a dusting of white edible glitter, another had swooping lines of frosting that loosely resembled fancy roof tiles, and the third ended up covered in frosting as well but then covered in tiny multicolored sprinkle balls (which Anna later told me were called "nonpareils"). The last house had whimsical swirls of frosting with the candy floss I bought earlier hanging from the bottom of the roof tiles like icicles. I added sprinkles and candies to any blank spaces throughout the roof designs to add some color, texture, and interest.

I popped over to the communal supplies table to see if there was anything worth adding and found an assortment of small, string-light-shaped candies. They were more appropriately sized for a larger gingerbread house, but I decided to use my marshmallow snowmen and snow-dog as a centerpiece, along with the lights sticking up from the ground around them like those comically large, fake, plastic lawn ornament lights.

I considered ditching the snowmen, given that they were the same size as the houses, but ultimately decided to leave them. Town center holiday displays were often gigantic in the movies, so why not in my little gingerbread village. It made me laugh, the thought of a town full of gingerbread people coming together to roll balls for and then assemble snowmen as big as their houses. Good thing the marshmallows wouldn't melt and flood the town.

As silly and cute as the centerpiece was as-is, the townspeople would obviously all get together for a tree lighting ceremony, so I needed to make a gingerbread tree. I cut out two pieces of the remaining gingerbread, smaller than the snowman because I didn't have much left to work with, cut one in half, and attached each half to the middle line of the tree to make a plus-sign shape when you looked from the above so that you could see the tree shape no matter which angle you were looking from.

The tree got frosted before being dusted with green edible glitter and adorned string lights in the form of piped lines of silver frosting and small candy balls. I surprised myself at how nice and, dare I say, sophisticated it looked. That is, until I added the tree to the town center, in front of the snowmen (and beside the snow-dog), which made it look like the snowmen were setting up the tree, and any suggestion of elegance disappeared.

I had nearly finished adding candy-lined walkways that led from each of the houses to the town center display when one of the organizers rang a bell and announced that there were only five minutes left to add finishing touches. There were some gasps and a bit of frantic murmuring around the room after that, and a few people ran, actually ran, to the communal supplies tables. Thankfully, I wasn't really planning on doing much else; even the walkways were just a result of still having time and wanting the little village to feel finished.

I added the last of the candies lining the walkways before opting to use the last of the silver frosting to make them more defined. I piped out a quarter of the remaining amount in each walkway and then used a spoon to smooth it down, differentiating the texture and color from the snow-covered ground around it.

Once that was done, I started packing up my remaining materials, putting everything I wanted to keep in the now-empty kit box and storing that in my bag. I threw away packaging from used-up supplies and wiped down my station with a napkin from the snack table before sitting in the chair at my station and admiring my little village and taking photos from all angles. I knew I wouldn't win this competition, but I was very proud of what I'd made.

I sent the photos off to my parents, brother, a few friends, and Adam. I bit my lip to keep from smiling when the first reply came from Adam only a minute later applauding my work. I was the type of person who usually texted back quickly (unless I was with other people or had put my phone away for some reason), so I loved that he seemed to be, too. He followed up his reply with a photo of his own gingerbread house, having added gingerbread crumbs around the side where the "bite" was, along with fallen decorations.

Haley: I love my little mini village. I guess now I owe you one.

*Adam: Hmm, I seem to remember releasing you from cor-
porate jail...*

Haley: Guess I owe you two then

Adam: I'll start you a tab

Not me, swooning. I was realizing that I needed to add "silly" to what I was looking for in a partner. I didn't want the class clown, but I'd dated so many men who thought that lightheartedness and silliness were juvenile or not masculine enough. They were exes for a reason.

Anna was still focused and working on her gingerbread house, and when I shifted my gaze to her gingerbread house, I audibly gasped. Her hands, stilled and she snuck a glance over at me, waiting until I waved her off before she went back to adding small silver star sprinkles, surrounded by multicolored sprinkles and then circled with small gold balls to make what looked like it could be a stained-glass window.

She must have also gotten green frosting in her kit box and had used it, along with white frosting, to make a checkered design on the roof. The green lines were thinner than the white and ran alongside them so that the entire design was two-toned.

Small red balls had been added where the lines of the checkered pattern intersected and larger red candies in a line to hide the top seam of the roof. Anna had added a beautiful brick design to her door and, having earlier asked to use a small piece of my gingerbread once it was already broken down, added ledges below each window, each of which she'd added frosting shutters beside. Trees were added, with snow caught on their boughs, alongside snowmen and the illusion of the entire house being strung with lights.

"Anna," I said, so low it was almost a whisper, "it's stunning." Anna smiled softly at me, the hint of a blush coloring her cheeks as she added her final details. When she stepped back, a full smile bloomed on her face, and she turned back to me.

"Okay, I think I'm done."

"How did you even do all that work in an hour? And it's so perfectly done. Have you been a gingerbread artist this whole time and just not told me?"

"Based on my attempt to make gingerbread earlier, I think we both know that's not true." She laughed at herself as she sat down in her chair beside me. "Part of the reason I was so rushed earlier was because I went down the rabbit hole of watching decorating videos specific to gingerbread houses. Once you have the idea and have seen someone do things like this"—she gestured towards the rooftop—"it's easier than you'd think, so long as you have a steady hand."

"I seriously doubt that anyone with a steady hand could do that. We've obviously just uncovered a secret talent of yours. You should enter into real contests."

"Nah, this was enough. It was fun, but I don't think I'll be ready to make another until next Christmas."

"Okay, everyone, time's up in five, four, three, two, one – *and we're done!*" One of the organizers rang the bell in her hand after she finished the countdown. A few grumbles came from the crowd, but a number of people had already finished and were cleaning up. "Please remove everything but your finished gingerbread house from your table. Our three judges will begin coming around shortly, but you don't need to be at your table, so you're free to grab a drink or a snack, use the restroom, or check out the rest of the finished pieces in the room."

I'd grabbed some water for us both at the snack table when I got napkins, so we stayed put at our stations, waiting for others to make their rounds before we did a lap. The organizer made a series of announcements, including details about the sponsorship tree tags, and before long, all the tags had been claimed. Anna and I had enough time to walk through the line of tables to see all of the different gingerbread creations and eat some of our remaining candy before the judges stood in the center of the room and announced that they were ready to crown the winners.

"In third place," one of the judges began, pausing for dramatic effect, "station sixteen." When we checked in, we were directed over to our table by the woman at the check-in table pointing at our table. She told us our numbers, but I'd promptly forgotten them, relying instead on her pointing and following Anna. The numbers were on the front of the table, so I couldn't see who'd won. When I looked over at Anna, she was sitting straight up, her mouth dropped open and eyebrows raised halfway up her forehead.

"Congratulations!" The woman on the other side of Anna clapped as she looked over at us. No, not us. Anna. Then it clicked.

"Wait...*Anna! You won!*" I was nearly yelling, clapping so hard that my palms stung, before Anna looked at me, shrugged, and laughed. I joined in, hooting and hollering, wrapping my arm around her shoulder before shouting, "That's my friend!" The crowd, whose applause had waned somewhat, started clapping again and laughed happily along with us.

Well, we were laughing happily. The event organizer rang her bell again, gaining everyone's attention as the judges announced the runner-up. There was a round of applause for him as well, though not so long as it was for Anna.

"I can't believe it," Anna whispered to me while the judges were announcing the first-place prize package and trying to create some suspense for the announcement of the winner.

"Are you kidding? I can! You made a work of art! Look! Look at it!" I pointed at various elements of Anna's gingerbread house. "You deserve this. I think you were robbed of first place, but I can admit that I'm a little biased." The winner had just been announced, and we looked to see what she'd created as it was being carried up to the middle, now-cleared supply table so that it could be shown off.

The woman holding the piece was smiling and then was presented with a basket full of baking tools and a gift certificate. She hadn't just made a normal gingerbread house; she'd made a three-tiered structure, each tier essentially a slightly smaller, stacked house that felt whimsical and magical. Each tier had a different theme, but they worked together cohesively. It was incredible. How she managed to pull that together in one hour was a mystery.

"Do you think she's a professional baker or something?" I looked over at Anna, but she was still smiling down at the yellow ribbon and gift card that one of the organizers had handed her after she was announced as one of the winners.

Anna was waved over to take photos with the other two winners, so I started assembling the boxes that were provided to bring our creations home in. I hadn't thought about this part when we'd made dinner reservations at a place down the street. We managed to fit Anna's gingerbread house inside the box provided. Mine fit with so much room to spare that I made a few cuts, creating new folds to shorten the height so that the box was just taller than the snowmen in my town center. We packed them both up after having someone nearby take a photo of us holding them. Thankfully, we left buffer time before our reservation, but we didn't have that long before we were meant to be at the restaurant by the time photos and packing were done.

"I still can't believe this," Anna said as we walked the few blocks over to the restaurant.

"Don't sell yourself short, even to yourself. I'm still blown away by how amazing your decorating skills are. I'll be expecting a very pretty birthday cake a few months from now."

"Would you accept a gingerbread house that is a few months old and has been sitting on the counter until then?"

"I would not."

"Tough crowd, but okay. I'll see what I can do."

"Admittedly, I really thought tonight was going to be an 'L' for both of us, dare-wise. Not that I didn't have faith in you, but it felt like a long shot."

"I didn't win, though. I got third place."

"What's that you're holding?"

"Umm, my gingerbread house in a box?"

"In your other hand."

"My ribbon?"

"That you *won*?"

"I... yeah, I guess I did."

"Come on, champ, I'll buy you dinner to celebrate." I looped my free arm through Anna's, and we walked the remaining block to the restaurant as I put on a fake accent and started interviewing her, sports announcer style, on her decorating process and creative vision. By the time we entered the restaurant door, Anna was playing up her role, giving exaggerated answers and thanking everyone she had ever known for their support and love.

We spent the next two hours drinking and eating our way through the restaurant's menu. At one point our waitress asked about the gingerbread houses, wanting to know if they were a yearly tradition. Anna and I started reminiscing, trying to figure out if we'd established any traditions over the years without realizing it. We hadn't, but we wanted to make some. We spent the rest of the night swapping ridiculous suggestions for things we could turn into new traditions.

By the time we got home, I couldn't tell if my stomach hurt from the multitude of dishes we'd shared or from laughing. Probably a bit of both. Anna and I had so many memories together, but spending time planning out things we'd do together for the rest of our lives was the reason that my cheeks hurt too. How lucky was I to have a best friend like Anna? Maybe I'd show my gratitude by letting her win tomorrow's dare...on second thought, nah.

DAY 11: BE THE FIRST TO GET KICKED OUT OF A GROUP OF CAROLERS

It was snowing. I loved when it rained, when I could sit in bed listening to the light pitter-patter of the raindrops hit my window, but when it snowed, although it was pretty, it just meant that cold would eventually blanket me and that getting around was going to be more difficult.

I actually liked the snow and knew that most of what fell overnight and this morning would melt as the day got slightly warmer, but I was chilly, had the start of a headache, and was a little grumpy. I checked my position to see if I was waking up on the literal wrong side of the bed.

Once I had taken some pain meds and had a warm drink in my hand, I wrapped myself in a blanket and slumped down on the couch. There really needed to be straws for when you wanted to lay on the couch sipping a drink without adjusting. Maybe I'd invent that today. Seemed like a lot of work, though.

After a few sips of my hot cocoa, I set the drink down and fell to the side to rest my head on the pile of accent pillows Anna had accumulated. Three per side probably wasn't necessary, but I appreciated them now for giving me a soft place to land. I let my eyes close, trying to breathe through the spikes of pain radiating from my temples across my forehead.

I woke up before noon, thankfully now headache-free, and made a big enough gap in my nest of blankets that I could pull my phone from the coffee table to aimlessly scroll. Still chilled, I forced myself up and into the shower, after which I heated up leftover tomato soup and made myself a grilled cheese sandwich.

By the time I'd finished eating, I'd fully woken up and was feeling a little antsy. Anna wasn't home—she'd mentioned something about going to try a new workout class with Maddie and then getting lunch with her after—so I couldn't see if she wanted to go bopping around with me.

A quick glance out the window showed that it was still snowing, but the snowfall had lightened considerably. My desire to stay inside and be cozy was warring with my restlessness. It only took a few minutes of considering where I could be cozy elsewhere before I landed on the yarn store. There would be a good chance that Bernie or some of the other Knittie Bitties would be there, and the atmosphere was always welcoming and fun. Mind made up, I bundled up and started the walk over.

I knew Bernie was inside the moment the door cracked open. She was loudly complaining about someone at the senior center refusing to let her teach a class.

"Do you even know how to paint? You've never mentioned it." An unfamiliar voice asked.

"No, but what does that matter," Bernie replied, "I won't be painting, just telling other people how to paint. They'd never have to know!"

"But how would you teach a class on painting if you don't know how to—you know what, never mind."

Bernie harumphed loudly in response as I rounded the corner. She and her friend, the only ones in the shop other than Jean, who waved to me as I entered the store, were sitting in two armchairs tucked into a corner of the shop near the specialty yarns, according to the sign hanging above them. "You better have picked a craft, young lady," Bernie said, spotting me.

"What's the thing where you knit but with only one stick?" The woman beside Bernie gasped. Bernie patted her arm lightly while narrowing her eyes on me.

"Don't let anyone hear you say that again, knitter or crocheter. You'll get run right out of the shop."

"Crochet! That's the one!" Bernie scowled at me. I knew what it was called, but when I'd been looking up different types of crafts and hobbies to potentially learn, there seemed to be a rivalry between people who preferred crochet and those who preferred knitting. Bernie seemed a safe person to test out whether that was all online bluster or not. Apparently not. "It's all yarn to me." Bernie rolled her eyes. "I was looking at all the little animals you can make, and I thought it would be fun to make a tiny dragon."

"That's a little advanced. How about a worm?"

"Ew, no. How about a fox?"

"How about a snake?"

"How about an owl?" Bernie paused at that suggestion.

"That's probably doable. A little oval for a body and then two flat wings?" Bernie tapped her knitting needles on her thigh before putting them, still attached to her project, down on her chair as she got up. "Come on, let's find you some beginner-friendly yarn."

Despite my impatience, Bernie made me practice stitches, unravel them, and practice some more before starting on my owl. For both, she created some kind of little knot circle thing before letting me make the stitches around it, but she promised to teach me that part later.

After about two hours, I had about half of a tiny little ball and was starting to get the hang of how to make the stitches. Jean joined the three of us once we'd relocated to the normal seating area that had enough chairs for everyone, where she and Bernie's friend discussed the pros and cons of some kind of wool that Jean had started stocking. Apparently, it was very soft but not very easy to work with.

I had mostly tuned them out, too focused on the task at hand, only half-listening to Bernie as she told me, in detail, about a television show from the seventies and eighties about an alien that came to Earth to observe humans and made weird noises. I mostly just hummed in agreement when Bernie paused, but the show sounded bizarre enough that I considered watching a few episodes.

I took a break for a bit to rest my hands and told Bernie about the recent dares and the scavenger hunt the next day. We'd be getting points for each of the items we collected from the song 'The Twelve Days of Christmas,' as well as a bonus point if we got all of the items for a particular day. For instance, on day two, for two turtle doves, we'd get a point for each turtle dove (or whatever we got to represent it), plus a bonus point if we got two. If we got six pipers piping, we'd get six points, but since that was for the eleventh day of Christmas in the song, we'd get twelve points if we got eleven pipers piping—one for each piper and then a bonus point for the set. Bernie started brainstorming things I could get to represent each thing, but I had to cut her off since Anna and I agreed to no pre-planning. Bernie shook her head, and I went back to my owl.

It took another hour for me to finish my owl's body, but I sat back to appreciate it once it was stuffed with fluff and the ends were tied off. Jean helpfully let me just keep track of what I was using and to check out whenever I was getting ready to leave so that I didn't need to keep buying things individually.

"Bernie, look! I made an owl!"

"The body of an owl," she corrected. "It'll need some eyes and a beak too. I think Jean has some plastic eyes that you can add somewhere. Go check and find some you like."

I headed down the aisle that Jean pointed to and found a few different options. There were plain eyes that were just little circles and a selection of eyes with irises painted on, both in a variety of different sizes. I considered picking some eyes that were half the size of my owl for the fun of it before realizing that it might just end up creepy.

Ultimately, I picked up some of the plain black circle eyes, assuming that they'd work well for a lot of crocheted animals, so I wouldn't be buying a bag of six to only use two. There were some with separate backs and some with little holes on a piece sticking out the back like fancy buttons, and when I brought both packages to Bernie, she plucked one out of my hands, tossed it on my seat, and told me to put the others back. I did as I was told. Bernie had her project on the table in front of her when I got back and walked me through how to attach the eyes, also explaining when, how, and why to use the other version if I needed to in the future.

As much as I wanted to stick around and make the owl's wings, my back was hurting from slouching over, and I didn't actually know what the plan was tonight for the dare with Anna. We were essentially going to see who could be worse at caroling while pretending to be good at it. I hadn't given it much thought but suspected that it would either be ridiculous and fun or an absolute train wreck.

I took everything I'd used up to the register where Jean was helping out another customer. Having paid, I said goodbye, promising Bernie that I'd be back shortly after the holiday to learn how to make and attach wings, and then left the shop, holding my little owl body to my chest as I walked happily home.

Anna was home when I got back, but she was on the phone with her mom. I ditched my coat and boots before tossing my bag of new supplies on the floor by the couch and sitting beside Anna, who gave me a bemused look as I silently held out my owl. "What is that," she asked after she hung up.

"The body of an owl. Bernie taught me how to crochet today. She's going to show me how to make wings and a little beak whenever I get some time to go back."

"Cute." Anna shifted on the couch toward me. "Mom asked if I could stop by her house tonight to help with some decorating. Want to come with? We could use your decorating skills." I ended up going over and decorating with Mrs. Koyama most years. Anna would sit on the couch and snack while Mrs. Koyama and I pulled out tubs full of decorations, hung lights, and pretended like we were considering putting decorations in new places before adding them to their designated spots.

"Sure. We should bring your gingerbread house so that she can show it off to everyone who visits this week."

"Oh, that's a good idea. It'll be a nice festive addition to the kitchen island where we put out snacks for everyone on Christmas. She'll be bummed if you don't bring yours too, though."

"Guess they're both coming with us then." I shrugged. Mine was just going to get stale out on our counter, so I didn't mind bringing it with us at all. "About today's dare." Anna winced. "I didn't think far enough ahead to figure out what we were doing."

"Neither did I. Although, since we'll be out in the 'burbs, it'll be easier to go from house-to-house caroling. Here, it'd just be us trying to get into condo buildings and then going door-to-door until we got tossed out. We'll have to pick a neighborhood a few miles from my mom's house, though. I'm not caroling to her neighbors."

"Are you sure? It would be pretty funny if your mom heard neighborhood gossip on Christmas about terrible carolers, and it turned out to be us."

"That wouldn't be funny at all."

"It'd be fun for me."

"Let's just avoid it altogether. Do you want to hang for a while? I'm pretty much ready to go. We could stop by Mom's to say hi and drop off the gingerbread houses, head out to do the dare, and then go back to help her decorate. She's making curry rice for dinner and said we could eat there."

"Why didn't you lead with that? Your mom's cooking is drool-worthy. Give me ten minutes." I jumped up off the couch and bolted into my bedroom to change into something nicer than the sweatpants I'd worn to loaf around the yarn store.

Mrs. Koyama's cooking was always good, but her homemade Japanese dishes were better and more authentic than anything you could order in from local restaurants. I was back in the living room, ready to leave, in six minutes. Anna was in her coat and pulling on gloves when I arrived. We grabbed our gingerbread houses and headed out.

"Okay, how are we doing this?" We'd just stopped by Anna's childhood home, unloaded our gingerbread houses (to Mrs. Koyama's delight and praise), and were back in Anna's car. I clicked my seatbelt on as she started backing out of the driveway.

"I know the general area where each of my mom's close friends live, so I'm just going to head somewhere else. There's a pretty nice neighborhood about fifteen minutes away that always has really nice Christmas lights up. If we go there, we could also drive through after to look at the lights on houses we don't walk past."

"Yes, please! It's always such a bummer in the city that the buildings aren't really decorated other than the city-decorated streetlights."

After a short drive, Anna parked in front of a house with no lights on, presuming that they might not be home and thus couldn't get annoyed about us parking on the street in front of their house. Since we obviously weren't going to be able to just conjure up a group of people to go caroling with, we decided to go on our own without bothering to try finding a group.

We also decided on some ground rules. The winner would be whoever ended up being asked to stop singing or had the door slammed on them to stop listening (an immediate door slam at seeing carolers didn't count), and we would take turns in our attempts at being the obnoxious caroler so that there wasn't any dispute about who was the cause of the abrupt end. We also couldn't both use the same method for being intentionally terrible, but we could switch it up whenever we felt like it.

I didn't have any ideas, so I was just going to rely on awkwardness and my sub-par singing. Anna won yesterday's dare, so she got to pick who went first: me. Great.

We walked up the driveway toward the front door of the first house we saw with lights on inside, two down from where we parked, but neither of us actually wanted to ring the doorbell or knock. Did anyone actually enjoy having carolers come to their door? I sighed and rang the doorbell.

"Wait, shoot, what songs do we know?" I looked at Anna with wide eyes, my mind erasing any knowledge I had of any songs that I knew well enough to sing without just singing along. The door swung open before Anna could respond, and we both looked at the elderly woman staring at us expectantly.

"Jingle bells, jingle bells!" I joined Anna, but despite actually knowing most of this song, I almost immediately stumbled over the words and replaced "jingle all the way" with "jingle every day." My brain caught up to me after that, acknowledging that carolers would be far more annoying if they didn't even know the words to the songs they sang, so I started purposefully singing over Anna but intentionally messing up a few words every other line.

The woman mostly looked at Anna, who was quietly singing the correct words, in between wincing at my (intentional) screw-ups. She actually sat there with the door open, listening politely until we were done. She thanked Anna before turning and telling me gently that I might want to practice a bit more with the lyrics at home. I had to hold back my laughter until she shut the door fully, and we were back on the sidewalk.

"How did she listen to that with a straight face?" Anna choked out through her laughter. "I could barely hold it together myself. Did you plan that?"

"I wish I had, but no. The first mistake was an actual mistake, but it worked out nicely. Do you know what you're going to do?"

"I do."

"Are you going to tell me?"

"I want you to experience it in real-time." We walked to the next house, this time ringing the doorbell straight away since our nervousness and awkwardness had largely abated.

Anna did not disappoint. We decided to keep the same song for each of our attempts to keep everything fair. When the front door opened, I started lightly singing, but Anna was just speaking all of the words. I glanced over to her, her face expressionless, as she spoke each word. Not a single word was sung.

If I didn't actually listen to what she was saying, she could have passed for giving an incredibly boring, monotone presentation at work or a lecture to a group of students. The teenager standing in the open doorway was looking at her in confusion, with one hand on the door poised to shut it, but he seemed shocked into inaction. When we finished, he didn't even say anything, just took a step back and slowly shut the door.

"Honestly, I expected people to shut the door in our faces right away," I said to Anna after we left our fifth house. Anna had the next attempt. "How are they listening to us butcher these songs?"

I'd gotten pretty close to having someone shut the door mid-song on my last attempt. A man had come to the door and, just as he lifted his hand and started saying something about not needing to hear more, a woman came up beside him and was thrilled about having carolers. When we'd finished our song, she mentioned that it was their first Christmas in their own home, and she asked us to sing another. The man didn't say anything. Anna and I quickly re-sung Jingle Bells, but this time, I sang correctly just to get it over with faster.

"Speak for yourself. I am providing these fine folks with a performing arts show."

"Sure. The people at the last house offered you tea. They probably thought you'd been singing so long that you couldn't sing anymore."

"I guess we're not great at being terrible." There was a gate surrounding the next house with lights on and three dogs in the yard. I liked dogs, but I didn't want to risk them not being friendly or opening the gate and potentially having them escape, so we walked on. "Do you hear that?" Anna jerked to a stop and clutched my arm. "It's singing."

I looked in the direction Anna was leaning and, sure enough, there was a group of people on a front porch, about six houses down where the road curved, singing. It wasn't as loud as I would have expected, given that there looked to be at least four of them, but what I could hear sounded pretty good. We skipped the next few houses, walking towards the carolers instead. They were done singing and were just about to go up the driveway of the house next to the one they'd left when Anna and I got close enough to draw their attention.

"Hi," I said, waving, "we didn't expect to run into any other carolers tonight!" As we got closer, we could see that each person in the group was wearing a matching shawl over their coat. It fell like a robe over their shoulders with a buckle in front, and they each held a songbook.

"Hello, there," the woman in the middle of the group said, "are you out caroling as well?"

"We are! Any interest in teaming up so that we can give the nice people of this neighborhood a full choir?" I was certain that teaming up would make caroling more awkward, so I wasn't sure why I asked instead of suggesting to Anna that we go to a different neighborhood.

"Well...hmmm." The woman seemed hesitant to agree. Based on their matching attire, I presumed that they did this often and seriously. A tall man in the back looked like he'd rather eat his songbook than have two strangers join, but everyone was deferring to the woman who'd spoken, so she must be the leader. "I suppose that would be okay, but we'll need to figure out where you should stand to best blend in with the group."

"Okay?" I wasn't sure what she was actually asking us to do; Anna apparently wasn't either because we just stood there looking at the woman, confused.

"You'll need to sing," she said slowly, clear by her deep sigh that followed that she was already regretting her decision to let us join. "Try 'Silent Night.'" Anna and I started to sing. I wasn't planning to screw up any words, worried that it would get the offer to join rescinded, but Anna clearly had no such reluctance. Instead of speaking the words, though, she sang them.

A few lines in, after the group seemed to release some of the tension gained from when we were offered the chance to join, Anna's voice changed. She started singing off-key; it was clear to me that it was purposeful, but she wove it into longer stretches of singing normally. It wasn't subtle, and I was enjoying the entertainment value of the horrified looks from everyone in the caroling group as it continued. When we finished, I pretended to cough, trying to get a hold of myself and not blow our cover.

Anna had a serene, hopeful look on her face as she asked, "So, where should we stand."

"Just, um, off to the side here, the woman gestured towards the open space near the person on her right. "And, hmm, maybe it's best if you were to hum along." She looked at Anna, whose face dropped. When did she become such a good actress? "You know, because it will tie everyone's voice together." She didn't leave any room for argument, turning on her heel and starting the walk up the driveway of the house that we'd been loitering in front of this whole time.

"I'm pretty sure I just won the dare," Anna whispered to me as we hung back far enough to stay out of the group's earshot. "I don't know how much earlier you can get asked to stop singing than before you even start."

"Seriously. The way you made it seem like you had no idea, and it was just every few notes? Perfect execution."

"Thank you, thank you very much."

"Do we really need to stay now?" I glanced up, and the group was waiting for us and staring at us impatiently.

"We're already here. Let's do one and then bail after this."

"Alright, ladies, get in place," the leader ushered us over to where we were supposed to stand before she looked at Anna, "and remember, we need you to hum." Anna nodded, smiling softly at the woman.

One of the others rang the doorbell and then knocked immediately as well. Eager, much? A little kid opened the door, followed by a man who was reminding him to not open the door to anyone without him or the boy's mother there as well. It occurred to me that we didn't actually know what we were supposed to be singing but joined once the group started the first lines of 'Deck the Halls.' Anna, however, was silent for the first few bars. The group leader seemed relieved until Anna started humming, just not the song we were singing.

At times, I thought her humming sounded familiar, but it kept switching up in tempo and octave. If someone could hum a guitar solo, I would swear that Anna did at one point. She was getting dirty looks from everyone in the group except me, and I eventually just stopped singing altogether, too busy biting my tongue to stop from wheezing out laughter to sing at the same time.

"We're only doing one song?" Anna asked the question with a completely straight face as the door closed in front of us. She didn't leave time for a reply before giving us an escape route, though. "Probably for the best; we really need to be heading home. You all have a great night!" She tugged the sleeve of my coat, and we nearly ran down the driveway. A look behind us showed the carolers still in the driveway of the same house, probably making sure that we got far enough away and didn't see an opening to rejoin them.

"What," I managed to squeak out between laughing so hard that I was tearing up and trying to catch my breath, "were you humming? I swore I recognized some of it."

"A mash-up of recent hits, interspersed with a little freestyling."

"I bow down to the champion. Did you see the snobby lady's face? I thought steam was going to come out of her ears."

"I was kind of hoping she'd stop us mid-song. Clearly, she is a professional caroler because I could barely keep it up myself."

"I wish we'd been able to record it."

"It would have made a weirdly festive but grating ringtone." I wiped the tears from my eyes as we walked back to Anna's car. Someone was pulling into the house we'd parked in front of just as we were arriving. Anna waved at them and got in. We stayed put for a few minutes, letting the car warm up, before Anna pulled out and started driving.

"You know what this means, right?" I looked over at her, not sure what we meant. "I'm in the lead—by a lot. Think you can get enough points tomorrow in the scavenger hunt to catch up?" She shot me a triumphant smile as we turned out of the neighborhood, our plan to look at lights forgotten as we headed back to her mom's house. Most of the wins I'd gotten had been shared with Anna, I realized, but she'd had a handful of solo wins. I was going to need all the points I could get.

Game on.

DAY 12: SCAVENGER HUNT

After a night of flip-flopping in bed, trying to sleep, and stopping myself from thinking through a plan for the scavenger hunt dare today before scolding myself that I wasn't supposed to be pre-planning anything, I expected to sleep through my alarm. At the very least, I expected to wake up to my alarm, hit snooze approximately seven times, and eventually get up solely from annoyance at listening to the beeping.

When I did actually wake, there was no gradual shift to consciousness; I was awake and alert so abruptly that my first thought was that I had slept through all five of my alarms despite the fact that the light that typically streamed in from the window through the cracks between my wall and curtains was non-existent. I took my phone from its place on my side table as I tossed aside my comforter and slipped my feet into the slippers next to my bed—it was 7:30 a.m.

On the one hand, I only got about five hours of sleep and should probably try to get a bit more; on the other hand, I was already up and may as well start my day. It was going to be a long one. Fun, but long. There was a sort of frantic energy running through me that I knew wouldn't let me get any extra restful sleep, so I started wiggling my fingers and toes before letting the movement extend to the rest of my body. I transitioned into some light stretching until I had dispelled my jitters and was calm and focused.

I needed to make a plan. First, I needed to map out what I had to find and what ideas I already had for each of the scavenger hunt items. Anna and I never made any rules about what would count for each, other than that we could take some liberties provided that we could explain their connection.

I wanted to make a point not to just go out and buy a ton of stuff that I didn't actually have any need for or didn't have a way to use or repurpose, but to some extent, that was probably going to be unavoidable. Although the sponsorship tree tags from the community center were all taken before Anna and I could grab a few, the drop-off cut-off for miscellaneous items that could be distributed to the families wasn't until tomorrow at noon, so maybe I could find toys that would work and then donate them. Once I wrote out my list, I re-read what I had so far:

12 – drummers drumming

11 – pipers piping

10 – lords a-leaping

9 – ladies dancing

8 – maids a-milking

7 – swans a-swimming

6 – geese a-laying

5 – golden rings: *jewelry*

4 – calling birds

3 – French hens

2 – turtle doves

1 – partridge in a pear tree.

Okay, so, not much progress, but I pushed back from my desk and walked over to my dresser, where a small jewelry box sat. I often received jewelry from well-meaning acquaintances who didn't notice that I didn't typically wear any, but I had a few nice pieces saved for special occasions.

As I opened the top of my jewelry box, I had a passing thought that it was a shame it wasn't a music box with a spinning ballerina, like I had as a kid to count as a lady dancing. I knew a few people with kids who might like them as gifts, and the rest could be donated, but I was already going to end up buying a lot. For now, I'd add that to my list of ideas and see if I could figure out something else throughout the day. It felt good to have a backup plan in case I didn't think of anything else.

Looking through the meager contents of my jewelry box, I found two sets of small hoop earrings and a few rings. One of the sets of hoops was yellow gold, but the rest were all white gold. The song didn't specify, so I was going to count them all. I walked back to my desk and put a checkmark next to "day" five. One done before 8:00 a.m., nice. I mentally gave myself a little pat on the back and looked back over my list.

Why were there so many birds? I wondered if Anna would kick me out of the apartment if I showed up tonight with live birds. However, a quick mental image of geese inside our apartment had me wanting to kick me out too, so maybe we should put a "no new pet birds" rule in place. Swans, though, might be doable. Not real swans, obviously, but across the city, there was a park next to a large lake that had paddle boats that looked like swans that you could take out for the day.

The lake was big enough that it didn't typically freeze over, and I vaguely remembered someone once telling me that they were out there all year round. I added it to my ideas list, the low dose of adrenaline from solving a puzzle buzzing through me as I pulled on jeans and a sweater and headed out to the kitchen, pulling my bedroom door shut behind me just in case Anna was inclined to go snooping. She was sipping on coffee and looking at her phone intently from one of the barstools at the counter when I entered, but she flipped it so that the screen wasn't visible when she heard me approach.

"Goooood morning, and happy scavenger hunt day!" She was smiling brightly and using her finger as a microphone. "How are you feeling this fine morning?"

"Ready to close the gap in points and leave you in my dust."

"I can appreciate the confidence. I just hope you won't be disappointed when I come back with every item."

"Today's going to be fun," I said, leaning over to bump my shoulder against hers after I sat down on the stool beside her. "But I do have one rule to add."

"Oh?"

"No bringing home pet birds."

Anna's face scrunched up in horror. "Can you imagine? This place would be overrun!"

"Okay, good. Phew."

"What are we thinking about for an end time, though? There's something that I might pick up that I would want to bring to the community center to donate since there were no sponsorship tree tags left the other night. The drop-off deadline is tomorrow, but I'd rather get them over there tonight before they close so that I don't have to deal with it tomorrow."

"I was actually thinking the same thing, but good point about not leaving ourselves a task for tomorrow morning. When do they close?"

"Eight o'clock, but we'll need time to wrap and label things and then get them over there."

"Do you think 6:00 p.m. would be early enough? That would give us the whole day and then we can wrap things after we go over our finds."

"Sounds good. Now, if you'll excuse me," she said, getting up, "I have a scavenger hunt to win." Winking, she turned and skipped toward her bedroom. Enjoying the challenge already, I got up, grabbed a banana for breakfast, and headed back to my own room to get ready for the day.

12.2

I was an idiot.

What part of my brain was malfunctioning this morning when I thought to myself, "yes, Haley, there will definitely be swan boats out on the lake in December! Why *wouldn't* the parks district let people get into a small paddleboat and go out to the middle of a lake where they could fall in and get hypothermia? Liability risk? Don't be a buzzkill!"

I really would have appreciated my common sense kicking in before I spent almost an hour waiting for and riding a bus to get to this park. Obviously, when whomever told me that the boats are here all year, they meant that they were stored here.

Looking around, I saw a small structure about three hundred feet to my left, butting up to the lake with a small dock next to it. There was a tarp covering the side facing the water instead of extending the wooden side walls around the back that I walked over to check out. As I neared, a sign on the front wall of the structure read, "boathouse." Excellent.

Casting a glance around me to make sure no one was looking in my direction, I walked out onto the dock next to the boathouse, glad that it was covered in slightly packed snow that provided some traction rather than just being covered in ice. I only needed to go a few feet onto the dock before I reached the tarped back wall.

The tarp was attached to hooks along the sides tightly using carabiners, but I managed to pull the on tarp just enough to see that there were racks of swan boats inside. Unfortunately, I couldn't make enough space that I would be able to fit my phone through to take a photo.

After another quick check for anyone watching me, I opened one of the carabiners and maneuvered it until it separated from the hook it was attached to. There were enough other hooks that the tarp largely stayed in place, while still having created a space big enough to sneak my phone-wielding hand inside. There wasn't enough room to pull back and get the whole group of boats in the photo, so I switched over to video and tried again, this time moving the phone to record as much of the space as possible.

Based on the number of boats stacked high and deep, I guessed that there were a dozen in total, but some weren't visible from my vantage point. I watched the video back that I took, and I counted out eight visible boats, even if just partially in the shot. I only needed seven, so I tucked my phone into my coat pocket, zipped the pocket closed, and grabbed the carabiner to reattach it. It must have been handling more pressure from the tarp than I realized because I had to fight to pull it far enough to re-hook it to the side of the boathouse.

As I stepped off the dock, I looked up to see a couple holding hands while out on a walk of their own, both of whom were staring at me. I smiled, waved, and high-tailed it out of the park before they could get any ideas about reporting me for what I assumed was trespassing. There wasn't a sign, though, so I just told myself that it was fine; I didn't need three security incidents in one week. Once I'd gotten far enough that I could no longer see the couple, I pulled a pen and the folded-up sheet of paper that I wrote my list on earlier out of my pocket and made a check mark next to day seven. Two down, ten to go.

On the bus ride to the park, I had been thinking about an old toy I'd seen from time to time of a monkey holding cymbals. You could wind it up and the cymbals would bang together. Cymbals were a type of drum...would that be close enough to be considered a drummer drumming? A quick search online from my phone confirmed that the toy was still made and that similar toys with other types of drums existed.

Figuring it was worth a shot, I mapped out directions to a popular shopping area where a large toy store known for carrying vintage toys was located. Fortunately, it was a shorter ride than the one I took to get to the park. Unfortunately, when I arrived, the store wasn't actually open. I really needed to start checking store hours, but I didn't expect a toy store to not be open until 11:00 a.m. two days before Christmas. If I ran a toy store, I'd be opening early and staying open late every day I could during the holiday season, especially now, knowing how many people left their shopping until the last minute. Looking through the window, it was clear that the place was huge and there was a good chance I'd find something inside, so I resolved to come back a bit later.

Hearing the faint chime of a bell across the street, I turned and watched as someone entered a bookstore. I could happily wait out the extra time there. Aisles created by floor-to-ceiling bookshelves led me to the back of the store where a used book section boasted deep discounts.

The groupings of books were less defined back here, but I found a collection of cookbooks and started flipping through. Four books in, I opened one that had the undeniable stamp of approval: pages smudged and splattered from obviously consistent use. I wasn't sure why a clearly loved cookbook had found its way back to the bookstore instead of being given to friends or family if someone hadn't wanted it any longer, but I was glad for my own luck as I flipped through page after page of recipes and photos of what looked to be incredible dishes.

I'd already decided that I'd be taking the book home with me as I looked back at the cover and saw the author's name, Claudia Piper. Claudia *Piper*. I took my list out to double check what I already knew, that I needed eleven pipers piping. Maybe I could rely on authors, since writing could be considered them piping up in conversation about whatever they were writing about. I rushed back to the front of the shop, getting turned around a bit as I tried to navigate through the bookshelves until I found the checkout desk.

"Hi," I said a little breathlessly to the teenager sitting behind the desk, "could you do me a favor?"

"Maybe," he replied, not saying more.

"Okay, well, can you run a search for books, particularly those in the used book section with authors with the first or last name 'Piper' for me?"

"None of the used books are searchable, since they're all just under the colored dot pricing system and we don't keep an inventory of what we have back there. I can run the search for the rest of the store for new books, though. Do you know the author's full name?"

"Uh, no, it can be any book written by an author with 'Piper' anywhere in their name." The guy looked at me like I wasn't making sense before he shrugged and typed something on the computer.

"Looks like we have three different books that would work, though there are a fair number of copies of each." He turned the computer screen slightly so that I could see the screen over the counter. The list he pulled up included the sale price of each book, and, oof, that wouldn't be happening. I could just buy the books and return them, but I didn't want to do that intentionally to an independent bookstore.

"Umm, I think I'll actually just stick to this one book for now, but thanks for checking." I put the cookbook I found on the counter and was pleasantly surprised when it turned out to be cheaper than expected, only three dollars. Probably because of how dirty the book was inside, but that didn't bother me.

"There's a library down a few blocks West of here," the guy at the register said as I tucked my new book into my backpack, "they might have what you're looking for." I had passed by the library he mentioned a handful of times, so I knew where to go when I got outside. It was thankfully only about two blocks down the road, and I entered to a gust of warm air and the sounds of excited kids. There was a sign for a story time event this morning that sounded cute, but I was on a mission now that I had a new lead.

The woman at the information desk gave me a friendly smile as I passed, heading toward one of the available computers. I searched books with "Piper" in their author's name and was rewarded with an extensive list. Since it was the library, I didn't need to be particular about what I checked out.

As I tracked down each book, there were some with multiple copies and some by the same author. I wasn't certain whether Anna would count either as separate pipers piping given that they were the same piper piping the same thing. I was spoiled for choice, though, so I collected ten books, each different and each by a different author before bringing my stack up to one of the self-checkout lines.

After I scanned my fifth book, I got a notice that I had hit my maximum. Nothing I tried worked to scan the remainder, including finishing checking out those I'd already scanned and starting over with the new books—I just kept getting a "limit reached" message when I scanned my library card.

"Excuse me," I said to the woman at the nearby information desk, "I want to check out these books, but the self-checkout system keeps giving me an error message. Something about a limit."

"I think I know what's going on, but let me scan your card and double check." I held up my library card for her to scan the barcode on the back. Having read whatever was on the screen, she nodded and then turned back to me. "It looks like you've reached the limit of what you can check out at one time. I see two books that were checked out a few weeks ago and then the five that you just checked out."

"I'm confused. I've checked out more books than that in the past."

"It's a new policy. Since we eliminated late fees this past summer, we've had a problem with people coming in and checking out ten, twenty, even thirty books at a time and then keeping them for several months or longer. It's happened enough that we've had inventory issues that are preventing other people from getting access to books as well, so we put a seven-book maximum at one time in place to test out whether that will encourage people to return the books they've read so that others can read them. I can process the return of any of the books you've just checked out if you want to replace them with some of the others you have there if you'd like."

"No, it doesn't really matter which I have. I just need things written by someone named 'Piper.' Is there any way you can make an exception if I promise to bring them back within the next week."

"Unfortunately, no, the system won't let me even if I wanted to. You could have someone else with a library card check out the extras, but then those books would count towards their maximum." I just stood there, staring at the books in my hand for a full minute before sighing heavily and letting my eyes close until the woman continues. "You said you needed authors with the name 'Piper.' Do you need them to be authors of books?"

"What do you mean?"

"If you don't, our computer databases are linked to search local, state, and national newspapers. I'm sure someone named Piper has written an article at some point."

"That's...that might work. Thank you!" I started speed walking back towards the bank of computers before realizing I left the books I checked out and the extras on the desk. Once I'd collected them all, and deposited the books I didn't check out on the re-rack carts, I logged in at one of the open computers and looked through the different search filters until I find those dedicated to newspapers.

There were more results than I expected, so I narrowed the search to op-eds, figuring that personal opinion writing might fit more closely with the idea of "piping up" with your own thoughts. One woman, Piper G., apparently had way too much time on their hands because there were several dozen op-ed results specific to them. I found a relatively short one about a conspiracy theory related to potholes not getting filled, before going back to the search results tab and pulling up another op-ed written by a different Piper.

It turned out that the vast majority of the op-eds in my search results were written by the same handful of people, so I ended up with eight op-eds that I printed out and put into my backpack. With my new finds, I only needed two of the five books I'd checked out earlier. I thanked the woman at the front desk for her suggestion on my way out as I stopped at the desk to return the three largest of the five books. The other two I zipped into my backpack on a bench in the library lobby.

"Haley?" Anna's voice surprised me, and I spun around so quickly that I lost my footing. Thankfully, the bench behind me caught me as I fell back.

"Fancy seeing you here!" Anna and I hugged, laughing at coincidence. "Are you working on a scavenger hunt item, or just stopping by on your way?"

"Wouldn't you like to know." Anna waggled her eyebrows at me. She was holding books that I'd seen her reading in our house, so I presumed that she was just returning books while she was in the area, but since this wasn't the closest library to home, she must be in this area for something specific. Anna and I had similar approaches to problem solving, it was one of the reasons we'd stayed friends for so many years despite having disagreements from time to time, so it wouldn't actually surprise me if we ended up with some of the same scavenger hunt items. I guess I'd find out when we went through everything later.

"I would like to know," I said as I put my backpack on and checked the time on my phone, "but, alas, I can't pester you because I have to go."

"Okay, see ya later." Anna waved and headed towards the front desk. She glanced at me, still in the lobby, and started paging through the first of her return books, seemingly checking if she'd left a bookmark or anything inside, before slowly feeding it into the return slot. I could see her looking to see if I'd left yet out of the corner of her eye before doing the same with her second book.

Before she started on the third, she turned back to face me. "You sticking around for something? I thought you had to go?" That sneak! She was here for something dare-related, I was sure of it. I was tempted to just stay put to see how long she'd make her book return take but decided against it. I waved once more and headed back out to the street to start the walk back to the toy store as my phone buzzed in my hand.

Raquel: Hey, any interest in grabbing lunch today?

I pulled out my list and glanced at what I had left to complete. I'd be able to go to the toy store before lunch, and I didn't really have any ideas about the rest of the dare items. Maybe taking a break to enjoy good food and good company would inspire some.

Haley: I'd love to! I'm on my way to that big toy store on 7th Street in the middle of all of the shops, but I'm not entirely sure how long that will take me. What time were you thinking?

Raquel: I actually live not too far from there, only about a mile away. Why don't I just walk over and meet you there and then whenever you're done we can find somewhere nearby? That way you won't need to rush.

Haley: That sounds perfect. I'll be there in a few minutes, so head over whenever you feel like it, or I can wander around in the area if you're not quite hungry yet.

Raquel: Will do, see you soon!

Bolstered at the idea of taking a break once done at the toy store and hopefully having completed another day's items for the scavenger hunt, there was a decided uptick of pep in my step. A few other patrons were already inside the toy store when I arrived, and the person working at the register was busy, so I just wandered through the store to see what I could find on my own. I knew generally where the throwback and vintage toy section was, so I headed back that way, glancing quickly at what else was on the shelves as I passed.

"Can I help you with anything, miss?" I turned away from the display of used toys in a glass case, labeled with their manufacture year dating back to the 1930s, to look at the person behind me. It was an older man wearing a green and red checkered cardigan. "My wife made this a few years back. It's my official holiday season sweater now." He must have seen me checking it out, appreciating the front pockets where candy canes peeked out.

"She's obviously very talented," I said with a smile.

"Oh, yes. My wife never met a hobby she didn't love for a few months, sometimes a year, just long enough to get good at it and make a trophy before moving on to the next." He chuckled before continuing. "Are you looking for anything in particular, or just browsing?"

"I am actually looking for something specific. The toy that's a monkey with cymbals that bang together, or something similar."

"Ah, a classic. We actually have a few here, unless they've sold in the last day or two while I've been gone. I'll take you over to them." He turned and waved at me to follow.

"I figured that it would be in the throwback section. I only remember seeing them when I was a kid."

"We rotate out what's back there, but we have quite a few toys that were originally released decades ago that are sprinkled throughout the store because they're still being manufactured. If I'm not mistaken, what you're looking for is right down here."

We rounded a corner into a new aisle of shelves. A selection of plastic instruments, piano mats, and microphones took over the first quarter of the aisle before we arrived at a collection of drums. There was everything from a single squishy-looking drum with a label boasting that it softened noise from being hit all the way up to professional looking drum sets in child sizes.

The man I'd followed reached up to a shelf above my head and pulled down a cymbal-clad monkey with a little red hat. "You just crank this lever here and it'll start up for a bit for you. Kindly, don't do much of it in the store. It's a bit obnoxious."

"Understood, thank you." Taking a step back, I could see the space that the toy previously occupied, but couldn't see any further back. "Are there any more up there? I can't tell." He backed up before stepping on a low shelf. He reached his hand over and came back to the floor with another of the same toy in hand.

"Looks like that's the last one. We could order more for you, though."

"No, this is enough for now. Thank you so much!"

"No problem at all. If you need anything else, I'll be around some-where, playing with toys." He waved before turning to walk back down the aisle. The toys were relatively inexpensive, but I still took a moment to appreciate that I was in a position to make these extra purchases, especially at this time of year. I'd spent so many years stressed about the financial implications of gift-giving and was glad to finally have a bit of room to breathe.

I was sure Anna wouldn't care if I just took photos of the toys as evidence, I certainly wouldn't if she came home tonight only with photos, but since I had the means to do so, I felt good knowing that I would be able to donate these gifts to families who didn't have the same resources.

I had been noticing more and more that, throughout the last twelve days as I forced myself out of my comfort zone and shook off the rut that I'd been stuck in, I was much more willing and excited to be generous and selfless. I was ashamed to admit that I hadn't been thinking far outside myself and my direct friends and family for a long while now, but I didn't want to let disappointment in myself cloud the positive changes I'd been making and taint the openness and willingness to help that seemed to be coming more easily lately.

Seeing no other drumming toys beyond the actual drums, and assuming that any other similar toys would also be in this section, I considered possible backup plans for the remaining ten drummers drumming that I needed to come up with. I walked up and down each aisle, ultimately ending up at the other side of the store in a section dedicated to toys for pets.

There were several aisles of shoulder-height shelves filled with toys for each dogs and cats, as well as an aisle dedicated to toys and enrichment items for bunnies, hamsters, birds, reptiles, and more. I checked some of the tags, and they all seemed to be priced more competitively than I'd seen before at pet stores.

The more I thought about it, the better an idea it seemed—get people, even those who didn't have kids, in the door to get discounted items for their pets, and then maybe they'd see something for the kids in their life that they wouldn't otherwise have gotten or would come back in the future if they ever needed something.

Amongst the rows of dog toys, there was a section of what looked to be stuffed animals that someone forgot to stuff. I picked one up, running my hands over the soft material and hearing the crunch of the crinkly material inside before squeezing a little squeaker in the middle. I put the toy back on the shelf, looking through the selection to pick out something for my brother's girlfriend who loved her dog possibly more than she loved my brother. I'd spent my whole life putting up with Jake, though, so I couldn't blame her.

One double-take later, I swiveled back a few toys. It was another of the crinkly toys, a duck. I mentally ran through the list of items I was looking for today and went through a quick internal debate about whether ducks were close enough to geese that I might be able to make it work. I was still struggling with justifying the leap when I heard Raquel say my name as she walked up behind me. There was a small stuffed bunny with comically large, floppy ears tucked under one arm as she waved with the other.

"Do you have a dog," she asked. "I don't remember you saying anything about one, only about one day wanting backyard chickens." During cookie decorating, Gloria had mentioned once that a famous friend of hers, one she refused to name despite our pestering, had rented goats as an alternative to mowing their giant lawn, and we'd gone down a long tangent of discussing what farm animals we'd be willing to adopt one day.

"I was looking for my brother's girlfriend's dog, but I think I might have just figured out a way to knock out another scavenger hunt item."

"Oh, today is the scavenger hunt! I can't believe it's the last day."

"Me neither, the time started to fly by after a few days. Let me ask you a question, though. Do you think that ducks and geese are similar enough that they could be interchangeable?"

"Hmm, they're both birds. I wouldn't confuse them if I saw one, but I still think you could make that stretch."

"I think I'm going to have to." That decided, I pulled six of the duck toys off of the shelf, all five of the available small ducks and one of the larger size. Raquel laughed as I draped them all over my arm and then picked back up the drumming toys.

"One to your brother's girlfriend, I'm assuming, but what are you going to do with the rest of them?"

"Donate them to the animal shelter. Dogs need presents, too. Unless...wait, do *you* have a dog? How did we talk about farm animals but not cover this?"

"I don't know about you, but I was pretty engrossed in Gloria's impassioned speech in favor of having a backyard highland cow. I'd love a dog but can't justify it with my work schedule. I do have a cat, though, Reggie."

Raquel was an anesthesiologist. When we'd met that first day at the yarn store she told me about having moved to the city because she'd transferred to a local hospital for a better job and to be close to her family after several years apart. She was working long hours and the times varied each week, so a dog was probably too hard to get someone to check in on as frequently as she'd need. "My sister and her husband are surprising my nephew with a dog for Christmas, though. It's currently being spoiled rotten by our mom, who's been taking care of her for a few days."

"One duck is coming your way then and you can bring it to them."

"I'd appreciate that, thanks. She's apparently going through toys like crazy. Puppy energy." Raquel shrugged before pointing at the monkeys in my arms. "Are those another dare item?"

"Yeah, drummers drumming, but I'm ten short."

"Were you really going to buy twelve of those?"

"I was planning to, but I didn't really think that through. I don't know what else to get for it."

"Well," Raquel said, holding the bunny out by its front paws and alternating them up and down to mimic drumming, "why not just get one little drum and then a handful of stuffed animals to sit around it? They could be drumming."

"That could work."

"Plus, there's a little bin of one-dollar mini stuffed animals up front near where I got this bunny, so the cost wouldn't be too unreasonable."

"You're brilliant!"

"Brilliant, maybe, but hungry, definitely. Let's get you some drummers and go get lunch." We headed back to the music section first to find a small drum. I'd been hoping to find something wide enough that all of the drumming animals could sit at together, but that didn't happen. There was a set of three that wouldn't be too onerous to carry around and would make a great donation for the community center.

Raquel carried the drums for me as I loaded up my arms with small stuffed bears, bunnies, and even a chameleon with a tongue sticking out and we went to check out. I managed to fit everything but the drums in my backpack, but only barely. The zipper was perilously close to bursting, but it would have to do. The drums were tucked snugly in a reusable grocery bag that I'd brought with me, though I had hoped not to need the overflow space. I'd need to head back to the apartment at some point to offload anything I'd picked up, but that could wait until after lunch.

12.3

Raquel led me to a sandwich shop that I'd never been to before. It didn't look like much from the outside, but the smells inside were enough to realize what I'd been missing.

We ordered at the counter, and Raquel's meatball sub and my jerk chicken sandwich were dropped off ten minutes later, exchanged with the paper towel holder holding a laminated square displaying a bright red number four. We didn't say much at first other than "oh my god" and "this is so good" every few bites. Eventually, we slowed down enough to actually talk, Raquel telling me work stories about the funny things people had said as they were going under and coming out of anesthesia and hoping that the next few days would be easy.

She'd shifted her schedule around at the last minute to help someone who had a family emergency, so she was stuck working over the holiday. Her family was going to have a second Christmas morning a few days after Christmas, though, so she would still get to spend a day with them all together.

"What else is left on your list," Raquel asked after we'd finished our sandwiches and were snacking on the homemade chips they came with. "Maybe I can help."

"Ugh, a lot, actually. Leaping lords, dancing ladies, milkmaids, calling birds, turtle doves, and the elusive partridge in a pear tree."

"I've never understood what was up with all the birds."

"*Right?*"

"You know that dance school over by the yarn store? I saw a sign yesterday that they were doing performances of The Nutcracker all day today." Raquel took out her phone and started typing something on the screen. She looked triumphant for a moment before reading off what she'd found. "Yeah, okay, so they're actually doing it three different times with different age groups. There's info here about how it's such a classic that they want everyone learning it and learning more advanced techniques each year, depending on which performance they're in. Looks like they started the first one about an hour ago, so it should be going for a while, even if some of them are abridged versions for the younger kids."

"Do you think we'd be able to get in to see it? There are tons of scenes with lots of people dancing at once; there's bound to be one with nine people on stage."

"I don't see why not. We can just pretend that we have family in the show."

"That's the plan for what to do next then. Let's hang for a bit, though. I'm assuming that they're starting with the younger kids and will go up in technique and age in the later shows. I'd feel weird about taking a picture of a bunch of little kids."

"Good point. Let's keep brainstorming."

When we left the sandwich shop, we opted to walk until we got cold rather than immediately hopping on the bus. Not my best decision given the amount of stuff I was carrying, but wandering the streets with Raquel, chatting the whole way, and periodically stopping into stores to look around made it worthwhile. Eventually, I called it and we headed to the closest bus stop on our route, which happened to sit in front of a bakery. We arrived just as a bus was pulling away from the stop, so we headed into the bakery in search of a treat rather than waiting outside.

"Haley," Raquel said as we were gazing at the confections lining shelves behind the glass wall above the counter, "do you see what I see?"

"Cookies? Cake? My healthy dinner plans going up in smoke?"

"Look at those brownies," she insisted.

"They look good. Are you going to get one?"

"Read the label, Haley."

"Dark chocolate turtle brownies." It took me longer than I cared to admit for my brain to connect the dots. "*Turtle* brownies!"

"Maybe you could cut them to look like birds."

I turned to look towards one of the people behind the counter that was hanging back until someone needed help. I raised my hand, and she walked cover.

"Hi there, can I grab something for you," she asked cheerily.

"Hi! Could I get two of the turtle brownies, and, umm, this is a weird question, but does the bakery have cookie cutters?"

"We have some for our own use, but we don't have any for sale."

"Is there any chance that you have some shaped like a bird? And, if so, is there any chance that you'd be willing to cut these brownies into the shape of a bird?"

"You weren't kidding about it being random. I'm not sure, but I can check in the back."

"That would be amazing! Thank you!"

Unfortunately, she came back empty-handed, so she packed up two still-square turtle brownies in a box. Raquel and I headed back outside after I paid for my brownies, she paid for a bag of bite-sized cookies, and we tried to figure out the best option for adding a dove element to the brownies.

Raquel suggested stopping at a craft or cooking store and getting my own cookie cutter or stencil to dust a powdered sugar dove. I made a mental note of both options but would probably end up just trying to cut them into a bird shape freehand later. I could manage a flying "v" bird shape as if they were off in the distance on a painting.

By the time Raquel and I got to the dance studio, the third performance was just starting. We were able to slip in with the crowd, and since the seats were already mostly filled, we stood behind the last row of chairs. When the lights dimmed and the music started, we watched as a group of what appeared to be college-age kids danced onto the stage, along with a few older dancers and a young girl.

As the performance began, I was riveted, in awe of how talented the dancers were, so much so that Raquel had to give my arm a small shake to get my attention. She held her hands up and mimicked taking a photo.

I turned slightly so that the light from my phone was minimal until I opened the black screen of the camera. One quick photo later, my phone got tucked back in my pocket. It was a large group dance, and a quick count confirmed that there were enough women on stage to meet the scavenger hunt requirement. As much as I wanted to stay to watch the rest of the performance, I didn't have the luxury of time today, especially since I still needed to come up with ideas for what to do with a few of the items.

We walked a route that passed by the yarn store, where we could see Jean inside so that Raquel could stop in to pick up more yarn for a project she was working on. I was getting tired of carrying around my earlier finds, so I said goodbye to Raquel and waved to Jean as I headed back to the apartment.

On the way, I received a text from Adam, asking how my day was going. I typed out a response with my free hand, lamenting about the number of things I had left on my list. A few thinking-face emojis popped up in response. Another message vibrated in my pocket as I juggled my bags, my phone, and my keys to unlock the apartment door. The contents of my backpack were emptied onto the bed, along with a bag of drums, but I brought the brownies to the kitchen.

Pulling out my phone to search for an easy outline of a dove, I was surprised to find a new message from Raquel, the lock-screen preview of which just showed about a dozen exclamation marks. She'd attached a photo where she was holding up a set of three buttons—buttons shaped like little white birds. Were they doves? Who knew. Would they work? Sure would!

Haley: Are those at the shop???

Raquel: YES!

Haley: On my way

I left the brownies in their box, but I put them in a brown paper bag that I wrote "do not open" on before putting them in the back of the fridge. I was hoping for a reprieve at home where I could put my feet up and maybe take a quick nap, but dove buttons waited for no one.

My coat got thrown back on, and I grabbed my mittens as I raced out the door and back down to the street. I started speed-walking toward the shop until I caught a red light and realized I really didn't need to be rushing. Maybe some of the Knittie Bitties would be there with Raquel and I could take a break with them. Those plans were dashed in the best way as I got another text, moving out of the way of the pedestrian traffic to read it.

Adam: Okay, I had to check when our return date was, but I may have a solution for one of your scavenger hunt items, provided that you can get it back to me in the next few days.

Haley: Is this when you tell me you and ten of your closest friends are lords who enjoy leaping?

Adam: Alas, only three of my friends are lords, and they've all sworn off leaping...would you take an earl?

Haley: I'd take a partridge, especially if it was sitting in a pear tree

Adam: Does the bird have to be alive?

Adam: And by that I mean can it be fake?

Haley: Anna and I have a no new pet birds rule, so it must be fake

Adam: My company rents Christmas trees that are rooted in pots for the office every year, and then after the new year we return them and the company we rent them from re-plants them. This year they offered rooted grafts of pear trees for rent as well, and they put a small, fake partridge on the branches of each one. We rented a handful of them.

Haley: Are you saying what I think you're saying?

Adam: If you think I'm saying that you could borrow one for the day, so long as you get it back to me before the end of the year, then yes, I sure am.

Haley: ADAM!

Adam: I've got a client call that's starting soon and should take about an hour. After that I'll just be finishing things up before I head home early. Do you think you could get down here before 4:00 p.m.

Haley: Definitely! I'll text you when I get there!

Adam: Try not to get thrown in corporate jail this time

Haley: No promises

I'd been standing on the sidewalk as I'd texted Adam to make sure that I didn't run into anyone while walking distracted, but I nearly jogged the remaining two blocks to the shop, throwing the door open and racing back toward where the Knittie Bitties always sat.

Raquel was there with two women I hadn't met before. She introduced me them, twin sisters who had moved from England together in their thirties and had been part of several knitting groups ever since. I bounced on my feet, trying to listen respectfully as they told me a bit about themselves before introducing myself and sitting down next to Raquel. She handed me the dove buttons as I told her what Adam had just offered.

"Breathe, girl," one of the sisters, Violet, told me, apparently concerned that I was talking twice as fast as any normal person would. I took a deep breath before leaning back in my chair, letting my eyes fall shut, and huffing out a laugh. Raquel gave the sisters an overview of what I'd been working on today and what we'd done together. I took the folded-up list out of my pocket and checked off a few more items.

"You know," the second sister, Audra, said as I told them what was left, "back home, they used to call us birds when we were young and fit."

"Haley," Violet sing-songed to me after she shot a look at her sister. "Oh, Haley!"

"Umm, yes?" I wasn't sure what was happening, but the women were giggling together.

"I was calling you, darling. Does that make me a calling bird?" We all laughed, and I looked down at my phone as it started to vibrate with an incoming call. I looked over at Raquel questioningly because it was her name listed as the incoming caller.

"Let it go to voicemail," she said to me conspiratorially as she held her phone to her ear. I clicked a button to do just that and let out a shocked laugh as she started to speak in a fake British accent. "Yes, hello, Haley. I'm just calling to tell you to have a good day. Toodaloo!"

My phone dinged with a notification of a new voicemail before starting to ring again with another call from Raquel's phone. She turned to the other ladies, passing them the device, and Violet took it, waiting until I'd sent her to voicemail as well before she left a similar message. Audra did the same before passing the phone back to Raquel. "Well, that's three. Where's Jean?" She called out to Jean, who came around the corner a few moments later.

"Need something?" Jean was focused on the clipboard in her hands, checking something off with a pen as she walked up to us before looking up.

"Would you mind leaving a voicemail for Haley?" Raquel held up her phone, my contact information pulled up and ready to be called again. "Oh, and pretend to be British and make sure you say that you're 'calling' for something."

"Do I want to know why?"

"It's for another one of the dares. This one's a scavenger hunt," I explained. She shrugged, reaching for Raquel's phone. I sent the call to voicemail, and Jean did an impressively convincing accent, leaving a message that she was calling to gossip about some yarn store drama. She made it sound like something scandalous had happened and then hung up, disappointing the rest of us when there turned out to be no tea to spill.

12.4

I managed to get to Adam's office within the hour, texting him that I had arrived as I pushed through the large glass front door. Three overstuffed chairs sat around a low table in the lobby, and I relaxed onto one, confirming out of the corner of my eye that neither the security guard nor the front desk worker were here to witness my stint in corporate jail.

No response came from Adam, so I expected to be waiting for a while as he finished his meeting, but no. An elevator dinged as one of the sets of doors opened, and I saw Adam step out. Well, I was assuming it was Adam. His face was obscured, given the small tree in his arms, but the brown leather messenger bag that hung from his shoulders had his initials stamped in small letters at the corner.

"Adam? Is that you behind the tree?" He leaned to the side and smiled at me from around the tree.

"Shh, don't give away my cover. I'm sneaking out." He went back behind the tree, raising it a little higher so that I could see him through the less dense lower branches. There was a small, fake bird just to the right of his nose, but no pears to be found. "I drove in this morning. Want a ride back to your place so you don't have to deal with this thing on public transit?"

"Yes, please! Lead the way." We walked in companionable silence until we got to Adam's car. He shrugged off my questions about how his day was going with a shrug and a "same old, same old" and instead asked about my dare progress. "With this one done and one more I need to stop at the store for, I'm only missing two. I have no ideas whatsoever for them, but I'm getting to the point of just calling it good with what I have. I don't expect to be getting any new ideas at this point, and I really want to take a nap."

"It sounds like it's been a long day. A long twelve days."

"It has been, but I somehow feel lighter. I've been carrying around the weight of feeling like I should be doing something different or putting myself out there and never actually doing it. I think I had convinced myself that I had waited so long that the only thing that would help would be some kind of monumental change where I overhauled a part of my life, but I really just needed to make an effort, have some fun, and meet some new people."

"I could see even that feeling daunting. We rarely notice how many people and opportunities are around us."

"It helps to have a dose of luck to find the good ones."

"Or roommates who flirt with my brother." Adam winked at me before focusing back on the road.

When we got to my building, Adam pulled out of traffic and turned toward me. "I don't suppose you've got time to go grab a drink or take a quick walk?" The war between wanting to spend more time with him and wanting to get the last few things done and then rest for a bit must have been playing out in my expression because he threw me a bone. "Alternatively, I would accept a raincheck."

"On most other days, a drink and a walk would sound great, but I am about to collapse. I'd love a raincheck for sometime soon, though, if that's okay."

"Of course it's okay. Plus, if this is anything like our last raincheck, I'll be seeing you in a few hours."

"I appreciate this," I said, holding the pear tree up a little higher. "I owe you one."

"I think you owe me two—one for the partridge and one for the pear tree."

"Not to mention the ride."

"I'll put it on your tab."

Adam waited until I got the front door unlocked and stepped inside before driving away. I trudged up the stairs and then kicked off my boots before walking into my room, dropping the potted tree on my desk, and collapsing on my bed. I wasn't done yet, though, and if I let myself settle in, I doubted I'd get back up, so I forced myself to stand, put my boots back on, and headed to the nearby grocery store.

12.5

"Gloria?" I walked over to my neighbor, who was juggling a bag of potatoes in one hand and a few different bundles of herbs in the other, both almost falling from her arms until she righted herself and walked to her cart.

"Hi there. Doing a little last-minute shopping? I got a bit ambitious tonight and decided to add a few more items to the meal I'm hosting on Christmas."

"I've just got one thing to get. Can I help you grab anything? If you don't mind the company, we can do our shopping together, and then I can help carry things back." Gloria's cart was already crowded with various items. I didn't like the idea of her trying to carry it all back herself.

"I'd love the company! There's something very underrated about grocery shopping with friends, don't you think?" Other than Anna and prior roommates that had come and gone, I hadn't ever gone grocery shopping as an outing with friends, but as Gloria and I wandered through the store together, pointing out items we'd never heard of and talking about our favorite foods, I realized that she was right.

I added a few items to the cart as cravings struck me in addition to what I walked over for, but I managed to keep my impulse buys to a minimum. Gloria liked to look around in an exaggerated fashion while putting items in the cart that weren't on her list, making me laugh as she pretended to not notice the treats being added.

By the time we got to the checkout lines, I was glad that I'd decided to stick around. I suspected Gloria was too, though she just looked at the cart, looked at me, shrugged, and gave a light, "whoops." I loaded up my backpack with my items and then helped bag Gloria's purchases while she paid.

We walked back to the building and up to our floor, but when I approached my apartment door, I could hear Anna inside talking to someone on the phone. I didn't want to give her ideas for the scavenger hunt item if she hadn't already completed them, so Gloria suggested that I come to her apartment to wait Anna out, presuming she was going to be leaving again or just waiting out the clock. I still wanted that nap, but I decided to go to Gloria's long enough to help her put away her things and give it about half an hour before going back to my place.

With my items in her fridge and hers strewn about her counters and tucked into corners of her fridge in groups according to what dish the ingredient was for, we went into her panic/movie room to lounge in the recliners.

"I'm disappointed that I couldn't at least get something for each dare, even if I am pretty impressed by what I did accomplish," I said as we sat, nestled under blankets and listening to music quietly reaching us from a speaker in the kitchen.

"Remind me, what are the missing items?"

"Lords a-leaping and maids a-milking."

"Hmmm, those are tricky." We sat in silence for a few minutes until Gloria turned to the wall beside me, where stacks of DVDs filled the shelves. "Haley, look at the middle shelf. See towards the far left, the spine with the sword and flowers?" I pointed to what I thought she meant. "That's the one. Pull that out. That can be your lords a-leaping, though I'm afraid you'll have to settle for just one."

"I'm confused."

"About halfway through, there's a scene where one of the characters, a lord in the 19th century, tries to jump—leap—over a creek and instead falls in."

"Is this something you wrote?"

"I did some re-writes after the original screenplay was purchased. Not one of my better projects, but I got a producer credit in exchange for a discounted rate since they were on a tight budget. I went in to watch filming sometimes, and I was there the day they were filming that scene. The actor had to keep getting dried off and then fall into the creek over and over. He was getting more annoyed with each take, but he was a bit of a jerk, so I had my suspicions that the director kept pretending to not be satisfied so that he'd have to keep doing it. If there was a blooper reel, it would have just been him falling in over and over again. Here, hand it over; I'll show you the scene."

I hadn't noticed the last time I was in here that Gloria had a DVD player set up under the table between the recliners. She said it was so that she didn't need to get up when she wanted to put something new on if she was already comfortable—top-tier forethought. We laughed while we watched and re-watched the scene she'd mentioned until I heard a door open and then close again out in the hall. I doubted I would have heard it from Gloria's kitchen, but the recliner I was in was right next to the door out to the hall.

"Peek out the door, see if you can spot Anna leaving," Gloria said when I asked her to pause the movie so that I could try to hear more.

There were definitely footsteps, and I managed to unlock the series of locks and crack the door in time to see Anna's navy coat disappear down the stairs.

"We're clear!" I started re-engaging the handful of locks that Gloria had on the door (she'd explained that she wanted this door more secure since someone could get inside and then just wait until she was asleep or left, and it would be less noticeable) before folding the blankets and heading to Gloria's fridge.

We said our goodbyes as I collected my things and brought them and the DVD back to my apartment. Once everything was put away, I collapsed on the couch, figuring that I'd wake up when Anna got home versus accidentally sleeping for hours if I went to bed. My eyes were closed, and my consciousness drifted the moment I laid my head down on a pillow and stretched my legs across the cushions.

<h1 style="text-align:center">12.6</h1>

The sound of keys turning in the lock and the door opening roused me from sleep what felt like seconds (but was actually about twenty minutes, if the clock on the television could be believed) later. Raised up on my elbows, I saw Anna standing in the doorway, trying to balance three rotisserie chickens in her arms. There was a beat of silence before laughter exploded out of me so abruptly that I nearly fell off the couch. Anna laughed with me, but she mostly was laughing at herself, not knowing what I knew.

"Wait," I said once I had collected myself enough to speak. Holding up a hand to have her stay put, I walked to our freezer and pulled out what I got at the grocery store with Gloria earlier. When I turned and she could see what I was holding, her laughter restarted with enough vigor that she nearly dropped the rotisserie chickens. We stood facing each other, Anna holding three cooked chickens, me holding three frozen chickens. Safe to say that we both nailed the three French hens portion of the scavenger hunt.

"What," she said after taking in a gasp of air, "are we going to do with *six* chickens?"

I opened the freezer and shoved the three I was holding back inside. "We should bring one of those to your mom's house tomorrow, and I guess we'll be eating a lot of chicken over the next few weeks." I took the top two containers of chicken out of Anna's hands and transferred them to the fridge. Anna had already taken the plastic top off the third and was cutting pieces off to eat when I turned around. I joined her, and for a few minutes, we stood there, eating chicken pieces in silence other than our intermittent giggling.

"Can I assume from you napping on the couch that you're done with the scavenger hunt?" I looked at the oven clock and saw that there was still almost an hour before the deadline.

"As done as I'm going to be. I'm out of ideas and motivation."

"Good, me too."

"I'm excited to see what you got today! Should we go grab everything?"

"Give me a bit. I want to wash my face, put on sweatpants, and decompress."

Eventually, we were both sitting on the couch, surrounded by the things we'd collected throughout the day. Anna was floored that I'd found an actual pear tree but then proudly presented me with a pear. Holding it out to me, she reasoned that the pear contained seeds which had the potential to grow a pear tree.

Pressed on whether it should count given that there wasn't a partridge inside the seed as well, she tried arguing that birds were incidental to trees and that once it grew, one would come. Even she knew it was a stretch, though, and she happily accepted one point instead of the possible two. I'd gotten both of the points since I'd gotten the item and completed the number of items for that day, even if it was just one.

As we sat eating the turtle brownies that I'd picked up (I'd added a dove button to the top of each, though we removed them almost instantly so that we could eat the brownies), Anna presented me with two drawings she'd made earlier: cartoon turtles with white wings. Looking closer, the turtles also had tiny beaks. I hadn't thought of trying to draw some of the items, but even if I had, my lack of artistic ability meant that my drawings wouldn't have been recognizable.

After we'd come down from laughing all over again about the six French hens in our kitchen, I played Anna the voicemails I had on my phone. Those were being saved until I saw Bernie and the rest of the Knittie Bitties again and could share them. Anna got out her phone as well, and I briefly wondered whether she had the same idea until she started playing bird calls and set four small, fake birds on the table. She'd apparently gone to the craft store in search of a partridge for her pear "tree" and decided to complete the larger item number day instead.

When I set my earrings and ring on the table, Anna's mouth dropped open. I wasn't sure why, given that she'd seen me wearing all the pieces before.

"Haley, I got up this morning and took the earrings I wore today out of my jewelry box. Are you kidding me? How did it not occur to me to just use my own? I must have been on autopilot."

"Wow, I figured this would be the item we did similarly. What did you end up getting for it?"

"These." Anna tossed a handful of gold scrunchies on the cushion between us. She picked each up and put them each on a different finger. "Unfortunately, I couldn't think of anything for the next one. I almost just got more fake birds, but I didn't want to do the same thing for two items."

"Why didn't you do it for the higher value item at least?"

"Because there weren't any that were sitting on eggs, and I didn't know of an easy way to make it seem like those birds were laying." Anna scowled before smacking her palm to her forehead. "I could have gotten fake birds that looked like they were laying down, though. In my defense, I picked those up just before the chickens, so my brain was already mush from coming up with other ideas." I made a good effort at not laughing, but a few chuckles snuck out, more when I flung my collection of dog toys onto the ground next to us, and Anna just stared at me blankly.

"Get it? They're laying there on the ground."

"Okay, that's pretty smart, but we don't have a dog, Hales."

"One's going to Jake's girlfriend, another to Raquel to give to her sister, and the rest I'm going to drop off at an animal shelter when I have some free time next week."

Anna called a pause while she went to get a notepad and pen to tally our scores. I was ahead by eight points, but I wouldn't be able to keep that lead if Anna had gotten everything else on the list. When she was done, she hopped up again and brought a small bowl of water back with her but wouldn't explain why.

I told her about my morning brain fart with the swan boats and showed her the video I took. She wasn't buying my explanation that they were all "swimming" in the air, so we agreed on half points, rounded up since I got all seven of the boats in the photo at least, and she added my four points to her tally.

She then put the bowl of water in my hand before reaching into a bag behind her; I couldn't see what she had until she opened her closed fist and dropped seven tiny white rubber ducks into the bowl. That was about as close to swans a-swimming as I could imagine either of us getting.

"Where did you even find these?" I watched the little ducks, each no bigger than the width of a quarter, float around in the bowl before putting it back down on the coffee table next to us.

"Some gag-gift store. I didn't just get seven, though. They only had the white ones that would pass for swans in variety bags of 100."

I had nothing for eight maids a-milking, but Anna showed me a few pictures on her phone, the first of which was Sita holding up a small bottle of milk. She scrolled through five more similar photos, this time featuring strangers, and explained that they were ladies, maidens, with milk.

She and Sita had gotten lunch together, and Sita had the idea and told a bunch of the nearby tables what they were trying to do. Most people were willing to take a photo, but a handful refused, and they started to feel really uncomfortable asking and decided to stop at six photos. Two more, and she could have gotten the bonus point, but apparently, after four people rejected them in a row, they decided to be done and move on.

"Now, here's why not using my own jewelry for day five is even more ridiculous," Anna said after I showed her the photo that I took at the ballet recital earlier. After a dramatic pause, she set her jewelry box in between us and opened the top. It was a sentimental item she'd received from her grandmother as a child. Cranking a key on the side, the ballerina inside started spinning. She set hers aside and then took eight more out of a bag sitting on the floor next to her, still in their boxes. "I figured this would be a good donation item for the community center to distribute since it can work for a wide age range. I'm going to put the scrunchies in a few, and I got a few packs of bracelets to add as well."

"That's incredibly generous."

"I'm assuming that if their families can't afford gifts, they probably don't have a lot of accessories and keepsakes since those aren't necessary items. Hopefully they'll like it."

Anna got up to use the restroom while I cued up the DVD that Gloria had lent me. Fast forwarding to the scene that we watched in her movie room, I pressed pause and waited until Anna returned. I hadn't expected her to be carrying ten books when she did, but she stacked them on the table before taking a pillow from the couch and tossing it on the ground.

I watched curiously until she noticed the movie paused on screen. I played it as she stood next to the couch, after which she started introducing me to the lords in the books she'd brought into the room. After pointing to their rank and title inside each book, she put them onto the edge of the pillow on the floor. Her fist thumped the pillow where the book was, making each book fly a few inches into the air before dropping back to the ground.

"Leaping lords." She went through each book before restacking them and coming back to sit on the couch.

"Is that what you were at the library for when I saw you?"

"Yeah. Most of these are books I already owned, but I had to return a few books anyway, so I got a few extra to round out the ten I needed."

"Good thing you already had some—did you know the library has a limit on what you can check out now?"

"I didn't. In that case, thanks, me, for having a regency romance collection already!"

"I was at the library for the next item." I spread out the books I'd collected as well as the op-eds I'd printed out. I held each one up, pointing at the author's name before moving to the next. Anna took the cookbook from the pile and started flipping through. She tore slips of paper from her notebook, and we spent the next ten minutes bookmarking recipes that we wanted to make soon. There were a lot. "We'll need to prioritize the ones with chicken..."

When we'd gone through the cookbook and set it aside, Anna showed me a photo of a group of five jovial older men sitting on couches and chairs in the middle of a cigar shop, each holding up an old-fashioned smoking pipe.

"And last, but certainly not least, do we have drummers? Are they drumming? Drumroll, please!" I made drumming sounds as Anna produced her phone with a bow. It was cued up to play a video focused on a set of drums. As soon as I pressed play, a woman walked onto the screen, tapped her drumsticks together three times, and then hit a quick combo on the drums before getting up and walking off-screen.

Just as she was exiting, a man walked on screen with a baby wearing noise-canceling headphones strapped into a carrier on his chest. He very lightly tapped on one of the drums before fitting the sticks in his baby's hands. He held the tiny hands that held the drumsticks and did another quiet pitter-patter of the sticks on one of the drums. Getting up, they both walked out of frame, exiting just as Anna appeared on the screen. Anna, hamming it up for the camera and off-screen crowd, attempted an elaborate series of beats, very few of which actually landed, before she too got up and walked off the screen.

This repeated twelve times over, looped so well that I barely noticed when the video restarted. It was silly and fun, and I kept watching, but on my third viewing, I realized that Anna was being a little sneak.

"Wait a minute!" I paused the video and turned toward her with an accusatory finger-point. "Did you think you'd get away with this?"

"I was hoping to." She just laughed, knowing that I'd finally caught on to everyone but her and the baby going through the drum line twice. She and the baby would have been too noticeable, but the man who had been previously carrying the baby was shown on the paused screen, and when I pressed play again, I could see where the same people showed up twice, the second time wearing (or having removed) a hat, jacket, or baby.

"You know we're only counting the first time each person plays, right? And you don't count!"

"Why don't I count? I was drumming my little heart out."

"You were the scavenger hunter, not the scavenged item."

"Yeah, yeah. There were only so many people in the music shop when I went, so I had to be creative."

"I applaud you, but you're still only getting six points for that one."

"Oh, you know what that means?" Anna was looking over her points tally. "You still have a fighting chance for this dare." She announced that with a sly smile as if she wasn't actually worried. I just got up and pulled out the drum set, setting stuffed animals around each drum before finally taking out the little monkey with its cymbals, winding the crank so that they banged together a few times. As it did so, I went around and showed each of the stuffed animals drumming.

"Count 'em! All twelve, which means thirteen points for me." I sat down on the couch next to her and leaned over her shoulder as she tallied up the remaining points. The final count had me at 67 points and Anna at 65 points. "I won? I won!" I jumped up on the couch, doing a little dance.

"You kicked that scavenger hunt's butt!" Anna held up a hand to high-five me, sitting back and laughing at my antics. "But…"

"But what? There should be no but!" I stopped dancing once I'd put it together. "Wait...what was the spread before today?"

"I was up by four."

"Okay...wait. Wait! You're telling me that I went bouncing all around town, won the scavenger hunt, but I still lost the bet?"

"Have fun with bathroom cleaning duty!"

I cringed, but two extra weeks of cleaning the bathroom was worth the last two weeks. I'd relit a spark that had been nearly snuffed out. I found new friends and a new hobby that one of those friends was forcing me to not give up on. I had *fun*. Heck, I even ended up on a date, hopefully with more to come.

I must have been staring at the pear tree on our coffee table for longer than I realized after that last thought because Anna nudged me in the thigh with her slipper-clad foot. "You have to return that, right? It's probably best if you check in about it. I hear potted plants are best returned quickly and followed by a date."

She gave the phone in my lap a pointed look before walking to a bag she'd dropped by the front door when she brought home the chickens and pulling out a few packs of gift bags and tissue paper, which she brought back to the couch. She sat back down, tapped my phone screen with an exaggerated "ahem," and started counting out how many bags we needed for the items we planned to donate. I guess it wouldn't hurt to check.

Haley: About that raincheck...

Vague? Sure, but while Adam may have been up for doing something when he was sneaking out of work early, now it was the night before Christmas Eve. He was probably enjoying what felt like an early Friday, or maybe he was out with family or friends. This way, I wasn't limiting the raincheck just to tonight.

After organizing stuffed animals, jewelry boxes, drums, and more into piles off the coffee table, I went to get a pen and some ribbon left over from wrapping gifts in my room. Anna had already started putting tissue paper in each of the gift bags, but there was a stack of paper gift tags on the table. I started writing out notes that we'd add to each bag saying that they were from Santa and then moved on to write out an additional tag for each item identifying what it was and what age range it was suggested for so that the center could organize them easily.

"Does this feel a little anti-climactic to you?" Anna asked after we'd been working quietly beside each other for a while. She'd moved on to putting the items each into a bag and then tying on the applicable item tag. "The end of the dares, I mean. Are we done with them, just like that?"

"Maybe we should celebrate somehow."

"How, though? The next few days are going to be chaotic, and a quiet night in sounds pretty good."

"Let's end the way we started: with a holiday movie marathon and an obscene amount of snacks."

"I seem to remember a great deal of wine, too."

"You've got yourself a deal. We can pick up more on the way home from dropping off the donations. Or we can try making some festive cocktails."

"Or just spiking hot cocoa."

We looked at each other for a beat before we both shouted, "All!" Leaning over, I hugged Anna to my side, and she rested her head on my shoulder.

"Okay," I said, letting her go. "Let's finish this, drop everything at the community center, and then it's nothing but pajamas, snacks, drinks, and movies." We got back to our task, and I felt a bit lighter. I wanted to celebrate my friend winning, even something as silly as these dares. The full-circle plan felt good after the long day.

Adam: I love how quickly you call in your rainchecks

Adam: Dinner, drinks, or otherwise tonight?

Shoot, how had I already forgotten that I'd sent that last message? Anna looked over and must have seen the disappointment on my face because she sat back and nodded down at my phone. "Adam?" I nodded. "We can have a movie marathon tomorrow night at my mom's house instead if you want. It's not like we won't have other chances." She seemed genuinely okay with it, but I wasn't.

"We will, but tonight we're celebrating. Would you mind if we made a second stop after dropping off the donations so that I could drop off the pear tree, though? That way, I can say thanks again and also not have to worry about that later."

"Why don't you go drop off the tree while I go drop off the gifts? I was going to suggest getting a ride to the community center so that we weren't carrying a bunch of gift bags on the bus, but there's no reason both of us need to go to drop them off." I was gnawing on my lip in indecision. I wanted to stay with Anna, but I also wanted to see Adam, even if just for a few minutes. "Seriously, Hales, I'm good with this, and I'll be better if you go have a cute little meet-up that we can dish on later." She started gathering up the bags and putting them on the bar counter before heading back to her room, shouting "go get your man" over her shoulder.

Haley: How would you feel about a pear tree home-delivery and a short walk together? I've got a bit of time, but then Anna and I are going to spend the night celebrating the dares being done

Adam: As much as I want to see you, you don't need to get the tree back to me tonight. You can spend it with Anna and we can meet up later

Haley: I could, but I do really want to see you, and she's going on an errand first as well

Adam: In that case, a drop-off and a short walk sounds great. I'm planning to hang at home for the night, so come over whenever

The message was followed by his address, and it turned out to be only a little over a mile away. I changed into a soft sweater and jeans before Anna and I walked to the nearby grocery store to stock up on supplies for the night so that we didn't have to do it after our excursions. We grabbed four bottles of wine, despite the fact that we were both lightweights and would probably only crack two throughout the night, any snack that caught our attention.

Waiting in the checkout line, we watched as the woman in front of us put a whole, frozen chicken onto the checkout conveyor belt counter. It took all of my self-control not to start laughing when the woman complained to the cashier that she needed two, but there was only one left. Anna didn't have as much luck holding it together, and the woman shot her a dirty look.

When the car that we ordered with two stops pulled over at Adam's building, I hopped out onto the sidewalk and waved as it pulled away again with Anna inside. The building was a beautiful brownstone, clearly a new build but full of small touches that added character. A quick text to Adam later, I was buzzed inside and heading up two floors to his door, meeting him as he pulled the door open, fully bundled up in his coat, boots, and hat.

"Oh!" He looked up, and his face transformed with a bright, genuine smile. "I was going to come meet you so that you didn't have to carry that thing up." Taking it from me, he shot a worried glance at the bundle in my other arm where a frozen chicken was cradled. It was a last-minute decision to grab one of the chickens from our fridge, seeming like a funny idea at the time. Adam was looking at the chicken with his head tilted, expression bemused and clearly reluctant to ask about it.

"This is for you." I held out the chicken and, seemingly only as a result of reflexively polite manners, he reached out to take it from me as my hand dipped from its weight. "You know, since I owed you one." I could tell the moment he caught on—shaking his head as he leaned back to look up at the ceiling.

"I was thinking more along the lines of you letting me take you on a date. Though, you do still owe me a few more..."

"I have more chickens at home," I suggested, trying to stay serious as horror crossed Adam's face, probably imagining me bringing him three more chickens.

"You know, I think we're all settled up. Your tab is cleared."

"Oh, good! But I'd still like that date."

"Deal. Let me just put these inside before we go for a walk." Adam walked a few steps backward into his apartment, inviting me in. The entryway opened up to a spacious living room with forest green walls and wood beams running along the ceiling. A quick tour proved the rest of the apartment to be just as nice, and I was suddenly imagining lazy Sundays on the couch together as the snow fell outside and the smells of comfort dishes wafted out from the kitchen.

"So," Adam said, shaking me out of my daydream, "since we don't live that far apart, I was thinking maybe instead of aimless wandering, I could walk you back to your apartment. That way, I get to steal a bit of your time, but you don't have to worry about how long you want to spend before heading back to meet up with Anna."

"That's..." Really considerate, I thought to myself as I trailed off. He'd driven me home earlier today, even though that seemed like it was days ago, so of course he knew how closely we lived, and I appreciated that he wasn't pushing for more of my time when he knew I was planning to spend the night hanging out with Anna. "I'd like that." And, if Anna wasn't back by the time we walked back, we could always circle a few blocks.

We headed outside, and I told Adam about the rest of my day. He was bummed for me that I'd lost the bet but celebrated me winning the scavenger hunt. We walked side-by-side, so close that his arm and my shoulder kept bumping up against each other until we found a good rhythm where we kept brushing lightly against each other, the backs of our hands gently finding each other's and taking our time to separate. I swore I could feel the heat of his body even through my coat and mittens, and it made me lose track of the conversation more than once.

I found out that Adam was, woefully, someone who left grocery shopping for Christmas until the last minute, as he told me about still needing to pick a recipe for a dessert to bring to his parents' house for Christmas dinner. That aside, I appreciated that he was really considering what everyone would like and what would go well with the meal instead of just picking up the first thing he could find.

When Adam asked me about my family and why I was going to Anna's mom's house for Christmas, I told him about the call when my parents dropped the news that they'd be gone, not realizing that I hadn't touched on it before now when talking about the dares. For the first time, it wasn't a story filled with bitterness, but rather, I retold it in the context of the last two weeks, starting out horrified and dramatically grappling with my feelings of betrayal and how it morphed into something wonderful.

Adam laughed along with me as I told him about my initial plans to replace all of the gifts I'd gotten for my family with coal (I silently cringed, knowing that it wasn't originally a joke) and then pointed out that doing some holiday dares might make for a fun tradition that in future years I could do with my family as well as dares with friends. I hadn't considered that, but as soon as it was suggested, I could imagine it so clearly, already making me excited for years to come.

"Well," I said, dragging my feet after we got back to the front of my building. We'd gone on a loop of three extra blocks, but now I could see lights on in the apartment and knew Anna had gotten home. Adam turned to face me, seeming to understand that it was time. "Thanks for walking me home." I shuffled my feet and searched for something else to say that didn't seem so final.

"Enjoy your chicken." That probably wasn't it. Adam just smiled lightly.

"Maybe I'll keep it until I can make it for us for dinner one night soon."

I smiled up at Adam, noticing that we'd both stepped closer to each other given how far I had to tilt my chin up. The bare fingers of his left hand moved to hold my own mitten-clad fingers as we otherwise stood still.

Mother nature intervened with a gust of wind that blew a small section of hair across my face. Adam reached up with his free hand, gently brushing back the wayward strand. He kept it woven between his fingers as they rested on my cheek before sliding back slightly to rest against my neck, his thumb lightly tracing the line of my jaw. His eyes were focused on my lips as he leaned down toward me, stopping just short of connecting with my lips.

His gaze shifted to meet mine, a question behind them as the tip of his nose brushed mine. I leaned forward, rising up on my toes as my eyes fell closed and our lips met. Adam leaned into the kiss, moving the hand holding mine to wrap around my lower back to hold me against him.

The pressure increased and decreased as we moved our lips together, a wave of connecting, separating just enough to feel a breath of air wisp between us before coming together again.

Eventually, we parted enough for me to see the flush on Adam's cheeks under his still-closed eyes as he rested his forehead against mine. He was still holding me close enough that I could feel his heartbeat as it raced, and when his eyes finally opened, he smiled at me before meeting me for one more brief kiss.

We moved apart slowly, each taking the slightest step back. The arm that Adam had wrapped around my back traced the curve of my hip before finding my hand and holding onto me in that small way still. "So," he said quietly, the lingering effects of the kiss evident in his breathless start that didn't go anywhere.

"So," I returned quietly. The sounds of the city seemed muted around us, and I was lost in the moment until I saw the apartment lights flip off in my peripheral vision. They were replaced by the multicolored light of the decorated tree inside. "Time to head up." Adam followed my gaze with his own and turned to walk with me to the front door. Our hands stayed linked until I had the door unlocked and propped open with my boot.

"I'll see you soon, Haley?" He asked it like a question, though the answer was obvious.

"I'll see you soon," I confirmed. Adam squeezed my hand lightly before letting go and stepping back. I looked out the window of the door as it closed and watched as he ducked his head against the wind that had started to pick up as he turned to head home.

My mittens came off before I'd stepped back into the apartment, the fingers beneath rising to meet my still-tingling lips. Anna looked at me as the door opened, the start of her greeting turning into her wiggling her eyebrows at me as she realized what had me so dazed.

"Go change into something comfy, Hales. I'll cue up the first movie." I followed her advice, heading to my bedroom to change into flannel pajama pants and a cozy sweatshirt. When I came back out, Anna was on the couch, remote in hand, scrolling through movie options as she sang lightly and swayed to her own music. Somehow, my parents going on vacation over Christmas, something that I was sure I was going to have to dig myself out of the disappointment and loneliness of, led me to twelve days of magic and an even more magical kiss.

Was it wrong to hope that your parents went on a Christmas vacation every year?

The end.

ACKNOWLEDGEMENTS

You would not be reading this book if it weren't for the people in my life. As much as I needed to start getting the stories in my head out to make room for more, there was a constant undercurrent of "am I really going to be able to do this" and "will anyone even care if I do" that tried to stop me from doing the work to get this out into the world. I'm immensely grateful to the people in my life who supported me and encouraged me. I didn't tell many people I was going to write a book, and even fewer still that I was actively writing it, mostly due to my fear that I would never finish, and I didn't want to fail. It was stupid, and I slowly started reaching out to more people who provided me with a safe space to try. I could not be more grateful.

There are many people to thank, but my parents need to be first. I consider myself extremely privileged to have been raised by two people whose love of life, each other, and me was so obvious. They've always given me a safe space to learn who I am and what I want, and I challenge myself to do more and try new things because I saw them do the same and knew that I could achieve what so many others tried to tell me I couldn't. To my brothers, who I don't think I've actually told that I've been writing a book, but who always just go with whatever new thing I'm trying and assume I'll make it work. Well, with a good dose of humbling me—they are older brothers after all.

Special thanks to my friends who provided me with encouragement, feedback, and a listening ear and let me ramble about anything and everything. Mackenzie Moy, who made me feel like every small step was huge progress and made sure I knew someone was proud of me (often with a string of four or more texts in a row, mostly in capital letters, cheering me on). Your support is a bear-hug come to life. Bethany Price, who jumped from hearing that I was thinking about writing a book straight to certainty that I would be hugely successful and achieve all of my dreams. You shut down any doubts I had and refocused me on next steps, and you were invaluable in helping me bounce ideas and revisions off you. To Molly Steere Ekelof, who rudely moved to a different state and yet was always there to talk about things I was worried about, helped me find direction, enthusiastically asked to be an alpha/beta reader. You kept me balanced and were my voice of reason, plus you let me ramble as long as I wanted. To Neetu Nair, who was there from the start of the idea and kept me excited about the story even when my own characters were bugging me. You're my port in the storm. To Anika Steffen, who received ramblings texts long enough to be their own novel and helped me fine tune things and brainstorm how to fill out gaps in the story. I promise I'll put more spice in future books—I know you're annoyed about it being non-existent in this one. To Esme Ogiyama, who helped me find an appropriate surname for Anna's family and spent an evening teaching me how to make curry rice after they suggested it as the dish Anna's mom makes in the book because they loved growing up making it at home. I'll be adding a reference to different Japanese foods in all future books if it means I can convince you to teach me to make them! There are too many friends in my life that supported and encouraged me to name here. If you're reading this, please know that you were invaluable to me.

An amazing thing about being an author and a reader these days is the community you can find online with people you would have likely never otherwise have met. The reader and writer communities have given me so much encouragement and advice. Self publishing means having to learn hundreds of tiny little things that would otherwise be taken care of for you, an overwhelming mountain that I was able to scale because of other authors being willing to share research and tips.

Thanks to Erin DeMoss for the beautiful cover and working with me through revisions even when I couldn't picture how anything would look.

Thanks to Charlie Knight who, despite their incredibly busy schedule and my tight deadlines, worked with me to provide outstanding editing. Knowing that my book was in such good hands gave me such a sense of relief and let me take a breath in this crazy process.

And to you, dear readers, whether you got through two pages or made it all the way here to the end, the fact that you picked up this book and saw something in it to give it a chance is hard to wrap my head around. I hope you liked the characters and their adventures, and I hope it inspires you to have some adventures and fun of your own.

About the Author

Lisa Maloney, now officially the author of at least one published book, lives in Chicago, Illinois with Albert, a tiny lion masquerading as a cat. An attorney by day, she spends her evenings and weekends reading, writing, baking, making lists, and making pottery. If anyone has tips on what to add to an "About the Author" section of a book, feel free to send them her way.